**"I WILL SUE," SAID CHIUN,
VOICE DEEPENING WITH ANGER**

"Sue who?"'

"The oil company, of course. The despoilers."

"That's not how it works. Oil companies are only responsible if they spill oil before they sell it. After that, it's not their problem."

"Then who do I sue?"

"Depends on who sunk the sub," said Remo. "If the North Koreans did, you can sue them. If it was an accident, you're out of luck."

"Why is that?" Chiun demanded indignantly.

"If it was an accident, it was an act of God. You can't sue God."

"Then I will sue the Vatican," proclaimed Chiun.

Also available in this series:

#95 High Priestess

Created by
WARREN MURPHY
and RICHARD SAPIR

THE

Destroyer™

INFERNAL REVENUE

A GOLD EAGLE BOOK FROM
W🦅RLDWIDE®

TORONTO • NEW YORK • LONDON
AMSTERDAM • PARIS • SYDNEY • HAMBURG
STOCKHOLM • ATHENS • TOKYO • MILAN
MADRID • WARSAW • BUDAPEST • AUCKLAND

First edition September 1994

ISBN 0-373-63211-8

Special thanks and acknowledgment to
Will Murray for his contribution to this work.

INFERNAL REVENUE

For Mel Odom, Brother in Pulp
And for the Glorious House of Sinanju
P.O. Box 2505, Quincy, MA 02269

1

From the moment he drove through the gate, Buzz Kuttner thought there was something spooky about Woodlawn Asylum.

Maybe it was the grim-faced stone lions whose disembodied heads perched atop the brick entrance posts, or the fact that the evening sky began crackling with a sickly yellow lightning as he passed through.

Certainly it wasn't the fact that the back of his Ford Econoline van was crammed with pilfered computer equipment. Buzz Kuttner cut deals like the one that had brought him to Woodlawn on this stormy early-September night all the time. These days a dishonest buck was about the only buck the Buzz Kuttners of the world could turn.

Another forked yellow bolt stabbed down into Long Island Sound as he sent the van circling the three-story brick building, looking for the freight entrance. The thunder, when it came, was a dull, distant thump too meek to echo with conviction.

The bulb over the freight entrance couldn't have rated more than forty watts. Still, its dingy light was enough. The voice on the telephone had told him to look for a light over a corrugated steel door overlooking a rust-stained concrete loading dock.

Kuttner stopped, got out and threw open the van's rear doors before backing up snug to the dock. He waited.

A warm rain started. It drummed on the van's roof with monotonous regularity. The windshield swam. Kuttner looked at his watch, fingered the horn and considered tapping out a toot. But the phone voice who had set this up had warned him not to call attention to himself. He had been very clear on that score. In fact, he'd been very precise about everything, as if setting up surreptitious deliveries of high-tech computer equipment was SOP at Woodlawn Asylum.

Maybe it was, Kuttner thought. These days the medical industry was taking a pounding, thanks to Washington. Not as big a pounding as the computer field, but it was getting to that point.

The owner of the telephone voice—he had claimed his name was Jones, for Christ's sake—had been extremely precise about the merchandise. Jukeboxes with WORM drives. Top-of-the-line with no commercial history or programs already installed. Jones had seemed very particular about that, too. Kuttner hadn't argued. If the guy wanted completely virgin drives, that was his right.

Jones was awful fussy for a guy who was buying expensive computer equipment off the back of a truck, Kuttner was thinking when the corrugated freight door finally rattled up.

Looking up, he could see the man in the door mirror. A tall, gaunt shadow standing well back from the wan light of the forty-watt bulb.

Kuttner got out. "Jones?" he asked.

"Yes," the shadow said.

It was the phone voice, all right. Jones. He tried to project a tough growl that couldn't quite disguise the dry-as-dust tonality of his natural voice.

Warily Kuttner mounted the concrete steps. The shadow immediately withdrew a pace, as if fearful of human contact. Kuttner immediately relaxed. If this was an FBI sting, the guy wouldn't be acting so spooky.

"Got the money?" Kuttner asked.

The shadow bent down briefly, and an attaché case skidded into view. Kuttner knelt, opened it and closed it after he was convinced that if there wasn't exactly thirty thousand dollars in the case, it was close enough for government work.

"Okay," Kuttner said, straightening, "we have a deal."

"Installation is part of the bargain," the dry voice reminded him.

"Just tell me where."

"Follow me."

The gaunt shadow abruptly turned and walked into the cavernous area behind the freight door, picking his way behind the weak web of a penlight. Kuttner followed, finding himself walking down a noticeable incline and into a cool area that was filled with great dark shapes of industrial oil furnaces. Once he passed a cobwebby old coal furnace in a corner and next to it steel barrels filled with cold gray ash.

"I didn't know people still burned coal," he grunted.

"It's for problem disposals," Jones said.

Kuttner grunted. "Who hauls your ashes in this day and age?"

Jones didn't answer. Instead, he said, "You told no one you were coming to Woodlawn?"

"Who would I tell? You know this is under-the-table stuff, I know this is under-the-table stuff. The fewer people who know about our transaction, the better. That's why I worded the classified the way I did."

"You don't seem like the sort of man who traffics in stolen merchandise for a living," Jones remarked.

"And you don't sound like a guy who buys it. But that's what the world's come to. Guys like me, who used to pull down the big bucks installing information systems, and guys like you, scouring the classifieds for equipment that won't bust your budget."

Jones came to a door and unlocked it using three different keys dangling from a key ring. They passed into a dark space that was much cooler. There was no drumming sound of rain in here.

A light clicked on. A twenty-five-watter hanging from a drop cord.

"There," said Jones. He did not turn around. He was pointing the penlight ray to a far wall where four very old mainframes stood in a brick-lined niche.

There was a lot of grit on the floor, and in a corner bits of loose concrete and mortar lay in a pile. In the ridiculously weak light, Kuttner got the idea that the niche had been enlarged recently.

Jones said, "I would like the—what did you call them?"

"Jukeboxes."

"Yes, the jukeboxes connected to the mainframes."

"A hybrid system, huh? That's smart. You know what you want."

"Yes, I know what I want. Can you have the new drives installed by morning?"

"I can try."

"They must be installed by morning. No one must know."

"You got it," said Buzz Kuttner, going back to the van. There was a handcart and a dolly out by the freight door, and he used them to trundle the jukeboxes and their optical WORM—Write Once Read Many—drives back to the cool room with the mainframes.

When he got the first one back, Jones wasn't there. Of course, he might have been lurking among the furnaces. Kuttner felt eyes on his back. Suppressing a shudder, he got the other machines in place and set about hooking them together.

From time to time he was aware of Jones hovering beyond the radius of the eye-stressing twenty-five-watt light like an expectant undertaker. He didn't know why that image jumped into his mind. Maybe it was the guy's hollow voice and gaunt look.

To keep himself from getting too edgy, Kuttner started talking a blue streak.

"You've made a smart purchase here, Jones. These optical drives are going to be state-of-the-art deep into the twenty-first century. You won't have to replace these units until the next depression—God forbid."

"I understand that a stationary crystal data-storage unit capable of being read by moving lasers has proven workable on the laboratory level," said Jones.

"That so? Well, if you ask me, it's a long way from the laboratory to the kitchen—if you know what I mean."

"May I ask you where you get your equipment?"

"Different places. A lot of computer outfits going under these days, or dumping product. I pick up what I can where I can."

"Can this equipment be traced?"

"Not through me. These are XL SysCorp juke-boxes. The best. A voice on the phone lets me know when they have some available. I meet a guy I don't know, cash changes hands, and I come away with my truck riding low on its springs." Kuttner stopped. "That reminds me, you in the market for a new terminal?"

"No."

"Sure? I got a nice one. Just happens to be in the back of my truck. I don't even know what they call them, they're so new. It's a terminal built into a tempered-glass desktop. Hit a switch and the screen lights up. Comes with a touch-sensitive keyboard."

"I do not need any upgrades beyond the optical drives."

"Suit yourself. Like I said, these are the best. You planning to store data permanently, a WORM drive is your best bet. Write it once and it's on the drive forever. No accidental erasures. No more screwing around with tape drives."

"I intend to keep my tape drives as backup."

"Reasonable choice for a careful man. And you, I can tell, are careful." Kuttner shook a cluster of connecting cables. "So which is the master unit?"

"The one beside the standpipe," the disembodied voice of Jones said.

Kuttner looked around. He saw the standpipe in a corner, next to the last mainframe in the line. It was vaguely rusty, but out of the open bottom trailed a flat ribbon cable.

"Man, this baby is old."

"I have no need for cable upgrade," said the disembodied voice of Jones.

Kuttner pulled the jukebox cables to the master mainframe and started to hook everything up in a cable arrangement called a star. He kept up his end of the conversation.

"How far up does that ribbon cable go?"

"To the second floor."

Kuttner blinked. He craned his neck around and addressed Jones. "You mean you've got two whole floors between your system and your terminals?"

"Yes."

"Okay. I guess you really don't want anyone to know about this hybrid system of yours," muttered Kuttner, suddenly wondering if the mainframes had been skimmed out of some warehouse, as well. If so, it was a hell of a long time ago. Still, they had been good in their day. IDC mainframes. Too bad about IDC. Kuttner had worked for them once, back in the days when if you knew computers you could write your own ticket.

As he attached the cables, Buzz Kuttner noticed that the standpipe wasn't a standpipe. From the outside, yes, but inside it was a double sheath. Looked like copper and some other conductive metal. Maybe a nickel compound. It was the perfect shielding to soak up radio emissions. They used shielding like this on CIA and NSA computer lines so no one could intercept the radio signals computers naturally emitted and reproduce them on a remote screen. The government had a word for it. Tempest. Yeah, these cables were Tempest shielded.

What the hell kind of hospital is this? Kuttner wondered. Then he wondered if it was really a hospital at all. He remembered that Jones had given him travel instructions to Woodlawn, but in fact there were no signs. Not even at the gate. He had only Jones's word that this place was in fact Woodlawn Asylum. And how much good was the word of a guy who stayed in the shadows and called himself Jones?

Kuttner put these thoughts out of his mind. Whatever this weird place was, he had a job to do and a deadline, and best of all a big chunk of change waiting at the end of one heavy night's work. Who cared what this place actually was?

He kept talking. "Once you dedicate these jukeboxes to their tasks and roll the data off the mainframes, you can junk all but one of these old monsters, you know."

"I know."

"You need a guy to off-load your data, I got the interface. Of course, I'll have to come back with a minicomputer. I can do a direct channel link. Take maybe two or three weeks, depending on how much data you got in these mainframes."

"Thank you, no," said Jones, his voice no longer a growl but very dry. There was the suggestion of an accent. New England, or maybe the South. They had a lot in common if you really listened.

"Anyway," Kuttner resumed, "you won't need but one mainframe. Each jukebox contains one hundred optical platters, and each platter can store one hundred megabytes. You got an even dozen jukeboxes, so you're talking terabytes, if not googolbytes, of data storage and retrieval. Hell, if these XL's hold out—and that's their reputation—you won't need to upgrade until your grandchildren are great-grandparents."

"That is an exaggeration," Jones said, his voice flat.

"But not much of one, right?"

"I am not in the habit of buying a pig in a poke," Jones said. "I understand what I have acquired. The jukeboxes are sealed units. Inside is an arrangement very much like that of a record jukebox. A robot arm selects the correct WORM disk from the disk array on command and places it on the carousel for reading. It is the perfect system for Wormwood Asylum."

"I thought you said this place was called Woodlawn."

Jones cleared his throat with such violence Buzz Kuttner clenched his teeth. It was a very nervous clearing of the throat. "I misspoke," said Jones. "I was thinking of the WORM drives."

"Yeah, anybody can forget the name of the place where he works," Kuttner said dryly.

Jones said nothing, so Kuttner continued installing. Going back to the jukeboxes—they looked like squat beige refrigerators all in a row—he noticed the ragged edge of the long niche where the mainframes stood. Bits of copper showed through the poured concrete.

Grounded copper mesh, he realized. These main-frames had been practically walled in and Tempest shielded.

Woodlawn Asylum, or Wormwood or whatever it was, was no run-of-the-mill nuthouse, Buzz Kuttner decided. That was for damn sure.

SOMEWHERE in the hours before dawn—reading his watch was not easy in the dim light—Buzz Kuttner finished installing the last XL SysCorp optical WORM-drive data-storage units.

They purred so softly that once the triple-locked door was locked, no one standing where he stood now would suspect that an incredibly powerful hybrid computer system was operating on the other side.

"Okay, it's all set," Kuttner said, brushing concrete dust off the knees of his denim work pants.

"You have completed your task?" a voice asked. It was a different voice. Buzz Kuttner whirled. In the weak light, he saw no one.

"Who's there?" he demanded.

"I asked you a question," the voice said. Buzz Kuttner felt his heart jump high in his throat. The voice was now directly behind him. And he hadn't seen or heard anyone move.

"Who...is...there?"

"I am but a servant who cleans up untidiness," said the voice.

His heart pounding now, Kuttner declined to turn around. The voice sounded vaguely squeaky.

"You mean you're the janitor?" asked Kuttner.

"I have told you what my duties are."

"Then you're the janitor."

"In which case," the squeaky voice countered, "you may consider yourself trash."

Kuttner turned then. He turned completely around. "Where are you?"

"Behind you."

Buzz turned again. "I don't see you."

"That is because I am behind you," insisted the squeaky voice.

It was crazy. Buzz Kuttner was turning in place, repeatedly making 360-degree turns, and the voice was continually behind him. Therefore, it could not be behind him. It was coming from somewhere else. A hidden speaker or intercom. Kuttner stopped turning in search of the source.

"What did you mean, I'm trash?" he asked the disembodied voice.

"You are a thief."

"I'm an out-of-work media consultant and technical installer just trying to make payments on a house that's worth less than the mortgage. What do you expect me to do, walk the floor in a department store?"

"Your wife would not like that," the squeaky voice suggested.

"What wife? She walked when the severance pay ran out."

"You must miss your children terribly," the squeaky voice clucked sympathetically.

"No kids. That was my one break in life."

"That is good."

"I'll say."

"For without a wife or children, a thief such as you will not be missed."

"Missed?"

The squeaky voice grew deep and sonorous, as if telling a story. "Men such as you were chosen by the pharaohs of Egypt for the important tasks of palace building. Men who would toil long days and nights, their efforts unbroken by thoughts of family."

Buzz Kuttner didn't like the way this was going, so he began backing out of the ill-lit room. The voice seemed to follow him. Now it seemed near his left ear, but that was impossible. There was no one there.

"And when their tasks were complete," the squeaky voice continued, "they could be disposed of without a second thought, taking the pharaoh's secrets with them."

"I don't know any secrets."

"You have entered the *sanctum sanctorum* of the emperor I serve."

"Emperor! You're a nut. Wait a minute, this is a nuthouse. Of course you're a nut."

"I am not a nut."

"This is twentieth-century America, and you're talking about pharaohs and emperors and secret palaces. Of course you're a nut. And this is an asylum. Some crazy kind of asylum, but an asylum just the same. I can't believe you got me so worked up over a pipe dream."

So great was Buzz Kuttner's relief that he started laughing. It was a nervous laughter, and he let it go on a long time.

He never felt the bladelike fingernail that slipped easily into his back between two lumbar vertebrae, severing his spinal cord like a soft strand of spaghetti.

Buzz Kuttner was still laughing when he collapsed on the hard floor in the grit of shattered concrete. The laugh became breathy, then trailed off into a long exhalation and ending in a rattle that sounded like a broken continuation of his laughter.

After a silent minute the gaunt shadow returned to the room. He wore gray. His hair was white.

"Your will has been done, Emperor Smith," said the owner of the squeaky voice. He bowed slightly, and a slice of light captured a flash of orange silk whose pattern resembled the stripes of a Bengal tiger.

"Good. Please dispose of the body."

"Where?"

"The coal furnace. Place him inside."

"If it is your will."

"I would help, but I must get rid of the truck."

A gnarled yellow claw with fingernails like ivory blades gestured toward the array of mainframes and jukeboxes. "All has been accomplished to your satisfaction?"

"Yes," said Harold W. Smith. "CURE is now ready to enter the twenty-first century."

"And once you have returned, you and I will be ready to enter negotiations for further service between your house and mine," returned Chiun, Reigning Master of Sinanju.

2

His name was Remo, and he was whistling into the teeth of the hurricane.

The winds had been clocked at seventy-five miles per hour, and Remo was walking against them. He was whistling "The Wayward Wind," and he could hear every note over the growing roar.

The waters off Wilmington, North Carolina, were flat and oily in anticipation of Hurricane Elvis making landfall as Remo walked along the Wrightville Beach beachfront, where plywood sheets covered the windows of upscale summer homes and cottages. People had spray-painted messages to Elvis on the plywood.

"Elvis Go Home!"

"Elvis, You're All Wet!"

"Go Back Where You Came From!"

As if hurricanes cared.

There was a mandatory evacuation along the beachfront, and almost everyone had left. Except Roger Sherman Coe.

Roger Sherman Coe had elected to ride out the storm in his beachfront home. That was just like Roger Sherman Coe. The law meant nothing to him. The hurricane warning had been posted while Remo was en route to his rendezvous with Roger Sherman Coe. Remo had put a call to the man from his first-class seat on Flight 334.

"Is this Roger Sherman Coe?" Remo had asked.

"Yes."

"This is Bernard Rubble from the Federal Emergency Management Agency, Mr. Coe. We're calling all citizens in your area to personally alert them about Hurricane Elvis."

"I'm staying," Roger Sherman Coe had snapped.

"You're sure?"

"Absolutely."

"Suit yourself," said Remo, who had then hung up and tried to keep the first-class stewardess out of his lap. Stewardesses were that way around him.

Assured that Roger Sherman Coe was determined to ride out the storm in the security of his expensive home, Remo had driven his rental car from the Wilmington airport and walked the last mile toward the beach because the state highway patrol was turning back cars on the main approach road.

Remo hadn't minded walking. The fresh air was good for him. And because this was a simple assignment and he was in a good mood, he couldn't help whistling.

There were a lot of reasons for Remo's good mood, not the least of which was that the man who had taught him to whistle into the teeth of a hurricane had been recalled to headquarters. Remo didn't know the reason for it, and it didn't matter. All that mattered was he had a solid week without complaints about the neighbors, having old soap operas constantly on the television, and carping. Remo especially didn't miss the carping. It usually took the form of Remo being told he didn't truly appreciate the person doing the complaining. Remo's comeback was that he never appreciated people who complained all the time. This invariably produced more carping and led to Remo's pointing out that it was easier to appreciate another person when that person carped less.

So when Upstairs had called him with instructions about the Roger Sherman Coe assignment, Remo had been only too happy to oblige.

The wind plastered the black front of his T-shirt against his lean but muscular chest as Remo walked along the sand leaving no discernible footprints. He would have to think about it to leave footprints because leaving footprints had been drilled out of him.

His chinos, snug against his trim legs, were also black. His dark hair was too short for the wind to mess it up, not that Elvis wasn't trying. Remo leaned into the oncoming wall of wind, walking at a slight angle the way he had seen people on TV news reports trying to negotiate hurricane winds.

Surprisingly it worked for him. The skills that had been drilled into him had taught him not to do the obvious Western thing when confronted with forces greater than he. He was doing the obvious Western thing and he wondered what Chiun would say about that. Maybe the obvious Western thing was sometimes the right thing to do after all.

Remo had no more time to think about it because he had come to the beachfront house numbered forty-seven. That was the number he remembered, but because he had no head for figures or trivia he pulled a sheet of paper out of his chinos pocket and verified it. He had the right house. He let the hurricane winds whip the sheet of paper from his loosening fingers, and it skimmed away like a chattering paper ghost.

Remo shifted direction, walking toward the beachfront house. Now he was walking with one side to the wind. His body, which understood these things better than he, adjusted itself, and Remo found himself walking at an angle, like the hunchback in an old Frankenstein movie.

The weathered-shingle house of Roger Sherman Coe was boarded up like all the others. Unlike the others, there was no spray paint graffiti defiance marring the wobbling plywood sheets. Not that the hurricane cared one way or the other.

Remo knocked on the door. The knock was surprisingly loud for the force Remo seemed to exert. The door shook and the house shook with it.

Evidently Roger Sherman Coe thought it was only the hurricane knocking because he didn't answer on the first knock. So Remo knocked again.

This time Roger Sherman Coe answered. The door whipped inward, and he thrust a pale, lantern-jawed head out.

"Good afternoon," Remo said brightly.

"I'm not leaving. I'm staying. You can't make me go."

"I'm conducting a survey for the National Weather Service," said Remo. He smiled. The obvious Western thing would be to scowl. Scowls triggered the fear response and risked flight or retaliation. Smiles relaxed people—sometimes right into the boneyard.

The man looked incredulous. "In the middle of a hurricane?"

"Hurricanes tend to focus the mind," Remo assured Roger Sherman Coe. "We get better answers that way."

Roger Sherman Coe looked at Remo's empty fingers at the ends of his unusally thick wrists, and asked, "Where's your questionnaire?"

Remo tapped his head. "Up here. It's all up here."

Roger Sherman Coe just stared.

"First question," said Remo. "Do you approve of the National Weather Service's new naming system for hurricanes?"

"What?" shouted Roger Sherman Coe over the growing roar.

"Hurricane Elvis," Remo shouted back. "It's an experiment. After we saw how popular the post office was with the Elvis stamp, we thought we'd try it. You know, try to improve the popularity of tropical storms. Do you approve of Elvis as a hurricane name? Please answer yes or no."

"No! I don't approve of hurricanes at all."

"Good. Now, the National Weather Service hopes that Hurricane Elvis will be just the first of a new series of celebrity hurricanes. We're considering the following names for the rest of the hurricane season— Tropical Storm Roseanne, Hurricane Madonna and Hurricane Clint."

"Eastwood or Black?"

"Black. Country music is big again. Now, could you rank the choices in order of preference?"

"Look, I'd like to get through Elvis before worrying about the next blow, if it's all the same to you."

"Got it. Now, the obligatory sexual-preference question. Do you prefer hurricanes named after men or women?"

"I prefer no hurricanes!" Roger Sherman Coe shouted, trying to hold the door open. Remo wondered why the man didn't simply invite him in, and decided some people just didn't know when to come in out of a blow.

"That wasn't a trick question. I need a sexual preference."

"Girl hurricanes sound better. I grew up in girl hurricanes."

"Same here," said Remo.

"Are we done now?" asked Roger Sherman Coe, squinting against the wind that seemed not to bother Remo at all.

"Stay with me. Just a couple more questions."

"Make it fast!"

"What about building so close to the water on hurricane-active areas? If Elvis smashes this place down, do you think FEMA money should be used to rebuild?"

"FEMA is a joke."

"Tell it to the Midwest flood victims."

"I almost lost this place to Hugo."

"No wonder you prefer girl hurricanes."

"I prefer no hurricanes."

Elvis's wail was building now. It didn't have the freight-train roar that characterized a full-blown tropical storm, but it was coming. Remo knew he would have to wind this up.

"Do you have any next of kin?" he asked.

"Why does the National Weather Service care about that?" Roger Sherman Coe wanted to know.

"Because you're not going to survive Elvis," Remo said in a casual voice.

Roger Sherman Coe saw the lips of the pollster from the National Weather Service move, but didn't catch the words.

"What?" he shouted.

"Do you believe it's a dog-eat-dog world?" Remo shouted.

"What kind of fool question is that?"

"A direct one."

"Yeah, it's a dog-eat-dog world."

"So if you're a dog that eats other dogs, it's okay?"

"It's the way the world works."

"And if another dog, a bigger dog, decided to eat you, you can't really complain, can you?"

"Not if I barked first."

"You ain't nothin' but a hound dog," said Remo.

"What?" said Roger Sherman Coe.

"I just wanted to see if you understood why they sent me to take a bite out of you."

"I'm not following you," Roger Sherman Coe screamed into the growing blow.

"You're Roger Sherman Coe. Right?"

"Right."

"The Roger Sherman Coe who makes his living as a contract killer?"

"What?"

"Who burned down an entire house with the family in it so they wouldn't testify against the D'Ambrosia Family?"

"Are you crazy? You have the wrong man."

"Not according to the National Computer Crime Index," said Remo, lifting an innocent-looking hand. He made a fist but left his index finger sticking out. He was very casual about it—because that was the Eastern way—and that gave Roger Sherman Coe time to slam the door in Remo's face.

But not enough time to step back from the door.

They say a hurricane can drive a straw through a solid tree trunk. Remo didn't need a hurricane to back him. His right index finger shot through the panel and caught Roger Sherman Coe directly over the heart.

When Remo withdrew the finger, the door slid open and Roger Sherman Coe's jittering body fell with it. When he landed at Remo's feet, he was already dead. His heart had burst under the piston-like power of Remo's single finger.

The wind was pretty wild now, and Remo decided to leave the body where it lay, with the front door open. The hurricane would sweep right in, and with luck, when they found Roger Sherman Coe's body after it was all over, his death would be blamed on Elvis. An act of God would have killed Roger Sherman Coe and not a force of nature or a secret arm of the United States government that had decided a criminal of Roger Sherman Coe's caliber deserved the ultimate sanction.

Remo was walking away when he heard the tiny shriek.

He turned.

Standing in the doorway of the beachfront house was a little girl with sad brown eyes and dirty blond hair. She had a fist up to her mouth and she was saying "Daddy?" in an uncomprehending voice.

"What is it, April?" a woman's anxious voice demanded. And a tall blond woman stepped into the wind. Seeing the body, she pulled the little girl away from the door, then fell on the body, crying, "Roger. Roger. Get up. What's wrong, Roger?"

By that time Remo Williams had disappeared into the howling wind whose freight-train roar was not long in coming.

At the height of the storm, a state police helicopter spotted a man in a black T-shirt standing firm at the end of a stone jetty against the incoming wind. That was incredible enough.

The part that was astounding, and ultimately decided the pilot against reporting the sighting, was the way the man stood up to the gale. Especially when airborne driftwood and other debris snapped toward him. Each time he lifted an open hand or the tips of his shoes he smashed the wind-driven wood into splinters that were carried, whirling and harmless, away.

He looked angry. He looked very angry. A person would have to be very, very, very angry to take on Hurricane Elvis.

Strangest of all, it looked as if the guy was trying to protect a single beachfront house from destruction. And he was winning.

3

Dr. Harold W. Smith arrived in his office as dawn broke, nodded to his private secretary and carefully closed the door to his Spartan office, whose picture window of one-way glass overlooked the dead gray expanse of Long Island Sound. It was usually a sparkling blue dotted with white sails. Today it was gray and strange and flat.

There was a hurricane watch from Charleston, South Carolina, to Block Island. Elvis had glanced off Wilmington and now was prowling up the East Coast like a howling wolf, pushing ahead of it heavy, oppressive air and sullen clouds.

Harold W. Smith was not concerned about Hurricane Elvis as he settled in behind his shabby oak desk and for the last time touched the concealed stud that brought the blank glass face of his hidden desktop terminal humming from its well.

Harold W. Smith didn't know that he had executed that action—one he had performed almost daily for most of the thirty years he sat in the director's chair of Folcroft Sanitarium—for the final time. He simply logged on and initiated the virus-scanning program. It ran its cycle in less than six seconds and announced the new WORM arrays, as well as the old IDC mainframe tape drives, to be virus free.

It had been almost a week now since he had had the new XL SysCorp jukeboxes with their WORM drives installed in the basement of Folcroft Sanitarium, the nerve center for CURE, the organization he secretly headed.

So far, Smith was pleased. It was rare for Harold W. Smith to be pleased about anything. He was a gray individual to whose dry, patrician visage smiles did not easily come. No smile actually touched his thin lips this morning. Something tugged at the corners, but only someone who had known Harold Smith all his life could have recognized the faintly constipated grimace as an expression of pleasure.

It had been a long, long time since Harold W. Smith had upgraded the CURE computer system. He had put it together himself, back in the early days of CURE, the government agency that offically did not exist.

Originally there was just one mainframe. Over time others had to be added. And other innovations had forced upgrades.

There was a time when, for security reasons, printouts slithered by under a desktop glass panel to a shredder, but even paper that existed for no more than sixty seconds before being committed to memory and shredded for consignment to the oblivion of the basement coal furnace represented a security risk. And so Harold W. Smith had pioneered the paperless office. The four great basement mainframes alongside the new optical jukeboxes were connected with Smith's desk terminal through the shielded standpipe, and no printer was dedicated to print its secrets.

When the Pentagon's Advanced Research Projects Agency created the first computer network, ARPAnet, by wiring thirty-two high-powered computers together by phone link in the early 1960s, not even the Joint Chiefs of Staff suspected there was a thirty-third system involved and Harold Smith was an unsuspected eavesdropper on all that was said and done.

When data transfer by phone wire took off in the early 1970s, it was old news to Harold W. Smith. He had been doing it since the inception of CURE.

When fiber-optic cable came in, the term *multiplexing* was already in Smith's vocabulary.

When the PC invaded the home market and America began dialing up bulletin boards, information services and other networks, Harold W. Smith had not only been there before, but his powerful mainframes continually trolled the net, gathering information for storage and eventual security analysis.

When a remarkable new software called Windows came on the market, Harold W. Smith never bothered to read about it. His version, called Doors, was ten years ahead of Windows five years before there was a Windows.

When on-screen technology brought in digital imaging, pull-down menus and other high-tech features, Harold W. Smith was already there. His monochrome terminal normally displayed green text against a black screen because it was more restful to his overtaxed gray eyes, but a touch of a key transformed it into a color monitor that could bring in TV signals. This feature was only now coming onto the commercial market, but Harold W. Smith had had the capability for years.

Now ARPAnet had mushroomed into Internet, and half of America was sifting through the mountains of hard information and soft trivia carried along the phone and cable wires.

The way Harold W. Smith saw it, he was one of the first hikers on the information superhighway back when it was the electronic equivalent of a unlit dirt road.

But lately the net had grown too large and too diverse, and the old Folcroft Four, although perfectly adapted to the mission of CURE, were no longer enough. Thus Smith had been forced to seek out a new high-performance system to augment the old. It had not been difficult. There was a ready black market in stolen information systems out there. Stolen was important. Folcroft, a private hospital, had not yet come into the information age. It would be awkward to acquire such powerful machines through its purchasing office. CURE had a vast operating budget, but it was a black budget, and unusual Folcroft purchases—especially large ones—would have to be explained to the AMA or the IRS.

And so Harold W. Smith had made a hushed call to a furtive purveyor of pilfered information systems, arranged a midnight rendezvous, overseen installation of the new equipment in the basement of a nonexistent asylum and, when it was all over with, had instructed the termination of the only security risk involved in the transaction. It had been unpleasant but absolutely necessary. Buzz Kuttner had given his life for his country—he just never knew it.

When CURE had been set up in the early 1960s, its mandate was very clear and very dangerous. Locate and eliminate threats to U.S. security, both domestic and foreign. It had been a lawless time, one calling for extreme measures. The President who had laid the problem before Harold W. Smith, a faceless CIA computer programmer whose background check showed him to be the only man the beleaguered chief executive could trust with the job, had explained it this way: democracy was not working. Corruption on all levels, combined with threats from the extremists on both sides of the political spectrum, threatened to sink the glorious experiment that was America. If this went on, the President had said solemnly, he might have to suspend constitutional liberties for the duration of the crisis—probably the remainder of the century—and rule by decree under martial law.

It would have been the end of the United States of America. Both men knew it.

So when the President—only months away from being struck down by an assassin's bullet—told Harold W. Smith about CURE, an autonomous secret agency sanctioned to circumvent constitutional restrictions to put America's social house back in order, Harold Smith saw the wisdom of it. He became the first and only director of CURE—not an acronym, but a prescription of a sick society.

Above the law, independent of the executive branch and licensed to neutralize anyone who was deemed a threat to America's continued survival, Harold Smith of the Vermont Smiths had run CURE in its first decade purely as an information-gathering agency. Enforcement was up to the justice system, which Smith frequently set on malefactors by anonymous tips and surreptitiously guided public exposure.

But as the justice system began to unravel during that turbulent decade and lawlessness only grew, Smith received Presidential sanction to kill.

It was a job that required a combination secret police and Superman, Smith knew. He also understood that CURE would not long remain a secret if he employed an army of agents. He found his solution in the legends of the House of Sinanju, an ancient guild of assassins who had for three thousand years protected thrones from Egypt to Rome. Every century or so the Master of Sinanju trained his successor in the sun source—so-called because it was the first and most potent of the martial arts, from which everything from kung fu to tae kwon do came.

Smith had sent an emissary to the fishing village of Sinanju on the bitter coast of western North Korea and recruited Chiun, the last Master of Sinanju, to train a white man in the ancient assassin's discipline.

Smith had already chosen his one-man enforcement arm in an ex-Marine turned beat cop. Remo Williams was an unmarried orphan whose cool killer instincts had been proved in the jungles of Vietnam, and it had been a simple matter to frame him for a killing he never committed and, by manipulating a corrupt judicial system, railroad him to the death house.

Over the years Remo Williams, code-named the Destroyer, had operated secretly, trained and guided by

Master Chiun, destroying America's enemies. They had performed effectively and ruthlessly, if sometimes messily.

Somehow, through it all, Harold Smith, CURE and America had survived.

Still, when it came down to it, Smith preferred his computers. They were tireless, efficient, predictable and virtually infallible. Best of all, they never asked for cost-of-living raises or vacations.

And now the new hybrid system promised to increase his data storage and outreach exponentially.

So far, all Harold Smith noticed was a marked increase in response time and ease of handling. The familiar plastic keys of the foldout keyboard brought information to his gray eyes at the slightest touch. But for an aging man who had toiled behind this desk for three decades managing the ultimate firebreak of American democracy as his eyesight steadily worsened, any improvement in capability was a godsend.

A faint breeze touched Smith's face, and he looked up in alarm, one finger flashing to the stud that would send the CURE terminal dropping from sight.

Standing before the closing door was the Master of Sinanju. He stood barely five feet tall, a little mummy of a Korean wrapped in a white linen kimono resembling a death shroud and no hair on his skull except a cloudy puff over each ear.

"Master Chiun!" Smith said. "Er, I did not hear my secretary announce you."

Chiun bowed slightly, his parchment features crinkling into a web of wise wrinkles.

"That is because she did not see or hear me pass her station," Chiun said in his squeaky voice, often querulous but now purring with good humor. "For what benefit to the Eagle Throne is an assassin who cannot enter his emperor's inner chambers unseen and undetected?"

Harold Smith swallowed his objection. If the President who had founded CURE could look down from the next life and see his handpicked director being addressed as "Emperor," he would have concluded he had given over the reins of ultimate power to a dangerous megalomaniac. The truth was that Chiun had taken to addressing Smith that way because the House of Sinanju had always worked for absolute rulers, and to act otherwise would mean risking the wrath of his Korean ancestors who might also be looking on from the next life.

"I see," said Smith. He adjusted his hunter green Dartmouth tie, the only spot of color in his otherwise gray wardrobe. Smith's suit, hair and even his face were all shades of gray. Adjusting his rimless eyeglasses, he went on.

"You have looked over our contract?"

"Yes."

"And it meets your approval?"

"The gold is no more than it was last year."

Smith repressed an inward groan. "We have discussed this," he said.

"We have discussed this," Chiun said, his voice growing thin, "but it has not been properly explained to me how it is that the greatest house of assassins in history is not entitled to increased compensation."

Smith did not remind the Master of Sinanju that the matter of the gold that was to be shipped to his village by submarine had not only been explained, but explained in exhaustive detail. Instead, he said with more patience than he felt, "We have a very great deficit in this country. An increase in the gold is impossible this year."

"But the next?"

"Next year is possible. Theoretically."

"If it is possible next year, why not this year? I would gladly forgo a significant raise next year for a modest one this year."

Smith blinked in the face of a flash of déjù vu. He was certain Chiun had spoken those exact words last year. He had got around it by providing a home for Chiun and Remo to live in.

"I am very sorry, it simply is not possible this year, and I cannot promise for next. But by waiting a year, the odds increase."

"It is the fault of the new President, is it not? The flint-skinned Democrat."

"The President is under great pressure from Congress and the electorate to slash the federal operating budget."

Chiun slipped up to the desk and pitched his voice low. "Perhaps it would be better for all of us if the stubborn Congress and insensitive electorates all die."

"Congress," Smith tried to explain, "in fact raises the money that enables America to pay you so handsomely. And the electorate are the taxpayers who give their money."

"Then let taxes be raised," Chiun cried, flinging one fist into the air.

"The President is under great pressure not to raise taxes any further," Smith countered.

"I am willing to accept campaign donations. Remo could go door-to-door on your behalf. I am certain he would not mind."

"Impossible."

Chiun flinched as if stung. "That is your final offer?"

"I am afraid so."

Chiun closed his clear hazel eyes. One old ivory hand lifted to brush at the tendril of a beard that clung to his tiny chin. He seemed to be thinking, but Smith knew otherwise. The old Korean was simply trying to psych him out.

Harold Smith had been through all this before. This time he was prepared. "I took the liberty of arranging for the submarine carrying your gold to depart for Sinanju, in anticipation of our coming to an understanding," Smith said in a neutral voice.

Chiun said nothing.

"If I was premature, I will need to know at once," Smith added. "It is very expensive to send a nuclear submarine across the Pacific Ocean without a mission."

Eyes still closed, Chiun remained still and unspeaking.

At length, his eyes popped open, and in a sorrowful voice the Master of Sinanju intoned, "I have a village to support. If some of the babies must be drowned in the cold waters of the West Korea Bay because the food is insufficient, so be it. I will instruct the village care-taker to spare the male children, and do away only with the surplus females.''

And the Master of Sinanju cocked a cold eye to-ward Harold Smith.

Smith wasn't buying. "I am certain it will not come to that," he said.

"If it does, you will be the first to know," Chiun re-turned in a chilly tone.

"If there is no other business, I will be happy to confirm the arrangements to ship the gold to Sin-anju," Smith offered, making a point of touching one of the telephones on his desk.

The Master of Sinanju hesitated. "We will have the formal signing of contracts this evening?" he asked at last.

"As you wish," said Smith, repressing a smile. He had been forced to send the submarine two days ago because it was the only launch window he had for the next two months. If the gold was not in the village of Sinanju on time, Chiun—and for all he knew, Remo—would refuse all assignments until delivery was made.

It was a gamble the parsimonious Smith had been loath to make, and he breathed an inward sign of re-lief that all had turned out. Perhaps, Smith thought, he was getting the hang of negotiating with the Master of Sinanju.

At his elbow a telephone rang. It was the blue con-tact telephone. Smith brought the receiver to his ear before the second ring could start.

"Yes, Remo?"

"I've had it."

"What?" squeaked Chiun, rushing to the desk.

"Is that Chiun?" Remo demanded.

"Yes," said Smith. "He is here with me. We have just concluded negotiations for another year of service."

"Well, I hope you and he will be very happy together, because I've had it with these piss-ant hits. Count me out."

Smith clapped his hand on the receiver mouthpiece and said, "Remo seems to be trying to resign. What do you know about this?"

"I know he is obligated to me for his every breath," snapped Chiun, snatching the receiver from Smith's hand. "Remo, stop behaving like a child. Speak! What is wrong with you?"

"From now on I only take assignments I agree with," Remo said tightly.

"This is blasphemy. You accept whatever assignments your emperor deems worthy of you."

"Change in plan. You can have my rejects."

"Remo, what has gotten into you? Think of the poor babies of Sinanju who look to you for sustenance."

"I'm thinking of the little girl I orphaned tonight. No more. From now on I see background checks on my hits. You tell that to Smith."

And the line went dead.

4

Harold W. Smith had already initiated the callback trace program before Remo could hang up. The new system offered up the number and location of the phone from which Remo Williams had called as if Smith had simply wished for it.

Smith hit a function key, and the number was automatically dialed through his blue contact telephone.

"Yeah?" Remo said when he picked up. His voice was unhappy.

"This is Smith."

"Don't tell me you bugged my B.V.D.'s," Remo said sourly.

"Hardly. My new computer system traced your call. You are at the Wilmington, North Carolina, Holiday Inn, I see."

"I'd be on the first flight out of here except Hurricane Elvis has the airport shut down," Remo growled. "Next time you send me to terminate a guy, make sure his wife and kid aren't hanging around."

"Are you referring to the Roger Sherman Coe matter?" asked Smith.

"No," said Remo. "I just did David Cassidy, and the entire Partridge Family is up in arms."

Smith cleared his throat to cover his confusion. "I don't quite follow—"

"Follow this. I found Coe right where you said, and I took him out just like you wanted. Only as I was walking away, his wife and daughter popped out in time to see him breathe his last."

Smith sipped a sharp intake of breath. "You were not seen, were you?"

"Forget security. Listen to me, I did a guy in front of his wife and daughter. I made that little girl an orphan. You know what that means? No, you wouldn't, you cold-blooded fossil. Well, I know what it means. I grew up in an orphanage. I wouldn't wish that kind of childhood on anyone. You know what my Christmases were like?"

Harold Smith cradled the receiver against a gray shoulder and attacked his keyboard. The plastic clicking of the keys sounded like hollow dice rattling.

"Are you listening to me, Smith?" Remo said angrily.

"Yes, I am pulling up Coe's file."

"He's dead. Why bother?"

"Because I do not recall him having a wife or daughter."

"Well, he does. I can vouch for that because I just spent the past three hours standing on the frigging beach protecting them and their house from Hurricane Elvis."

Harold Smith didn't respond. He was moving digital packets of data at high speed, his face tight with concentration. The Master of Sinanju hovered nearby, his features anxious.

At length Smith gave out a dry groan.

"What?" said Remo.

"What is it?" said Chiun.

"Remo," Smith said in a low, horrified voice, "are you certain you had the correct house?"

"I went to the number you gave me."

"What number?"

"Forty-seven, I think."

"Think! You were supposed to write it down."

"I did. I threw away the paper after I was done. It was 47 Ocean Street. Yeah, I'm sure of it now."

"That is the correct address of Roger Sherman Coe. Did you ask him his name?"

"I'm a Master of Sinanju. I know enough to identify a target before I do him."

"Hear! Hear!" said Chiun.

"And he identified himself as Roger Sherman Coe?" Smith pressed.

"Yes."

"Something is wrong," Smith said hoarsely. "Something is very wrong. According to my data base, Roger Sherman Coe is not and never has been married. In fact, he is a homosexual."

"Then he deserved to die," said Chiun loudly. "Hobosexualism is a despicable crime—unless one is a soldier in the U.S. Marines."

"The Roger Sherman Coe I killed had a wife and daughter," insisted Remo. "She couldn't have been more than five years old."

"The Roger Sherman Coe on my data base in fifty-six years old, red haired, and has committed an estimated sixteen contract killings that have been tied to him.''

''This guy was on the sunny side of forty.''

''Oh, my God. You may have killed the wrong man.''

''Smith, don't say that. Don't tell me that. Making a widow and an orphan is bad enough, but don't tell me I hit the wrong guy.''

Chiun bustled up to the telephone. ''Remo, take heart. If a mistake was made, it falls not on your shoulders.'' Then, in an urgent voice, Chiun added for Smith's benefit, ''Take responsibility. Quickly. Remo is in a very fragile state of mind. We must not lose him to this tragedy.''

''But my computers do not make mistakes,'' Smith said dully.

''Yeah? Well, they did this time,'' Remo Williams said bitterly. ''Thanks a lot, Smith. Remember what I said earlier about picking my assignments? Cancel that. I quit. I'm through. Take CURE and shove it up your tight New England ass.''

''Remo, you do not mean that!'' Chiun wailed, seizing the phone. ''Tell Emperor Smith you did not mean that! Smith, do not sit there like a ghost-faced white. Say something to absolve my son and my heir of this terrible guilt that overwhelms him.''

''Stuff it,'' said Remo. And he hung up again.

Harold Smith sat in his cracked leather executive's chair and stared into space. He seemed oblivious to the buzz of the dial tone in his ear. He seemed oblivious to the Master of Sinanju as he tore at the puffs of hair over each ear and paced the room in frustration.

"My contract! That implusive white idiot has ruined a perfect negotiation," Chiun wailed.

And all Harold W. Smith could do was mutter as if to himself, "My computers have never been wrong before. Never."

He sounded like a man who had lost faith in the sanity and order of the known universe.

If he was aware of the Master of Sinanju leaving his office, it was not reflected in his shell-shocked face.

5

Hurricane Elvis had skirted Long Island, started out to sea and run into a cold-air mass that stalled it thirty miles out in the Atlantic. It couldn't go forward. Unable to go back, it festered over the water, churning up ocean brine and recycling it as hard, bitter rain that flattened spirits and human activity from Eastport to Block Island.

One by one airports up and down the affected area reopened, and Remo Williams was on the first flight out of Wilmington. Maybe it was the dampening effects of the overcast skies and the relentless rain, or maybe it was the hard scowl he wore on his face, but the stewardesses all left him alone during the short flight to Boston.

At Logan Airport Remo recovered his car and drove south to Quincy, Massachusetts, and home.

Home had long been an unknown concept to Remo Williams. In his pre-CURE days, a succession of walk-up flats in Newark, New Jersey, and after that, motel rooms and hotels all over the U.S., had served as temporary residences. Every time he and Chiun had settled down in a condo or a house, security considerations beyond their control drove them out.

For the past year home had been what Remo mentally thought of as a Swiss/Gothic/mock-Tudor stone church converted into a condominium. Chiun had dubbed it Castle Sinanju. It looked enough like a castle that at the last contract negotiation, Smith had been able to foist it off on the Master of Sinanju as a pre-Revolutionary War American castle. And Chiun had happily accepted it. Remo had not. But he had grown to enjoy having its sixteen units and accompanying parking spaces all to Chiun and himself.

Now Remo thought of it as home, and in his pain, it was where he was retreating to.

Chiun would not be home. Knowing the Master of Sinanju, he would be on his way to Wilmington to talk sense to him. Remo didn't want to talk to anyone right now. He just wanted to be alone. He just wanted to think. He had a lot of serious sorting out to do.

As he sent his blue Buick coupe into the handicapped parking slot, Remo thought of how for the past twenty years of his life he had been pulled in two opposing directions. There was his duty to CURE and his country. And there was his growing and unwanted responsibility to Chiun and the House of Sinanju that he would one day inherit. He used to feel good about being the first white man to master Sinanju, but as he unlocked his front door, he felt only a cold emptiness in the pit of his stomach.

The inner door surrendered to his key, and he stepped in.

Instantly his senses, numbed by his grief, came alive.

Someone was in the building.

His highly attuned ears telling him that no one was on the ground floor, Remo floated up the stairs. On the second floor the distant heartbeat clarified. He did not recognize it. But the second floor was empty. So was the third.

That left only the tower. The church, when it had been a church, had had a crenellated square tower instead of a steeple. Each face was dominated by a great window facing the four compass points.

A flight of steps led up to this space.

Remo went up like a ghost in a tight black shroud, making no sound, giving forth no scent of fear or other warning of his approach.

If it was a burglar, he was going to be one sorry burglar.

The door was ajar. Remo moved off the top step and without pausing went through the door, ready to meet any threat.

Except the one that grasped the exposed front of his T-shirt and used his forward momentum to propel him across the room and into one of the great windows.

Caught off guard, Remo came off his feet and literally flew acoss the space, headfirst.

His training kicked in then. There was nothing to grab in flight to arrest him. The windows were too wide for Remo to splay his arms and legs and catch the edges.

So he closed his eyes and willed his body full of air until he felt light in every bone, soft as a pillow and weighing no more than a marshmallow.

He bounced off the glass with no more sound than a nerf ball rebounding off glass. Landing in a crouch, he snapped to his feet, hands jutting like spear points.

"You entered like a water buffalo blundering into quicksand," a cold voice said.

"Huh?"

"But you acquitted yourself in the end. You entered western and you preserved your life by the Eastern way. A balance has been struck, and given the circumstances, neither blame nor shame will attach themselves to you."

"Chiun," Remo breathed, straightening to his full height. "I don't get it. That wasn't your heartbeat I heard."

"Nor was that the Remo I trained whom I flung like a soggy sack of potatoes," countered the Master of Sinanju. "But the Remo who made his body the consistency of a feather—that is the Remo I trained."

"You screwed around with your heartbeat."

Chiun nodded slightly. "Inelegantly put. But accurately put."

Chiun regarded him with opaque eyes as his hands came together, fingers wrapping around the opposite wrists and the wide sleeves of his tiger-stripe kimono coming together to hide all from view.

Two tatami mats had been placed in the center of the room. Chiun indicated them with a tipping of his bearded chin.

"If you will sit, I will sit with you," he offered.

Remo hesitated.

"I came here to be alone."

' "You came here thinking your teacher was a fool who would chase you to the far provinces of this backward land."

"I wouldn't have come here if I'd known you'd beat me back."

"I do not expect gratitude from an ingrate, but I would not dismiss a compliment directed at my foresight."

Remo folded his lean arms. "Okay, you were way ahead of me. Big deal."

"I will always be ahead of you, Remo Williams. And that is a very big deal. Now sit."

Face hard, Remo stepped up to his mat. Chiun did the same. In unison they crossed their ankles and scissored their legs down into the classic lotus position. They faced each other, spines erect, heads up, eyes locked without outward expression, the Reigning Master of Sinanju and his rightful heir and pupil. Two cultures, two worlds and two sets of conflicting responsibilities between them.

"Great pain, like a cruel raven, has set its talons into your heart, my son," began Chiun.

Remo hung his head. "I killed the wrong man. Practically in front of his family."

Chiun nodded sadly. "This is a tragedy. For them and for you."

"No matter what I do, I can't take it back."

"We give death. Like our best strikes and blows, they can never be taken back once unleashed."

"I don't know if I can do this anymore."

"Mourn?"

"No. Kill."

Chiun wrinkled up his parchment face. "You do not kill. Any fool can kill. Amateurs kill. Soldiers kill. Executioners kill. We dispense correctness. If an evil man vexes a kingdom and there is no army or soldier capable of ending this evil, we are the remedy."

"You sound like Smith."

"All men die in their time. The man you dispatched may have died in his rightful time or ahead of his time. In two, three hundred years, who will know or care?"

"I will. I robbed him of life, of the chance to see his daughter grow up. I ruined the rest of his wife's life."

"Perhaps they will all be reunited in their next life."

"Don't run that reincarnation crap past me. I had a bellyful of it last time out."

Chiun allowed his clear eyes to close briefly. "We will not speak of your last assignment. It ended badly. We are not perfect. Not when we work for whites."

Chiun's bony fingers tightened and came to rest on the draped knobs of his knees. He was silent.

Remo was silent. They stared at each other, faces unreadable.

"What do you wish to do?"

"I'm through with the organization."

"Over one mishap?"

"Twenty years is enough. Smith took from me what I took from that guy, Coe. His life. The only difference is I'm still above ground. But I never got my old life back."

"You wish to be a policeman again?"

"I want . . . I don't know what I want. My old life wasn't great. I was going nowhere unless it was toward a desk sergeant's post and early retirement."

"I see," said Chiun.

The gray light of the day filtered through the four high windows, washing out the color of their faces. They might have been two stone idols facing each other down through an eternity of unresolved pain.

"It is Smith's mistake," said Chiun. "You must understand this fully. You were the instrument of his error, but the error was his. You cannot lose sight of that. You are a sword, and a sword has no conscience."

"Let someone else be Smith's sword."

Chiun was silent. At length he said, "I have entered into a new agreement with Smith."

"You sign it?"

Chiun hesitated. "No," he said. And Remo was surprised. He was sure Chiun was going to fib.

"Then don't," said Remo.

"I must. Emperor Smith is the only emperor worthy of us in these evil modern days."

"What evil days?"

"There is peace breaking out everywhere."

"There are dozens of brush-fire wars going on."

"Mere incidents. The Russian Empire is no more. China wallows in making money, and Persia has sunk into religious anarchy. I am too young to retire."

"You're one hundred plus."

"And my village needs me. If you will not agree to another year's service, I must do so alone."

Chiun paused. Remo looked at him suspiciously. Always in the past the Master of Sinanju had found ways to manipulate Remo through trickery, sympathy or plain guile. But Chiun seemed sincere, almost resigned, to Remo's decision.

"Leave me out of the contract," said Remo.

Chiun stiffened a little, but his face betrayed no pain. His hazel eyes lifted slightly as if seeking his ancestors above.

"I will do this because it is my duty. Perhaps when your pain is less, my son, you will see things differently."

"Don't count on it."

"I will not," said the Master of Sinanju. Abruptly he came to his feet and departed the room.

Remo stared after him as he slipped down the tower steps, trying to read his body language. He couldn't.

Alone in his personal darkness, Remo Williams let out a slow, hot sigh that welled up from the hurtful knot in the deepest pit of his stomach.

His life would never be the same again, he knew.

And the knowledge made his throat constrict painfully.

HAROLD W. SMITH'S age-gnarled fingers trembled above the gray rows of keyboard keys as he prepared to plunge into that invisible universe of electronic data some called the net, others called cyberspace but to Harold Smith was such familiar territory it never occurred to him to give it a name.

And if it had, he would have been stumped.

One of the reasons the President who had conceived CURE had selected Harold Smith to head it up was a disarmingly simple one: Harold Smith was a man utterly without imagination. This quality was just as important a qualification as Smith's rock-ribbed patriotism and his unimpeachable rectitude of character.

Only a man completely honest and devoted to his country could be considered to head up CURE. But only a man hopelessly lacking in imagination could handle the job in the long term and not begin to consider taking over the nation. For CURE was almost autonomous. The President of the United States could suggest, but not order, missions. Unlike the executive branch, Harold Smith wielded ultimate power to exert his will. There was no congressional oversight, no budgetary restrictions beyond the limits of his yearly operating fund, and no voter or special-interest group could recall, impeach or abrogate Smith's office.

The President had only one recourse if CURE should exceed its mandate. He could order Smith to shut down. Smith understood that to mean erasing his computers utterly and himself personally. He kept a poison pill in the watch pocket of his vest for that purpose. Remo would likewise be disposed of, and the Master of Sinanju sent back to Korea. CURE would cease to exist as completely as if it had never been created in the first place.

Only America's survival would stand as evidence of a job well done. But only the most recent President would know.

Smith understood that only the threat of exposure or his own failure of mind or body could trigger that order. In the beginning he had hoped that CURE could fulfill its mission in his lifetime, allowing him to slip into the obscurity of retirement. That comforting fantasy had long ago died. CURE would perish with Harold Smith—unless the President elected to install a successor in his chair.

There had been failures in the past. Their most recent mission, to rescue an American actress who had been deluded into believing she was the reincarnation of Tibet's Bunji Lama, had gone badly. Remo had been sent to pull her out alive and head off an open revolt, but the actress had been killed by Chinese agents. U.S.-China relations were strained as a result, and the President had expressed his extreme disapproval to Harold Smith personally. The actress had been a close personal friend of the First Lady.

The distressing matter of Roger Sherman Coe had come at a difficult time. The President had already cut CURE's operating budget by a serious fifteen percent. Other cuts were threatened.

More ominously the Commander in Chief was now threatening to put CURE on deep-standby status.

But it was not any of this that caused Harold Smith to reach into a desk drawer, uncap a bottle of aspirin, tear open two foil packets of Bromo-Seltzer and plunk all four tablets into a paper cup of spring water before drinking down the bitter, fizzy concoction in one face-contorting gulp.

He would have to report this matter to the President. There was no avoiding it.

In the big picture the death of Roger Sherman Coe was not significant. CURE was not perfect. God knew that Remo and Chiun had made mistakes in the past, and casualties had resulted. That was not the problem.

Smith had ordered the man's death based upon an automated computer program designed to rove cyberspace for leads on elusive criminals. Roger Sherman Coe's name had bubbled up during one such search. Smith had checked the facts and determined that the Roger Sherman Coe in Wilmington, North Carolina, was the same Roger Sherman Coe listed on the National Computer Crime Index as a wanted felon. Ordering Remo to terminate the man was routine. Smith issued such instructions often and gave them no thought afterward. He had ultimate faith in his computers, their data bases and his software.

Someone or something had made a mistake. If it was not Remo, then it was either Smith or his computers. If it was Smith, it could mean he was reaching the upper limits of his ability to do his job. If it was the system, then CURE was finished.

So it was with trembling fingers that Harold Smith prepared to plunge into cyberspace to seek answers he would rather not know.

But because he was Harold Smith, he did not hesitate to go after them.

First he called up the National Computer Crime Index. Not the data base in Washington, but his own copy. Smith had downloaded it onto one of the WORM arrays after the new hybrid system went on line, along the entire Social Security database, IRS files and other important repositories of information. No longer would he be dependent on phone lines and his ability to infiltrate protected government files to do the work of CURE. New electronic-privacy laws before Congress, if passed, would not impede his work.

The particulars on Roger Sherman Coe were as Smith remembered them. A fiftyish man with red hair. Satisfied that his memory had not betrayed him, Smith next asked his computer to check the name Roger Sherman Coe against current news feeds and wire service reports. In the aftermath of Hurricane Elvis, the casualty reports had no doubt begun to trickle in.

Smith expected a several-minute delay, and he was pleasantly surprised when he got a scrolling transcript right off the wire.

The report was brief. The body of Roger Sherman Coe, thirty-six, of Wilmington, North Carolina, had been extracted from his beachfront home, along with his surviving family, Sally, thirty-three, and April, five. According to Coe's wife, rather than evacuate, the family had elected to tough out the storm in a rein-forced bedroom. But a strange noise had brought Coe out to investigate. When he failed to return, Sally Coe had gone to check on her husband's whereabouts only to find him sprawled in the open door of the home, dying, without a mark on him, but a hole punched through the door.

A preliminary report cited heart failure as the cause of death. The hole in the door was blamed on a piece of storm-driven debris.

The only remarkable circumstance, according to the report, was the fact that of the beachfront properties on Ocean Street, only the Coe house had come through unscathed but for the damage to the door. Every other house along the beach for a mile in either direction had been destroyed or washed out to sea.

It was being called the Miracle of Elvis.

"Remo," Smith said softly. "He protected the house."

Smith logged off the wire services, his face growing long. If the facts were as he had them, then the Roger Sherman Coe who had died at the height of Hurricane Elvis was not the same Roger Sherman Coe who was listed on NCCI.

Smith next pulled up Roger Sherman Coe's Social Security file and ran a comparison program with the NCCI data. He knew what he would find. He had done the identical cross-check at the start of the assignment.

The files matched. The same Social Security number was present. Other statistics matched, except for age, marital status and Remo's description of hair color. One Roger Sherman Coe was a redhead. The other was black haired.

But hair dye and plastic surgery could explain those discrepancies. And a common-law marriage could be converted to a legal one virtually overnight. The little girl might easily have been the product of a previous marriage, and would not show up on the NCCI file.

Lips compressing to a thin bloodless line, Smith plunged deeper. Perhaps they were one after all. The answer lay in his vast data base.

And if not, then beyond. On the net. In cyberspace.

6

Hurricane Elvis died in mid-Atlantic, his fury spent. Only a steady rain remained of his incredibly destructive force.

Remo Williams walked the sandy part of Wollaston Beach, not far from his house, oblivious to the rain. It was a warm rain, and the wind off Quincy Bay was unseasonably cool. He felt neither.

Second to Chiun, he was the most powerful human being to walk the earth in modern times. He didn't feel that, either.

All he felt was numb. Empty and numb.

As he walked along the beach with the pattering rain knocking tiny craters in the sand, Remo took stock of his life.

He looked ten years younger than his actual age, thanks to Sinanju. He could have any woman he wanted, thanks to Sinanju. There was no feat of skill a human being could accomplish that Remo couldn't do, thanks to Sinanju.

He breathed with his entire body, saw with every sense fully and, unless violent death caught up to him, he could expect to live a hundred years easily, or more. All thanks to Sinanju.

The gifts the Master of Sinanju had bestowed on him were staggering.

Oh, there were drawbacks. He couldn't eat meat, processed foods, drink alcohol or smoke cigarettes. But these days he didn't miss any of that. And after the first few years of having any woman he could want, that began to bore him, too. Women reacted to the confident rhythym of his walk, the graceful harmony of every bone and muscle operating to the peak of perfection, just as nature had intended, or to the irresistible pheromone scents he gave off without realizing it. They didn't come on to Remo because he was good-looking, or a nice guy, or honest or because they thought he'd make a caring lover or faithful husband. It was raw sex.

All his life Remo had been looking for love. He had found it in a way in an elderly Korean who treated him with a harshness that sounded like scorn but was really love.

He owed Chiun everything.

But in a way Remo had nothing. No wife, no family. And his job was something he couldn't even whisper to his most intimate lover. If he had one, that is.

There had to be more to life than this. It had taken the death of Roger Sherman Coe to bring it home to Remo.

Twenty years of being America's secret assassin had not made America a better place to live. The schools had become shooting galleries, the streets were ruled by fear and drugs and automatic weapons. Even the nation's capital had become ungovernable short of declaring martial law.

Chiun had always warned Remo that America was doomed. Relying on rule of, by and for the people was folly. What America needed was an emperor, Chiun had always said. Otherwise, it would slip into mob rule. Chiun had insisted America would slip into oblivion anyway. All empires did, ultimately. It was just happening faster here because idiots ran things.

It sometimes seemed that way to Remo. Successive Presidents had been hamstrung by the press and Congress, and it would take mandatory testing to convince Remo that Congress itself wasn't on drugs. America wasn't going forward into the next century. It wasn't even standing still. It was unraveling.

Remo could wash his hands of it without a second thought.

Except for Chiun. Chiun would hector him into an early grave, play on his sympathies and, all else failing, rain guilt down on his head the way the weakening ghost of Elvis was raining on him now, if Remo walked away from the latest contract.

Maybe, Remo thought, it was time to put some distance between himself and the Master of Sinanju. The thought made him cringe inwardly. Chiun had been like a father to him. More than a father, really. But his training was over. He had mastered Sinanju now. Maybe, Remo thought as he looked out over the rain-dimpled bay, it was time to make a clean break with everything. Maybe he needed to find himself, make some decisions that had nothing to do with CURE's mission, America's needs or a tiny fishing village in North Korea that hadn't changed in the three thousand years since it had first sent its sons out into the world to kill in support of its people.

Maybe it was time to stand on his own feet and live his own life. If Chiun cared about him, he would understand that. He had been young himself once, seventy or eighty years ago.

Remo had reached the rocky end of the beach as he came to his decision. He kept walking, his soft Italian leather loafers finding and pushing him along the great granite blocks that had been placed there to hold back the relentless erosion of the Atlantic. He felt the obdurate hardness of the stone even through his leather soles, and it seemed to suggest the rockiness of the path he was about to set out on.

Remo stopped on one of the largest stones. He looked down. Where others saw hard granite, he saw a flawed chunk of the earth's mantle. There were chisel marks at the edges where it had been cleaved from the old Quincy quarries untold generations ago and dressed into a rough oblong. It had rested on this beach since before Remo had been born, and even Hurricane Nornan couldn't move it.

With his left foot Remo traced circular patterns in the stone face, sensed a weak point and without any further thought dropped to one knee, bringing the flat edge of his right hand in contact with the weak spot.

Flesh met granite, and a sharp crack like a peal of thunder resulted.

With a grinding separation, the granite cube split along a perfect line. The two sections fell away from each other, and Remo leaped onto the next stone.

If nothing better came along, he could work as a stonecutter, Remo thought wryly.

The wry grin faded from his face when a squeaky voice called out his name.

"Remo! Is that you?"

"Chiun?"

BEYOND the sprinkling of stones, near a shaded beachfront park, the Master of Sinanju lifted his bird-like head. He was seated on a bench. Spying Remo, he flung the remnants of popcorn to the wheeling cormorants and sea gulls he had been feeding.

The Master of Sinanju crushed the popcorn container into a ball, and it disappeared up one sleeve for disposal later. He padded along on his sandaled feet to meet his pupil. There was the hint of a smile on Remo's face. Perhaps his mood had improved.

But as they drew near each other the Master of Sinanju saw his pupil's features settle into unhappy lines. How often they did that, he thought. It had been Remo's lot to suffer many hardships in life, and the gift of Sinanju bestowed upon him had not erased all cares.

As Remo came to a stop before him, Chiun searched his eyes and said, "You have been thinking."

"I have come to a difficult decision, Little Father."

His voice was sad. And the Master of Sinanju decided to make this moment easier on his pupil. "You wish to seek other horizons?"

"How did you know?"

"A father knows his son."

"No offense, Litt— I mean, I don't have a father."

"Not so. You simply do not know your father. You stand here breathing and tasting of Earth's sweet grandeur. The truly fatherless have no such luxury, for they have never been born."

"Point taken. What I meant was you're my teacher and my friend. Not my father."

Chiun cocked his head to one side. "Yet you honor me with the title—when the mood strikes you."

"I have been honored by your teachings and your guidance. But I have come to a place in my life where I must find myself."

"Find yourself? But you are here. Standing on a beach in the land of your birth." Chiun looked out over the rain-troubled bay. "I sometimes long to be standing on a beach in the land of my birth. But alas, this is not for me at this time."

"If you're about to lay a guilt trip on me," Remo warned, "don't."

"I was merely musing on my lot in life. As were you."

"Touché. But I gotta move on."

"I cannot go with you, my son. You know that."

"Where I have to go, I have to go alone."

"And the contract I have yet to sign?"

"That's between you and Smith now. It's only a year. Maybe after a year, I'll be back."

"I can keep Smith happy for a year."

"I expected more of an argument."

"That explains the disappointed expression on your sad-sack face," said Chiun. "Heh heh. That explains the disappointed expression on your sad-sack face. Heh heh heh."

And to the relief of the Master of Sinanju, Remo found spirit enough to smile at his poor joke.

"I'm glad you're not giving me a hard time about this," Remo said.

They began walking back toward the sandy end of the beach, the Boston skyline at their backs.

"You are old enough now to make your own decisions," Chiun allowed.

The rain lessened, and behind the endless gray expanse of storm clouds, the sun slid toward the horizon. Shadows grew long and lean as the light began to fail.

"Where will you go?" asked Chiun in a quiet voice.

"I don't know. I don't have any roots to go back to. The orphanage burned down long ago. I can't go back to Newark. Someone might recognize me. I'm supposed to be dead."

"It is good that your thoughts are not of returning to places you have been before."

"Why's that?"

"Because one looks for one's future in places he has yet to go."

"Good point."

"There is one thing that concerns me, however."

"What's that?"

"Shiva."

Remo was silent a long time. Their feet in the sand made no sound. No footprints appeared behind their track.

"I don't believe in Shiva."

"You are the avatar of Shiva the Destroyer, according to the legends of my House. The dead night tiger made whole by the Master of Sinanju."

"The legends are dead wrong," Remo said with more than a trace of an edge in his voice.

"It is not only the death of this innocent man that troubles you, is it?"

"It's been building a long time," Remo admitted.

"It has been especially troublesome since your last assignment. Tibet seemed very familiar to you, yet you had never before visited that land. A land legends tell is the abode of Shiva the Destroyer. A land your brain remembers from a past life your mind does not."

Remo shook his head in annoyance. "I don't believe in Shiva. I don't believe in reincarnation. I'm Remo Williams. Always have been, always will be."

"Not always."

"Correction. Before I was Remo Williams, I wasn't alive. After, I'll be dead. End of story."

Chiun's sparse eyebrows lifted in mock astonishment. "What, no Christian Heaven for Remo Williams? No angels in white to expiate your earthly sins with their many graces?"

"Not after Roger Sherman Coe," said Remo.

"If the error was not yours, the retribution is not yours, either."

Remo said nothing.

"You have one problem, not two."

"Yeah?"

"You are trying to find yourself but you do not know who you are."

"I just told you. I'm Remo Williams. No more. No less."

"And how do you know you are Remo Williams?"

"What do you mean?"

"Did you come into this world with the name Remo Williams stamped upon your backside? Or tattooed to your arm?"

"That's what they called me at the orphanage."

"And you believed them? Just like that?"

Remo frowned. "You're trying to confuse me."

"No, I am trying to unconfuse you. You have been confused by the virgins you call nuns. This happened before I first heard your ridiculous name. You say you have no roots, but what you mean is that you do not know what your roots truly are."

Remo stopped in his tracks. "You mean my parents?"

"Perhaps."

"I've gone through that. Smith says there's no record. And as I recall, you've always steered me away from this line of thought."

"You were younger then. Perhaps you are old enough to seek them out."

"What do you mean, seek them out? You don't think they're still alive, do you?"

"I did not say that," Chiun said quickly.

"I always figured they they must have died in a car accident or something," Remo said slowly. "Why else would they give me up for adoption?"

"Why do you think that?"

"Because," said Remo, with a suggestion of tears starting in his eyes, "I couldn't bear to think they just abandoned me like a stray dog."

"And this fear has haunted you all your life?" Chiun asked gently.

"Yeah."

Chiun nodded sagely. "Then it is time to put it to rest. Seek out your parents, Remo Williams, be they living or dead. And put the darkest fears of your childhood behind you."

Remo brushed a single tear away. "I can't believe you're being so understanding about this. From the bottom of my heart, thank you, Little Father."

"It is nothing. I may not be your father in truth, Remo Williams, but I have tried to be one in spirit."

"Thanks again."

Chiun regarded his pupil with understanding eyes. "When will you leave?"

"I don't know. Tomorrow. The next day. I don't know where to start."

"I do."

"Yeah? Where?"

"Begin with Smith. His oracles have proved exceedingly accurate in the past."

"Not in the past few hours," said Remo darkly.

7

Harold Smith prided himself on being logical.

Logic ruled his life. Long after he'd stopped attending church services regularly, logic had remained the driving force in his waking life. Every mystery had a solution. Any column of numbers could be added, and the result was predictable, unvarying, and the end product as sound as money in the bank. The product of a mathematic operation was subject to division, multiplication, addition or subtraction, and the answer could be looked up in a table and verified.

As the sun set on Long Island Sound, Harold Smith sat in his leather chair, his Dartmouth tie loose at his throat, fine gray stubble on his lean cheeks, his face dappled with the phosphorescent green glow of his monitor.

He was also sweating.

It was a hot, creeping sweat, and from time to time Smith felt flashes of a chill deep in his logical bones.

"This makes no sense," he mumbled as he manipulated his clicking computer keys.

Just as two plus two always and invariably totaled four, the two Roger Sherman Coes did not add up.

The dead Roger Sherman Coe of Wilmington, North Carolina, had an electronic trail that went back to his Selective Service file.

The Roger Sherman Coe of the National Computer Crime Index was a ghost. Smith could find nothing about him. There was no IRS record, no listing in any motor-vehicle registry in any of the fifty states. His credit cards had all been overcharged and abandoned, the balances unpaid.

Yet according to his computer, these two men, sharing one name but utterly different life-styles, were one.

They could not be one, Smith saw as darkness clamped down on Folcroft Sanitarium and the shaky fluorescent lights of his office automatically came on.

Smith paused in his search to sip mineral water. It was after hours and his secretary had gone home for the day. The night shift had come in, and no one would disturb him while he was at his work.

At an impasse, Smith logged off his search and switched to monitoring other areas of CURE activity.

Out there in business, government agencies and other walks of life, ordinary Americans routinely sent anonymous tips on ongoing or suspicious activities. They thought they worked for various government agencies—the FBI, the CIA, OSHA and many others—as paid informants. The checks came in the mail at the same time every month. And they filed their reports electronically.

Only Harold Smith received them. These ordinary citizens helped satisfy CURE's vast need for raw information.

Smith paged through the latest reports. They were unremarkable. A warning of a crooked state senator in the far west. A coal-mine owner who was routinely ignoring federal safety standards. Price-fixing among New England dairy farms. In the old days Smith would simply drop a dime on these people and hope the justice system did its job. Now it made just as much sense to tip off one of the proliferation of investigative-news television shows, trusting in the resulting broadcast exposure to coax the proper authorities into doing their jobs.

One report caught Smith's attention because it involved XL SysCorp, the computer giant that had manufactured the WORM arrays Smith now relied on.

It said that XL SysCorp was being picketed by a black special-interest group that accused the computer giant of discriminatory hiring practices. The matter did not fall under Smith's purview, so he passed on.

Another report emanated from within the Federal Emergency Management Agency, which had already moved into the area of North Carolina struck by Hurricane Elvis. The complaint accused FEMA of not addressing the situation quickly. It was an old complaint about FEMA. Smith passed on.

In the end there was nothing CURE sensitive. But the respite had cleared Smith's stymied thought processes. He returned to the vexing Roger Sherman Coe conundrum.

Smith ran audit trails from every angle. Nowhere did the two Roger Sherman Coes intersect. As the night wore on, it became more and more obvious that they could not be identical.

That left only one possibility: that the criminal Coe had appropriated the identity of the other Coe. It was a not uncommon ruse. And in this computer age, anyone with access to the net or computer-generated mailing lists could compile the basic information on an individual through IRS and DMV records. Those alone were sufficient to allow a hired killer to create a shield identity called Roger Sherman Coe and, when it had been milked for all it was worth, drop it for another.

It made sense. It was logical. It explained Smith's error. He began to breathe more normally. The tightness in his ribs loosened.

It was only a matter of proving it.

Somewhere in the hours past midnight, Harold Smith's faith in a universe of logic shattered forever.

Smith had just returned to his chair after a bathroom break. The sweat of his early-evening's toil had turned clammy, and his pants legs were sticking to his skin. His tie was on the desk now, and the top button of his shirt lay open.

A routine message came over the screen. It was a report from COMSUBPAC that the USS *Harlequin*, which had left San Diego Naval Terminal for Pacific maneuvers, had declared radio silence.

Smith nodded to himself and returned to the task at hand. Only he and the captain of the *Harlequin* knew that the sub was in fact heading for the dangerous waters of the West Korea Bay, where, as scheduled for every year for the past twenty or so years, a cargo of gold siphoned from the federal emergency reserves would be off-loaded and left on the beach of the tiny fishing village of Sinanju.

By now it was a routine mission. The *Harlequin* commander had his sealed orders, his superiors were instructed to ask no questions, and nothing was ever said about it.

So Smith settled down to a final effort at finding the false Roger Sherman Coe.

The world of reason collapsed in on him when, frustrated at the interminable dead ends he kept reaching, Smith decided to log onto the National Crime Computer Index in the National Crime Information Center. It was routinely updated. It was a long shot, but perhaps in the handful of days since he had downloaded the massive data file, new information had been added.

Smith accessed the data base with the coded passwords he had on file and called up the Roger Sherman Coe file.

It would not come.

The glowing green read simply, mockingly, NOT FOUND.

"Impossible," Smith said tightly. "I have that file in my own data base."

On the theory that the file had been closed, Smith called up the inactive portion of the data base records.

NOT FOUND, the screen read.

"Impossible," Smith repeated in a low, almost tremulous voice.

Smith tried again. He knew it would be a waste of time, but he tried again. A computer does not make logical errors, he knew. Ask it to find something, and as long as the operating system and its logic circuits were functioning, it would find the object of its search—this time, next time and every time, just as a calculator would always report the sum of three plus seven as the number ten. There was no room for error, uncertainty or what people like to call fuzzy logic these days.

NOT FOUND, reported the monitor.

Smith stared at the screen, oblivious to the drop of sweat being squeezed out of the tightening notch between his tired eyes. It rilled down the bridge of his patrician nose, slowed at the tip and clung by static tension until it fell on his unfeeling left hand.

A hand that trembled uncontrollably.

Smith hesitated. Less than a week ago, there had been a file on Roger Sherman Coe in the NCCI. Smith had downloaded it. It was now in his own duplicate of the NCCI data base. He had called it up just hours before. Read it with his own eyes.

Files do not uncreate themselves. Computers are not thinking, creative mentalities, he knew. A clerk had keyed the Roger Sherman Coe file onto the NCCI data base. Smith had merely vacuumed it up through the magic of fiber-optic cable and dumped it onto an optical WORM disk through the medium of laser writing. It was now permanently written onto a CD-like platter.

It was on his data base; therefore, it was on the NCCI data base. Such files are not erased, only moved into inactive memory or stored on tape drives for later referencing.

Smith pulled down a program of his own devising, initiated a brute-force search of the orginal NCCI data base and settled back into his chair for what he expected to be a protracted search.

In his concern he had forgotten the power of his new hybrid system.

The program executed in less than ninety seconds. It had scoured the NCCI data base for any file name that included the three component names in Roger Sherman Coe's name, in any combination, in any variant spelling and even allowed for the absence due to clerical error of any one of the three names.

Smith expected a long list of variants and a difficult night of culling out the variables.

Instead, at the end of ninety seconds he got a single name.

When it came up, he blinked twice, thinking somehow the system had made a mistake. The file had come up after all, impossible as that was.

Then Smith looked again. And he saw what he'd missed the first time.

A low groan escaped his tight lips. It might have been pulling his very soul out through his teeth. In a way it was. The cry of despair was Harold Smith's faith in life and, more importantly, in his own computer system, escaping forever.

On the screen glowed a name. It mocked Smith. Mocked his logic, his faith in the logic of mathematics, the reliability of computers and the subroutines and algorithms and binary codes that governed them.

The name was: ROGER SHERMAN POE.

Harold W. Smith sat frozen in his chair, a stricken expression on his bestubbled, phosphorescence-spattered features, his red-rimmed eyes boring holes into the monitor screen as if by an act of sheer will he could change the one thing that mocked his trust in his computers.

The common consonant *P.*

The letter remained *P.* It was not *C.* The file name remained ROGER SHERMAN POE. Not ROGER SHERMAN COE.

A nervous laugh escaped Smith's parted lips. It was an impossibility. If he had seen a blue elf emerge from the screen to gulp down his tie, it could not have been more mind-boggling.

And because he was a logical man, Harold Smith downloaded the Roger Sherman Poe file onto the WORM drive dedicated to the NCCI data base. Once he had captured it, he set it off on the right-hand side of the screen with urgent keystrokes.

Then he called up the Roger Sherman Coe file from his version of NCCI.

The two files sat side by side on the glowing screen.

Several days ago they had been identical. Now they were not.

One listed Roger Sherman Coe. The other, Roger Sherman Poe. Their Social Security numbers were completely different. Other particulars did not match.

There was only one logical explanation, he knew. A clerk had updated the file in the past few days. Smith went to the bottom of the Roger Sherman Poe file, looking for the date of the last update.

In the fleeting seconds when the file scrolled before his eyes, the lines a greenish blur, hope rose in Harold Smith's battered soul.

Then it died. The last update had been posted three months ago. The date was identical to that of the Roger Sherman Coe file. The NCCI computers were programmed to automatically record the current date on the day a file was changed or altered in any way.

According to the NCCI file, the Roger Sherman Poe file had not been altered since Harold Smith had first downloaded it days before.

Smith groaned once more—a short, mournful sound. It was the sound of a man in intense, uncomprehending pain.

"This is not logical," he said aloud. "This makes absolutely no sense. Files do not change themselves."

And yet it had. Somehow, during the transfer the Roger Sherman Poe file had become Roger Sherman Coe.

The instant the thought crossed his mind, Smith was forced to dismiss it. Computers are dumb, brute machines—superfast digital calculators. Give them numbers—and in the binary language of computers, all data is reduced to numerical equivalents—they will always and invariably add, subtract, multiply or divide in precise ways. Computers cannot think. They cannot correct factual data. They hadn't that capability. Even computers driven by artificial intelligence had so far attained at best a dumb, mulelike reasoning power.

Computer error likewise could not be blamed. A transmission glitch might omit data or add data—usually nonsense strings.

Smith looked at the Social Security numbers. He knew that the first three digits corresponded to the geographical region in which a person first obtained his Social Security card.

Roger Sherman Coe's area number was 220. That signified Maryland. It matched Smith's information that Roger Sherman Coe had been born in Chevy Chase.

Roger Sherman Poe's first digit cluster was 447, which designated Oklahoma. This, too, matched up. Poe had grown up in Tulsa.

Had there been a transmission error, the odds that the numbers would make sense were astronomical.

Add in the fact that with twenty-six letters of the alphabet, the last name Poe might as easily come out Toe or Xoe—or even 4oe.

No. There was no escaping it. Something had gone awry within Smith's new system after he had captured the Roger Sherman Poe file.

And because of it, an innocent man had died.

Smith made one last desperate stab at solving the mystery. He ran the computer-virus scan program. It was the only possible explanation.

The program ran. It checked every data string on every tape drive, disk and microchip in the massive and complicated CURE hybrid system. Each time the system came up clean. Smith ran it again, with the same result. And again.

Normally one scan would have satisfied even the supercautious Harold Smith. Because he no longer trusted his system, he scanned it four times for errors or problems.

Other diagnostic programs reported the system checked out clean.

Under the circumstances, it was the worst news he could have received.

Shaken, Harold Smith closed out the two files, and for the last time sent the CURE terminal slipping back into its desk well. The folding keyboard retracted as the screen automatically winked out and the entire unit dropped below desktop level. A much-scarred oaken panel clicked into place, showing no seam or trace of its existence.

Woodenly Harold Smith stood up and removed his gray coat and vest. He hung them on a wooden coat tree and walked over to the one concession to comfort in his Spartan office, a couch.

He turned off the overhead lights and went to sleep on the couch. He was too shaken to risk the drive home, and he desperately needed sleep.

It was well after midnight, too late to call the President with the horrible news. But Smith resolved to do it first thing in the morning. He would have to. The President must know that CURE's data-gathering arm was no longer reliable.

Without it, CURE had been maimed, perhaps crippled.

Harold Smith dropped off to sleep almost instantly. And for one of the few times in his life, his sleep was troubled by vague, inchoate nightmares.

They took no concrete form. That was beyond Harold Smith's subconscious powers. To have vivid dreams and terrifying nightmares would require imagination.

8

The first week of September is the slowest time of year.

The beaches are crowded. Air flights are packed. Business and government slows to a lazy crawl, and the stock market sleeps.

In workplaces short-staffed offices and factories try to struggle through to Labor Day. Projects are put off. Other tasks are done slowly and not finished until after Labor Day.

Enjoying the last dwindling days of a summer that it will never see again, America is at its most relaxed. And most vulnerable.

While the three people who comprise the supersecret agency called CURE slept fitfully, concerned about their future, four seemingly random and unconnected events were taking place.

In Georgetown, Grand Cayman Island, money began flowing out of the Grand Cayman Trust in a torrent. The vault remained shut, its time lock undisturbed. Its burglar alarms failed to sound. In fact, its night clerks continued updating transaction files all through the looting, oblivious to the catastrophe that was silently, invisibly, inexorably throwing them out of work.

An electonic red flag appeared on an active computer file in the vast IRS data bank in Arlington, Virginia. No human fingers placed it there. It simply appeared.

A Consolidated Edison supervisor posted an innocuous work order, instructing a crew to connect a Harlem office building to a long-dormant Con Ed gas line, after first being assured by DigSafe that no phone, cable or electrical lines were threatened by the excavation.

And on the North Korean frigate *SA-I-GU,* somewhere in the Yellow Sea, a telephone rang.

Captain Yokang Sako of the Democratic People's Republic of Korea Navy was asleep when it rang. The phone was a portable satellite unit, smuggled into North Korea by the captain's cousin, Yun, who regularly traveled to Japan on the cruise liner *Mankongbong.* It was a very useful item to have, especially on patrol.

One could call almost anywhere and receive calls from almost any spot on the globe without one's superiors knowing of it.

Captain Yokang lifted the receiver and said, "Yes?"

A warm, generous voice answered in impeccable Korean, "I have a proposition for you, Captain Yokang."

"Who speaks?"

"One who is willing to offer you as much gold as your crew can carry away."

"Gold? Whose gold?"

"Does it matter whose gold?"

"It matters if someone is trying to give it away."

"Of course, I wish something in return for this information," the voice said with calm assurance.

"Hah! What can I, a captain in the North Korean navy, offer in return for such gold?"

"Half the gold."

"Half?"

"I will tell you where the gold can be found, and you will seize it. Contact me then, and I will provide you with instructions as to where to ship exactly one half of the amount. The remainder is yours."

"Hah! So there is a catch."

"Not a catch. I am trading information, and you are trading the brute force needed to seize this cargo."

"The risk is all mine," Captain Yokang pointed out.

"The gold is half yours."

"How much gold?"

"Five million. Pure bullion."

Captain Yokang clucked thoughtfully. "This is enough to pay off my crew for their silence."

"There is no need to inform your superiors, either," said the smoothly reassuring voice.

"If this can be done safely, I will do it," said Captain Yokang.

"A United States submarine is steaming toward the West Korea Bay. It carries the gold."

"I cannot commandeer a United States submarine!"

"You can once it enters Korean territorial waters illegally."

"Why is it doing that?"

"It is better that you not know."

"Better or safer?"

"Both."

"Understood. Tell me where this submarine can be found."

As he listened over the satellite telephone, the smooth voice related everything. Course, speed and the exact position at which the USS *Harlequin* intended to surface.

Captain Yokang looked at a map as he took down the information. The area was off one of the most industrialized portions of west North Korea. An area of steel mills and coal mines and rice paddies. Along the coast lay only rock and a few fishing villages. Nothing of importance.

Yokang noticed a broad three-lane highway that swept up from the capital of Pyongyang to a certain point on the western coast. The highway went right to the edge of the water and stopped dead. There seemed to be no purpose in this. The map showed nothing but a blank area where the highway terminated. No doubt it was one of the Great Leader's many extravagances. North Koreans were not permitted to own motorized vehicles, yet the state boasted of its progressive highway system.

After he had all the information he needed to make himself fabulously rich, Captain Yokang asked the voice a reasonable question. "Who are you, comrade?"

"Call me Comrade," said the smooth voice.

IT WAS just after dusk in the West Korea Bay when Naval Commander John Paul Seabrooke was interrupted by the voice of his executive officer coming over the boat's intercom system.

"Captain, we're approaching Point Sierra."

"On my way," Seabrooke said. He wolfed down the last of his evening meal, wriggled his stocking feet into his spit-polished shoes and pushed his way past rushing seamen through the smelly steel innards of the USS attack sub *Harlequin* to the control room.

In his hand he clutched his sealed orders. Ripping as he ran, he extracted a single sheet of paper.

The orders were brief. They instructed him to look for a particular beach landmark and, once sighted, deploy his cargo on rubber rafts and simply leave it there on a beach.

The orders were signed, "Admiral Smith."

Seabrooke had never heard of Admiral Smith. But the U.S. Navy was full of admirals. It was full of Smiths, too, and Seabrooke wondered why the man hadn't bothered to use his first name or at least his initials.

The instructions were simpler than he could hope for. With luck the boat could surface in utter darkness, do its duty and slip back through the Yellow Sea without being detected by North Korean gunboats.

"All secure, sir," the exec reported as Seabrooke entered the bridge. The *Harlequin* was running submerged at periscope depth. The periscope was down in its well.

Seabrooke ordered it raised.

A snap of a switch brought the viewer rising to meet him. He seized the handles and turned them. The scope rotated easily as Seabrooke moved his body around.

The viewer showed black water under a thin slice of yellow moon. He looked for the Horns of Welcome, as the landmark had been called in his sealed orders. It had not been described. Evidently, whatever they were, they would be hard to miss even in the dead of the North Korean night.

The thought of where he was sent a shiver through Commander Seabrooke's rangy body. North Korea was practically the only Communist holdout left standing these days. It was also the most insular and danger-ous. Estranged from both Moscow and Beijing, Pyongyang was going it alone. The ruler, Kim Il Sung, was nearing the end of his life, and his son, Kim Jong Il, was anxious to take over.

It was well-known that while Kim Il Sung was a des-pot, Kim Jong Il was a dangerous megalomaniac with delusions of grandeur far beyond the petty vulgar dreams of his father.

There were rumors of food riots and insurrections all over North Korea. The long border with South Korea was tense. Intelligence reports predicted that when the elder Kim finally passed on, the son might make a grab for the south. Because only by involving his people in total war could he hope to hold on to his crumbling country.

No, it was not a good time to be in the West Korea Bay, Seabrooke mused. And it would be an especially bad time to be caught there.

Still, the U.S. Navy would not have sent the *Harle-quin* into off-limits waters unless it was for a damn good reason and the odds of success were great. The

Navy still remembered the *Pueblo* incident. Or Seabrooke fervently hoped Admiral Smith did.

They were running parallel to the coast. Seabrooke scanned the moonlit swatch of land. It was as forbidding as a moonscape. Mud flats and rock ledges. Nothing moved. Not even a sea gull flew. That meant the waters were bare of fish.

Then he saw them. Twin rock formations, one at either end of a particularly dead-looking stretch of mud flat. If they had been closer together, they would have made a pretty fair natural arch. Set apart as they were, they made Seabrooke think of the buried horns of some Precambrian dragon.

The Horns of Welcome. Had to be.

"Captain of the watch, rig controls for black and prepare to surface," Seabrooke barked, snapping up the periscope handles.

"Aye, aye, sir."

Instantly the order was repeated, and the red illumination lights were doused. The bridge became a claustrophobic space in which the tense faces of his executive officers moved in and out of the creepy illumination of control indicators.

"Blow main ballast tanks."

"Blow main ballast tanks."

Air hissed in the tanks. The sub began to rise, its stressed hull plates groaning.

"Contact, sir!" a voice shouted. "Bearing mark 056."

"Belay that blow-tanks order," Seabrooke cried, running to the sonar.

The scope showed a large object cutting across their bow.

"A surface ship, sir."

"Looks like a damn gunboat or something," Seabrooke hissed.

It was. They realized that when the sub suddenly lurched in place. Everyone grabbed for something solid. Men were thrown about the control room.

"Depth charge!" Seabrooke cursed. "Dive, damn it!"

"Dive! Dive! All dive!"

But they were in less than one hundred fifty feet of water over an ocean floor choked with monolithic stones and sandbars. There was no place to hide, and everyone knew it.

A second charge detonated over the stern. The *Harlequin* bucked like a great horse stung by a hornet. Hull plates groaned and popped. Damage reports began coming in from all quarters. The lights winked out, coming back on only when Seabrooke called for backup generators. The screws refused to respond.

Dead in the water, the *Harlequin* crew waited, all eyes on the sonar scope operator.

"The contact is coming about, Captain," the sonar officer said nervously.

It was. In a long slow arc.

"They have us dead to rights, no question," Seabrooke whispered.

The battleship, whatever it was, slowed on the approach.

"Looks like they're going to take another whack at us," the exec muttered.

Captain John Paul Seabrooke watched the green blip on the sonar scope, his face like a death mask. He had two options, both grim. Try to run and risk North Korean battleships converging on his small boat, or surface and surrender.

His orders had contained no instructions for that eventuality. Now that he thought about it, that was unusual. It was as if COMSUBPAC had expected no problems.

"Surface," he rasped.

The orders were carried out smoothly and efficiently. The *Harlequin* groaned anew and, leaking at several seams, clawed for open air. She broke the surface with a gushing hiss of cascading sea water.

"Pop hatches," Seabrooke ordered. "Sparks, alert COMSUBPAC that we are challenged by North Korea battleship and have surfaced to hear terms. XO, you're with me."

The exec followed Commander John Paul Seabrooke to the main bridge hatch. They grabbed their oils on the way and put them on.

"Maybe we can bluff our way out of this," the exec said with a nervous laugh.

"Don't expect miracles," Seabrooke snapped back.

They went up the hatch and stepped out onto the slippery deck atop the *Harlequin*'s great sail.

IT WAS A FRIGATE, Najin class. Seabrooke recognized its bulky lines, which closely resembled the old and obsolete Kola-class frigate of the former USSR.

A spotlight sprang to life and blinded Seabrooke and his exec as an amplified voice bellowed, "USS *Harle-*

quin, this is Democratic People's Republic of Korea frigate *SA-I-GU.* You must surrender.''

''They know who we are!'' the exec exploded.

Seabrooke decided to bluff it out. ''By what right do you attack a United States submarine in open waters?'' he shouted through his megaphone.

''You must surrender at once. Do you do this?''

''He isn't buying it, skipper,'' the exec muttered dispiritedly.

''We offer no resistance,'' Seabrooke called back.

Boats were lowered, and they waited in fist-clenching silence.

The first boatload of flat-faced Korean sailors secured the deck and sail. The second off-loaded the captain of the *SA-I-GU,* a squat man almost as wide as a Sumo wrestler with eyes that were unnaturally round for a Korean.

''I am Captain Yokang Sako,'' he announced. ''You are Commander John Paul Seabrooke?''

Seabrooke tried to hold back his surprise. He swallowed and said, ''I am permitted to give you my name, rank and serial number only.''

''I know these things,'' Captain Yokang growled. ''Do not waste my time with them, and this present difficulty will not be prolonged.''

''What do you want?''

''Your cargo, Commander,'' said the North Korean captain.

Seabrooke and his exec looked at one another with stark, sick eyes. Meeting, their gazes said, We've been set up.

''Is that all?'' Seabrooke said quietly.

"Once we have possession of your cargo, we will have no further use for you."

"I don't like the sound of that, skipper," the exec undertoned as the circle of rifles closed around them.

"Maybe he doesn't mean it the way it sounds," Seabrooke said with more hope than he felt.

"Do you surrender your vessel, or must it be taken by force?" Yokang demanded.

"If you guarantee no harm will come to my crew," Commander John Paul Seabrooke said, his ears ringing with humiliation. No sub commander in modern memory had ever been forced to hand over his boat to an enemy. His career was finished. Saving his crew was all that mattered now.

THE NORTH KOREAN seamen secured the *Harlequin* with hard looks and harder rifle barrels. Not a shot was fired. Not a harsh word was spoken by either side. It was very professional, very efficient, very civilized. Neither side wanted the incident to escalate any further than it had.

Commander Seabrooke led the Korean frigate captain to the weapons storage area and unlocked a storage room. He himself did not know what his cargo was. He had watched the crates as they were lowered through the weapons shipping hatch by crane back in San Diego and came away with the idea that very heavy machinery or weapons were housed in the crates.

The Korean captain proved him wrong when he stepped up to one crate and attacked it with a short crowbar he had picked up along the way.

The crate was stout. It took considerable struggle before nails shrieked as they came out of the wood, and the boards themselves cracked and splintered.

"Gold?" Seabrooke said when the shiny ingots tumbled out.

The Korean captain turned, his flat face twisting. "You did not know?"

"No."

"But you know where you were to drop this cargo?"

"No."

"You lie!"

"My orders were to drop the cargo on the beach and go. We were to meet no one."

The Korean captain stared long into Commander Seabrooke's unhappy face. Evidently he was satisfied that he found truth written there, even if he did not understand it.

A Korean seaman stepped up to Captain Yokang and whispered in his ear. The Captain frowned as he listened. One word escaped his mouth in surprise. "Sinanju?"

The other nodded gravely.

Looking up, Yokang glared at Commander Seabrooke and asked, "Have you ever heard of Sinanju? It is a fishing village near here."

"No."

"Never?"

"Never."

The Korean captain stepped close, standing toe-to-toe with Commander Seabrooke.

"I give you my word as a North Korean officer that if this gold is intended for the village of Sinanju, I will leave it and your vessel to complete your mission without further interference.''

Commander Seabrooke blinked. It was an absurd offer. Even if the man had that authority, surely he had already radioed his superiors that he had intercepted a United States submarine in North Korean waters. He could not have depth charged the *Harlequin* without express orders to do so, not in the rigidly controlled hierarchy of the North Korean Navy. It was a trick question. It had to be a trick question.

So Commander John Paul Seabrooke answered it truthfully. ''I'm sorry, I have never heard of any Sinanju.''

''It could not be Sinanju, anyway,'' Yokang muttered to himself, rubbing his blocky chin. ''Sinanju would never work for America, even if America knew of Sinanju. I did not think it was possible. But I had to ask this question. I had to be sure.''

As he spoke, the captain drew his service revolver. ''You see, if this gold belonged to the village of Sinanju,'' he continued, lifting the weapon to his right temple, ''I would be better off if I shot my brain from my skull than face the wrath of the Master of Sinanju.''

Commander John Paul Seabrooke registered the name of the Master of Sinanju and wondered if he was some local warlord. His wondering ended abruptly when the service revolver suddenly snapped out and pointed toward him.

''I thank you for your honesty, fool.''

Commander Seabrooke looked into the black barrel of the pistol, thinking, ''He wouldn't dare shoot me,'' when the end turned red three times in quick succession and his rib cage was smashed to kindling.

They left him to bleed to death there in the bowels of his boat as the crated cargo was lifted out through the weapons shipping hatch and taken aboard the frigate *SA-I-GU.*

Commander John Paul Seabrooke was still alive, but only in the clinical sense, when all hatches were secured and the *Harlequin* crew were beginning to think they'd see their families again.

While that happy thought was still sinking in, the plastique charges affixed to vulnerable points along the *Harlequin*'s hull went off in unison.

The Yellow Sea poured in cold and black and bitter. Commander John Paul Seabrooke drank more than his fill in the last thrashing minutes of his life, his final thoughts more bitter than brine.

I should never have told the truth. I should never have told the truth, his mind kept repeating like a broken record.

He was throughly drowned by the time the *Harlequin* settled to the rocky seafloor.

9

Flashlight in hand, Harold Smith picked his way through the basement of Folcroft Sanitarium. The light roved among the furnaces and came to rest on the glowing grate of the old coal furnace in one cobwebby corner.

Smith approached, knocked the wood-sheathed iron handle upward with the thick barrel of his flash and gingerly pulled open the grate.

The ash-caked coals smoldered resentfully. Smith picked up a poker and stirred them. Sparks flew and hissed. Broken lengths of scorched human bone swirled up from the coals, showing the fractured ends of femurs and tibia.

Buzz Kuttner was coming along nicely. In another night or two, he would be one with the coal ash. Only then would it be safe to pour his cremated remains in an ash can for hauling to the dump.

Closing the grate, Smith continued his rounds. The triple-locked door guarding his computer system was secure. There would be no need to check the machines. No point to it now. They ran, scanning the net, but Smith did not expect to ever access them again.

But from behind the doors, Smith heard furtive sounds.

He pressed an ear to the door, and the sounds became more distinct. They were impossible to describe. Muted organic sounds, like hamburger plopping from a meat grinder.

Fumbling for his keys, Smith got the blank door unlocked and pushed open the door.

His light filled the room.

He saw the Folcroft Four, tape reels turning in quarter-cycle jerks. They were as they always were.

But the refrigeratorlike jukeboxes stood ranked like dumb beige brutes. There were no moving parts, no ports, so there was nothing outwardly different or disturbing about them.

But inside, some thing or things moved and squirmed and made soft, indescribable sounds.

Horrified, Smith approached. He pulled away a panel to expose the WORM arrays and stepped back with a pungent curse escaping his lips.

The WORM platters were literally alive with crawling earthworms. Blind, limbless things, they crawled among the circuit boards, writhed among the microchips, tiny mouths munching on the disk drives that were stacked around the central spindle.

The drives had been literally gnawed like lettuce leafs.

"My God!" he said hoarsely. "So that's what's wrong with the system. The worms have not been fed properly."

SMITH SNAPPED AWAKE with the first red rays of dawn setting Long Island Sound ablaze.

It was not their gory light coming through his sealed eyelids that finally wrenched him out of sleep. It was the fact that his nightmares had for once taken the shape of concrete images. That had never happened before, and it startled his brain to wakefulness. More than anything else, this frightened Harold Smith, who disliked change.

In all the years, from his days with the OSS through the CIA to CURE, Smith had been able to count on untroubled sleep. No man he ever killed in the performance of his duty or had ordered executed in his capacity as head of CURE had ever returned to plague his dreams.

But the failure of his computer system had shaken him to his core. As he sat on the long couch fumbling his shoes on, Smith understood that he might never know a decent night's sleep for the rest of his days. He had failed his country and his President. He didn't know how, but he had. It was intolerable.

Smith walked stiffly over to his oak desk, retrieving his coat and vest on the way. Staring unseeingly over the sound, he put them on, patting the watch pocket of the vest for his coffin-shaped poison pill. It was still there. For thirty years it had been there.

Woodenly Smith took his seat. Reflexively he reached for the concealed stud that would bring the CURE terminal humming into view. He caught himself in time. Thirty years of routine was a long habit to break. There was no need to check the system again. He had been through that.

Instead, he cleared his throat and opened the right-hand desk drawer after unlocking it.

He brought out an AT&T desk-model telephone. It was as red as a fire engine, and instead of a dial there was only a blank face.

It was the dedicated line to the White House. For thirty years, Smith had used this as a secure communications link to eight sitting U.S. presidents.

Now he was about to call the White House for what he feared would be the final time.

It was 6:00 a.m. Not too early to call a President. They were usually up before first light. This latest President had a habit of rising later, but Smith felt certain that he would be up by now.

Smith placed an unsteady hand on the red receiver. He had only to lift it and automatically an identical phone in the Lincoln Bedroom would ring in sympathy.

He hesitated. Smith had reported many successes and failures to many Presidents over the long decades. But he had never been in the position of having to report the catastrophic failure of CURE. He sat there, sweat building up in his palms as he groped for the proper words.

He cleared his throat again.

And the telephone rang. His hand came away from the red receiver as if stung. Adjusting his tie, Smith picked it up and spoke.

"Yes, Mr. President?" he said unemotionally.

The voice of the President was hoarse. "Smith, I need you."

"What is the problem, Mr. President?"

"We've lost a U.S. submarine in enemy waters."

Smith frowned. "Enemy?"

"The submarine was on routine maneuvers in the Pacific. It must have strayed into North Korean territorial waters. They radioed that they had made contact with a Korean naval vessel. Then nothing. That was ten hours ago."

Smith's eye went stark. "The *Harlequin?*"

"Yes. How did you know?"

"My God!"

"That's how I feel about it," the President said bitterly. "It gets worse. We've contacted Pyongyang, and they claim their ships report no naval contacts. They claim they've not captured a U.S. sub or encountered it."

"My God," croaked Smith.

"When I heard it was North Korea, I thought of you. One of your people hails from that neck of the woods. I thought maybe he could do something for us."

"Mr. President," said Harold Smith. "The *Harlequin* was in North Korean waters on my authority."

"Your authority! You're not Navy." The President caught himself. "Are you?"

"No, I am not. But as you know, it is my responsibility to make yearly payments to the Master of Sinanju. At his insistence, these are made in gold bullion and dropped off at his village."

"We pay in gold. How much?"

"Several million. The exact amount needn't concern you."

"You don't have a deficit the size of the Pacific to contend with," the President said testily.

"I am aware of the nation's financial difficulties," Smith said bitterly. In all his life he had never owed more than the balance of his mortgage and monthly utility bills.

"How long has this been going on?" the President asked tightly.

"Since you first shook hands with the President who set up CURE," Smith said crisply.

The President was silent. In the background Smith could hear the muted sound of a classic-rock radio station.

Smith said, "There is an understanding between Pyongyang and Sinanju, Mr. President. The submarine is not to be molested."

"Was that understanding with Premier Kim Il Sung?"

"It was."

"Intelligence reports that he is failing and his son is wielding more and more power these days."

"Kim Jong Il is mentally unstable," Smith said. "It could explain this development."

"Development! Smith, this in a full-blown crisis. I've just lost an attack submarine with a full crew, and no one knows where it is. Do you realize what this means?"

"I do. But we have a deeper problem, Mr. President."

"Don't say that."

"The essential question is not whether or not the *Harlequin* has been lost, but whether it was lost before or after it off-loaded the gold."

"Why is that more of a crisis than the loss of a Narwhal-class attack submarine?"

"Because," said Harold Smith, "if the gold was lost with the sub, we will have to send another submarine with an identical amount if we are to retain the services of the Master of Sinanju."

"Damn," said the President. "We can't risk another submarine. The North Korean navy's probably got their own subs out in the Yellow Sea looking for ours."

"Exactly," said Harold Smith in a grim voice.

"Are you saying we can't use your people?"

"It may come down to that," said Smith.

"Smith, your country is depending on you. You've got to come through for us."

Harold Smith hesitated. This was a development as grave as the failure of his computer system. It had international ramifications, and the lives of over a hundred U.S. seamen hung in the balance.

The time may have come to dissolve CURE. Only the President could make that decision. But it was abundantly clear to Harold W. Smith that the President of the United States would not give that order until the *Harlequin* matter was resolved.

"I will do what I can, Mr. President," he said at last.

And Smith hung up.

REMO WILLIAMS was awakened by the distant sound of the telephone ringing.

Three telephones, actually. The one in the downstairs kitchen and the second one in the upstairs meditation tower. The third was two rooms away with its ringer shut off. Still, Remo could hear the electronic pulses futilely trying to trigger its bell. Since he had decided to sleep on the farthest room in the eastern wing of the condo, and Remo was hearing it all through many layers of wall and ceiling, he simply willed his acute hearing not to hear the ringing anymore and rolled over.

An hour later, when he got up, the phone was still ringing. It hadn't stopped when he stepped out of the shower. It continued ringing while Remo picked out a fresh white T-shirt, donned tan chinos, slipping his feet into loafers of handmade Italian leather.

The Master of Sinanju was boiling tea in a ceramic kettle in the kitchen when Remo walked in. He wore morning gold.

"I have been waiting for you," Chiun said unconcernedly over the telephone's insistent ringing.

"Why don't you answer the phone?"

"Because I have been waiting for you to answer the phone. I am the Master of Sinanju. I do not answer telephones."

"Well, I don't work for Smith anymore, so I'm not talking to him."

"If you talk to him, you will be able to ask for assistance in finding your roots," Chiun suggested.

"Nice try, Chiun. But there's no way I'm answering that phone."

"Very well."

The phone continued ringing. The ceramic kettle began steaming.

"How long has this been going on?" asked Remo, taking a bowl of cold white rice out of the refrigerator and sitting down at the breakfast nook to eat it with his fingers.

"For the past hour."

"Could be important."

"If it were important, Smith would have hung up a half hour ago, and be even now winging his way to a personal audience with me," Chiun said.

"Smith may not have that kind of time," Remo pointed out, eyeing the phone. His expression grew tense. The Master of Sinanju noticed this and said casually, "I am making longevity tea this morning. Is longevity tea satisfactory with you?"

"Longevity tea will do," Remo said, his eyes going to the telephone with every third ring.

"It will be ready soon," said Chiun, pouring the hot water into a green celadon teacup in the shape of a sleepy turtle.

"That ringing is starting to drive me crazy."

"You know what to do."

"That's right, I do," said Remo, walking over to the phone and lifting the receiver. He dropped it back again with a clattery clunk.

"Aiiiee!" Chiun screeched. "Ignorant white, what did you do?"

"I stopped the ringing."

"You insulted Emperor Smith!"

"How's that?"

"If we did not answer, he would naturally assume we are absent. But to hang up on him is unforgivable."

Remo returned to his rice. "Hey, I don't care what Smith thinks of me."

"Nor do I!" Chiun snapped. "But what if he wrongly concludes that I am the rude hanger-upper of telephones?"

"Simple. Blame me like you always do."

The telephone immediately began ringing again. Chiun's startled-wide eyes went to it. "Answer that!"

"No way. I'm retired."

"Then you will earn your keep by answering the telephone!"

"Not me," said Remo, chewing his rice into a liquid prior to swallowing it.

The phone continued ringing. It seemed to be getting shriller with each blast of sound.

At last the Master of Sinanju flung himself at it, crying in a loud voice, "Hail, Emperor Smith. Please accept the House's apologies for the incorrigible behavior my wayward pupil has just exhibited in hanging up, which I only this minute learned of upon returning from being out for the past hour."

"Master Chiun, we have a dire emergency," Smith said breathlessly.

"I will swoop to the site of this emergency and dispatch America's enemies without mercy, Emperor Smith. You have only to command me, for I will gladly do the work of two now that I alone serve you."

"The submarine carrying the gold is missing."

Chiun was clutching the receiver in both clawlike hands.

They clenched in unison. "Did the gold arrive safely?" he gasped.

"We do not know."

"Do not know!"

"Master Chiun, the sub with all its crew is missing."

"Not the gold! Remo, did you hear? My gold is missing."

Remo did not look up from his rice.

"We don't know that for certain, Master Chiun," Smith protested. "The sub may have encountered difficulties after it dropped off the gold."

"There is only one thing to do in this hour of darkness," Chiun cried, lifting a hand ceilingward.

"Yes?"

"I will call my village." And Chiun hung up. Immediately he dialed his personal international toll-free number, 1-800 SINANJU, first dialing the country code for North Korea.

A reedy old voice responded after a dozen rings, "This is the House of Sinanju. Whom do you wish dispatched?"

"Faithful Pullyang! Quickly, has the gold of America arrived yet?"

"No, Awesome Magnificence."

"Check the beach."

"I have just returned from the beach. There is no gold."

"If the gold arrives, call instantly."

"As you wish, Awesome Magnificence."

Chiun hung up, his face stiff. "You heard all?" he asked Remo.

"Yeah," Remo said worriedly. "I hope nothing happened to those sailors."

"They are unimportant," snapped Chiun, dialing so furiously that the nail of his index finger obliterated the black numbers with each whir of the dial. "It is the gold that is important. Have you learned nothing of what I have taught you?"

Remo continued eating his rice with his fingers, knowing that it was considered uncouth by Korean standards.

"Emperor Smith," Chiun shrieked into the telephone. "The gold did not arrive."

"It must be recovered."

"Or replaced."

"My information is that the sub was challenged by a North Korean gunboat somewhere in the West Korea Bay before it was lost."

"Impossible."

"That was their last report."

"Ridiculous. The minions of Kim Il Sung would not dare challenge the vessel designated to carry the gold of Sinanju."

"It is our understanding that Kim Jong Il is running Pyongyang during his father's convalescence."

"That whelp! He would not dare order this outrage."

"Please go to North Korea immediately and learn the truth, Master Chiun."

"This will be done with utmost dispatch and great zeal," said the Master of Sinanju.

"Here it comes," Remo muttered.

"—once the gold is replaced."

"This is no time to replace the gold," Smith protested.

"You are the secret emperor of America. You can work wonders. I know you can do this, Smith."

"Master Chiun, please."

"The contract has been signed. But the gold has not been delivered. Thus, we have no contract. I would dishonor my ancestors if I were to undertake service under these conditions."

Smith was silent for a breath.

"Is Remo there?" he asked at last.

"No," Remo called out through a mouthful of rice.

"He is lying," Chiun spat out the words. "Of course he is here. But he does not wish to speak with you, therefore it will do you no good to appeal to him."

Harold Smith's voice was pleading now. "Please, Master Chiun. We must act quicky while there is still time."

"Yes, by all means. Act quickly and replace the gold of Sinanju."

"But it takes three days to cross the Pacific by sub."

"What is this? Yesterday you told me that you only then sent the gold. Now you say it reached the West Korea Bay before being lost. How can this be?"

"I, er, fibbed," Smith admitted.

"Hah!" said Remo. "Caught at last."

"Fibbed?" demanded Chiun.

"I, ah, had sent the gold ahead of schedule. It was necessary because the *Harlequin* was the only sub available for the next three months."

"What if we did not reach an agreement?" Chiun asked suspiciously.

"I could have signaled the boat to turn around at any time. This was done in the interests of efficiency."

"And because of your impatience," Chiun flung back, "my gold has been lost at sea. It must be replaced at once."

"I can possibly have a down payment drop-shipped to your home by late afternoon," Smith offered.

"Unacceptable," said Chiun. "If I accept the gold on American soil, I will be responsible for transporting it to Sinanju and possibly for paying usurious income taxes, exorbitant customs fees and other burdensome levies imposed by your new President, the flint-skinned one, and his grasping consort. Thereby being cheated of full tribute. Only in your barbarian country are such things done, Smith. Do you think the pharaohs handed my ancestors a sack of gold, only to demand one third back in taxes? Or the Romans? Not even the Chinese would stoop so low, and they are notorious thieves."

"Even as we speak, your gold may be in the process of being confiscated by North Korean authorities," Smith pointed out.

"Your gold. It is not mine until I have taken delivery. I have not."

"Would you accept a cash surety until the gold is replaced?"

"Possibly," said the Master of Sinanju, and seeing that he had Harold Smith on the ropes, promptly hung up on him.

"Why'd you do that for?" Remo demanded. "Now he knows you hung up on him."

Chiun lifted his indignant chin defiantly. "If necessary, I will blame you. In the meantime he will move heaven and earth to scrounge up replacement gold."

"I don't think even Smith can scrounge up a boat-load of gold ingots on short notice, Little Father."

Chiun made a face. "Why do you care, retired one?"

"Because there's a submarine full of U.S. sailors missing, and somebody's gotta do something."

Chiun leveled a warning finger at his pupil. "You are retired. Remember that. I will have no sunlighting from you."

"That's moonlighting and don't worry. I'm through with Smith."

"Yeah. But is Smith through with you?"

10

Harold Smith stared at the blue contact telephone in his white-knuckled hand. His office, spacious but Spartan, seemed to be closing in on him.

First his computers had failed him. And then the submarine had been lost. Now this.

In the past, when the Master of Sinanju had been recalcitrant, Harold Smith could count on Remo's stubborn sense of duty to his country. Not after the Roger Sherman Coe incident. When Remo, as he sometimes had, refused missions, Chiun was always there to take up the slack.

Sitting in the chair he had occupied for thirty of the most difficult years of his life, Harold W. Smith understood with a sinking coldness in the pit of his stomach that he commanded virtually no resources.

Except, he realized suddenly, the instrument in his tremulous hand.

Smith brought the receiver to his ear and punched out an international number with quick stabs of his forefinger.

A crisp, vaguely British voice replied, "Grand Cayman Trust."

"This is account number 334-55-1953," Smith said.

The plasticky clicking of a keyboard came over the line, signifying the account number was being inputted into a workstation computer.

"Password, please."

"Remedy," said Smith.

The clicking came again. Then the voice asked, "How may we help you?"

"I would like a cashier's check in the amount of five million dollars drawn against my account and couriered to Boston's Logan International Airport," said Smith, figuring he could be in Boston within three hours and present the check to Chiun in person by late afternoon.

"I'm sorry. The account shows insufficent funds for us to issue that check."

"Insuff—"

"Our records indicate that all but the minimum deposit, twenty-five dollars, was wired to Chemical Percolators Hoboken Bank in New York City overnight."

"Impossible. Only I know the password and account number."

"Our records are quite clear on this."

"To whose account was my money transferred?"

"I am sorry, but since you claim to be the owner of the account and you do not yourself know, I cannot tell you."

"But I *am* the owner of the account!" Smith said in a heated voice.

"Yet you seem unaware that you wired the bulk of the account to New York."

"Chemical Percolators Hoboken, you say?"

"Yes."

"I will get back to you," said Smith, and hung up. Reflexively he reached for his computer stud to look up the bank phone number. He caught himself and instead dialed the operator.

"AT&T."

"I would like to place a long-distance call to Chemical Percolators Hoboken Bank in New York City," Smith said tightly, thinking, Was the entire world going mad?

The line began ringing, and the operator asked, "What party?"

"Station to station," said Smith, who knew it would save him money.

"Thank you," said the operator, who went away once a female voice said, "Chemical Percolators Hoboken. How may we help you?"

"I would like to speak with the manager," said Smith.

The bank manager possessed a lockjaw WASP voice that reassured Harold Smith with his first clipped vowel. "Yes?"

"I am calling about a wire transfer your bank received from my account."

"Of course, sir. If I could have your account number?"

"I do not have an account with your bank," Smith said crisply. "I am calling to inquire about a wire transfer of some twelve million dollars you people received from the Grand Cayman Trust yesterday."

"Grand Cayman Trust. Where exactly is that?"

"In the Cayman Islands," said Smith. "Obviously."

"Of course," said the manager. There was a pause. "Would you mind identifying yourself?"

"My name is Smith."

"First name?"

"I would prefer to leave it at Smith."

"I see," said the bank manager, his voice cooling. "Well, Mr. Smith, I can assure you that you've been misinformed. We have received no wire transfers in that amount in several weeks and certainly not from an institution of the Grand Cayman Trust, uh, sort."

"They assured me down there that the transaction took place late yesterday."

"And I am assuring you that it was not received at this branch," the bank manager said pointedly.

"Have you any other branch in New York City?" Smith asked.

"No, we do not."

"Someone is not telling the truth here," Smith said through tight teeth.

"That may be, but if you have a problem with your account at the Grand Cayman Trust, then I suggest you take it up with them."

"I will," said Smith, ringing off. He called the Grand Cayman Trust and, reaching the manager, quickly summarized his problem.

The manager brought up Smith's account on his own desk terminal and said, "All but twenty-five dollars was wired to Chemical Percolators Hoboken yesterday."

"Do you have a written record or authorization?"

"I see by my screen that you expressly waived the need for debit tickets or other written authorization on transfers of any type or amount."

Smith swallowed hard. He had. Using the Grand Cayman Trust, notoriously lax in their oversight and regulations, enabled him to move and launder vast amounts of money without leaving a paper trail to Folcroft Sanitarium or him personally. The system had worked perfectly—until now.

"According to Chemical Percolators, they did not receive the wire transfer of funds," Smith said.

"According to our records, it was sent *and* received."

"Chemical Percolators is a very large, very reputable institution," Smith pointed out in a tone that could not be misinterpreted.

"Yet you chose *our* fine institution," the bank manager answered in a frosty tone.

"A mistake."

"Would you like to close out the remainder of your account, then?" the manager said in a thin voice. "All . . . twenty-five dollars of it?"

"No. I will get back to you."

"Always happy to serve."

Smith hung up. He removed his rimless eyeglasses and rubbed his eyes. This was impossible. Money does not disappear en route. Then Smith realized that the money had moved electronically. In a physical sense, it had not moved at all. Only electrons, sent by computer and backed up by a voice confirmation, had moved.

Someone had raided the CURE bank account and, during the transfer, redirected and misappropriated nearly twelve million dollars in taxpayer funds.

That someone would have to be tracked down. Smith still had the matter at hand to resolve.

He would have to replenish the CURE operating fund.

OVER THE DECADES CURE operations had grown exponentially. Just as Smith had been forced to upgrade his computer system to its present state, so had his operating budget mushroomed. In the first decade of CURE, it had been possible to draw millions of dollars out of various off-the-books CIA, DIA, NSA and other Intelligence-community operating funds undetected because there was little or no congressional oversight on such black-budget expenditures once appropriated.

But CURE had one day outgrown the ability to do that undetected by its sheer voracious financial need. A blind had to be created, a federal agency whose mandated purpose was too important to ever be closed or suffer budget cutbacks, one with an annual operating budget vast enough that CURE could siphon off funds at will without arousing suspicion.

Smith normally moved funds from this agency by computer to the Grand Cayman Trust—a notorious haven for money laundering—to ensure absolute security. There was no avoiding it. He reached for the concealed stud that would bring his terminal humming up from his desk well.

Smith pressed the stud. Almost at once the intercom buzzed, and his secretary said, "Dr. Smith. There's someone to see you."

"I have no appointments this morning," said Smith as the desktop panel dropped slightly before it was to slide to one side.

"It's Mr. Ballard."

"Ballard? I know no—"

"He's from the IRS, Dr. Smith," the secretary said.

Smith hit the stud again. The scarred oak panel reversed its mechanical course to return flush to the top of the desk and vanish from casual inspection.

"The IRS?" Smith said dully.

"Shall I send him in?"

Smith hesitated. Lips thinning, he said, "Yes." He did not sound enthusiastic.

The door opened and a balding pear of a man wearing bifocals entered, carrying an imitation-leather briefcase.

"Dr. Smith. My name is Bryce Ballard." He put out a pudgy hand.

"Is that your real name?" Smith said without warmth.

"No, actually it isn't."

"But you do claim to be with the IRS?"

"Here's my identification."

Ballard showed an IRS revenue agent's card that appeared genuine.

"I have reason to believe you are not who you say you are," Smith said flatly.

"You can check with my office," said Ballard. He waved toward the couch. "May I sit down?"

"Yes," said Smith, dialing the number the man gave him.

"Internal Revenue Service," a voice announced.

"Ask to speak with Mr. Vonneau," Ballard called over.

"I would like to speak with Mr. Vonneau."

"One moment, sir," a switchboard operator said crisply.

Smith regarded the man Ballard. He looked harmless enough.

He might easily pass for an IRS revenue agent, but Smith had excellent reason for thinking him an impostor.

"Vonneau speaking," an unemotional voice said.

"This is Dr. Harold W. Smith at Folcroft Sanitarium, Rye, New York," said Smith. "I have a man in my office who claims to be here to audit me. He gave his name as Bryce Ballard, although he admits that is not his true name."

"Describe him, please."

Smith described Ballard in flat but accurate terms.

"That's Ballard. As you know, Dr. Smith, IRS agents for their own personal protection are allowed to assume authorized pseudonyms."

"Then I am being audited?" Smith said in a disbelieving voice.

"You are."

"Impossible."

"Actually, we're auditing quite a number of medical facilities. Don't worry, you're in good hands. Ballard is thorough and, of course, fair."

"What I meant to say," Smith said, "is that I received no official notice of an audit."

"Give me your business-taxpayer identification number."

Smith rattled off the number from memory. There was silence on the line. Then Vonneau came back to say, "According to my files, the notice was sent out a week ago, and an appointment was arranged for today by telephone."

"I did no such thing," Smith said tartly.

"According to our computerized logs, you did. Perhaps one of your staff handled it."

"I do not delegate such matters," Smith said stiffly. "There must be a mistake."

"IRS computers," Vonneau said just as stiffly, "do not make mistakes of this scope."

"Thank you," Smith said without emotion, and hung up.

Ballard stood up and said, "I will need to see all your in-house financial records to start."

"Why is Folcroft being audited?" Smith demanded suddenly.

"Routine. Your return popped up on the random-audit list."

"I happen to know that random auditing has been suspended for the next two years while the new IRS computer system is being installed."

"True," said Ballard, offering a weak smile. "I might as well tell you, word has come down from the top. The President's health-care program has to be paid for somehow. Waste and fraud in the medical profession are rampant, as you know if you watch any of the news-magazine shows. The IRS has been asked to look into this very thorny area. We've already collected substantial sums in back underreported taxes, FICA payments and fines, all of which will be earmarked to pay for the health-care program. Of course, I'm sure that won't be the case here."

Harold Smith heard all this with his ears ringing. He was being audited by the IRS. It was a virtual impossibility. Smith had continual access to Folcroft's IRS records by computer. He knew the mathematical formulas the service used to target institutions for auditing and every year carefully made out his returns, underreporting legitimate deductions and not taking others so that no red flags triggered the random-audit process.

And just in case, his computers were programmed to monitor the IRS master file in Martinsburg, Virginia, for this very eventuality. Smith should have been warned Folcroft had been targeted for an audit. He could have headed it off by remote manipulation of the IRS's own computerized files.

The Folcroft Four had failed him again. And he was forced to sit numbly in his chair as IRS Agent Bryce Ballard droned on about his needs. Harold Smith stared at the scarred corner of his desk that hid the system he could not access and now no longer trusted if he could.

"First," Ballard was saying, "I will need to see your computer system."

Smith looked up, startled. "System?"

"You do have financial records?"

"Yes. On a standard three-book ledger."

Ballard's round face slackened into stunned lines. "Do you mean to say, Dr. Smith, that a facility of this size has never been computerized?"

"I have never seen the need for it," retorted Smith.

11

If Jane Kotzwinkle didn't have three children to raise and an ex-husband who believed child-support payments were due only when he won the daily number, there was no way she'd put herself through the many indignities of wearing a Con Ed hard hat and snug uniform in broad daylight. The night shift was fine by her, and usually it was enough. But she needed the overtime, her babies needed new clothes, and with so many of her colleagues on vacation, Manhattan needed her services.

What Jane Kotzwinkle didn't need was the stares. Not from the passersby who did a double and sometimes triple take when they happened upon her digging up a section of New York City pavement in her Con Ed blue-and-gray coveralls, nor from her fellow workers who stopped what they were doing to appraise her rear end whenever she bent over to look down a manhole or pick up a tool.

And especially she did not need the wide cow eyes she got whenever a NYNEX rep came out to check on the dig.

This one looked fresh out of CUNY or some damn place. He pulled up in a NYNEX company car that was no more than three months old and, spotting her hard hat with its Con Ed symbol, walked right up to her and asked, "Where can I find Kotzwinkle?" The brainless mutt.

"I'm Kotzwinkle."

This one didn't even try to hide his surprise. "You?"

Duh, Jane Kotzwinkle thought. Like this wasn't the 1990s.

She got down to business using her best ramrod voice, the one she used on her boys when they wouldn't turn in at bedtime.

"We're digging in back of this building," she said, walking away. "Come on. I'll show you."

"My name's Larry," he said, clutching his rolled-up blueprints. "Larry Lugerman."

Like I care, you waxy-eared dip, Jane thought. She took him around to the side and pointed to the spot. They were in the shadow of one of the few new buildings in upper Manhattan. Her crew stood around drinking Dunkin' Donuts coffee, looking bored in the early-morning light.

"Is this a line break?" Larry asked, his voice a little nervous.

"Client wants a gas line put in. That's what we're going to do. Hook him up."

They came to the spot. Jane Kotzwinkle indicated it with a disdainful toss of her head. "We've got a gas pipe that runs north-south, right here," she said. "We're going to tap it and run a line into the basement. According to DigSafe, we're okay."

Larry looked at the spot and unrolled his blueprints, holding them so Jane couldn't read them over his shoulder. Like the location of NYNEX trunk lines was a fucking national-security secret, she thought.

"Let's see..." he muttered. He looked from the blueprints to the spot in the concrete that Jane was impatiently tapping with her work boot and back to the blueprints.

"You're in the clear if you don't disturb anything beyond twenty yards in either direction," he said finally.

"Good. Thanks," she said dismissively. DigSafe had told her the exact same thing.

Larry Lugerman looked stricken. "I'm supposed to stay."

"Fine. Can you manage a jackhammer?"

"No."

"Then what's the use of you staying?"

"In case there's a problem with the phone lines."

"You just said if we stay within a forty-foot box, we're okay."

Larry swallowed. "Sometimes the blueprints aren't updated as well as they should be."

"Then what's the point of all this hoop jumping?"

He took a step backward. "I'm just doing my job."

"Fine. Just stay out of the way while *men* are working."

Jane walked away from his melting face. She knew he had been thinking of asking her if she was free for lunch. He had that gooey look in his eye.

Like she'd date a guy who wore a coat and tie to work.

An hour later the stuttering of the jackhammer had died down, and they were into the shovels and pick-axes portion of the excavation.

"Got something here," Melvin Cowznofski called out.

Jane beat the NYNEX suit to the hole. Partially buried in the dirt was a braided steel cable, half-severed. Twisted strands of copper wire lay exposed to the early-morning light. The strands were protected by bright red rubber tubing.

"Looks like a phone line," Jane muttered.

"Let me see," Larry said anxiously, pushing through the ring of gas company workers.

"That look like a phone line to you?" Jane demanded.

"Yeah. But an old one. It's a copper analogue line. All the cable on the island is fiber-optic."

"Is it a problem?"

"I gotta call this in. Don't do a thing till I get back."

Three minutes later Larry Lugerman came back, relief on his youthful face. "It's okay. They have no record of it."

Jane Kotzwinkle looked at him pointedly. "So?"

"That means you can cut through it, work around it, do anything you want."

"Just because they don't have a record of it?"

Larry shrugged. "If there's no record, it doesn't exist, as far as we're concerned."

"But it's a phone line. You said so yourself. How can it not exist?"

"It's probably an old test line upgraded or abandoned years ago that some lazy SOB forgot to remove."

"You're the authority," Jane said aridly, picking up a pickax and chopping away. The line parted. Nothing happened. There was no spark of complaint, not that anyone expected a spark.

As a piece of the copper wire came flying out of the hole, Larry picked it up and said, "Boy, this is really old. They haven't used two-wire lines like this for carrying voice since I don't know when." He noticed the red rubber sheathing, looked into the hole and saw that every line in the cable was protected by the exact same red rubber coating.

"This makes no sense," he muttered. "They always color code the individual lines. Otherwise, how would the linemen know which lines were which?"

Nobody paid him any mind. They were busy excavating the gas pipline. After a while Larry dropped the utterly fascinating copper telephone wire and stared at Jane Kotzwinkle's ass as she bent to her work.

He was wondering if she was up for lunch.

12

After Harold W. Smith got IRS agent Bryce Ballard squared away and out of his office, ledgers in hand, he returned to his desk to punch the concealed stud of the CURE computer system.

His finger stopped short of the button when a muffled ringing came from the right-hand desk drawer. It was the red presidential phone.

Smith dug it out of the drawer and brought the receiver to his ear. "Yes, Mr. President?"

The Chief Executive's tone was hoarse and urgent. "Smith, I need an update for the hounds of hell."

"Who?"

"The White House press corps. Someone leaked the *Harlequin* story. I've gotta to issue a statement to settle things down."

"Mr. President, I regret to say I've not been able to get to the matter."

"What?"

"Sir, an IRS revenue agent unexpectedly walked in."

"For God's sake, why?"

Smith cleared his throat unhappily. "Er, it appears I have been targeted for audit."

"What the hell do you do up there that the IRS would want to target you? Scratch that. I don't want to know. If I don't know where you operate out of or your cover, I have limited deniability."

"Very wise, Mr. President."

The President pitched his voice low and conspiratorial. "Want me to pull a few strings? Squash the audit? I can do that—I think."

"I am tempted, Mr. President, but for the White House to order the audit squashed would be so highly unusual as to call undue attention to my cover operation."

"Yeah. Good point. Now, let's get back to this submarine thing."

Smith hesitated. "Mr. President, there has been another difficult development."

"Yeah..."

"It appears that the CURE operating fund has been possibly, ah, embezzled."

"Embezzled! I thought you and only you controlled that fund."

"I do. It appears to be a bank embezzlement."

"Well, can't it wait until this *Harlequin* incident is dealt with?"

"Without operating funds, I cannot replace the missing gold the Master of Sinanju is demanding in order to start the next contract."

"You telling me you don't have any agents?" the President asked sharply.

"I'm afraid so."

"And you're caught between contracts?"

"Yes."

"Smith, what kind of operation are you running there?"

"One that has suffered a regrettable cluster of setbacks," Harold Smith admitted, trying to keep the embarrassment out of his voice.

"Well, they couldn't have come at a worse time."

"I know."

"You know I have serious reservations about this operation," the President continued. "If it wasn't for the fact that the past President I most admire set you up, I would have shut you down my first week in office."

"I have had that sense," Smith admitted.

"Goddamn it. The country is spending a billion dollars a day servicing the national debt, and you've let twelve million slip through your fingers. Not to mention another five million in gold bullion lost with that sub."

"I am certain it will be recovered."

"Well, recover it."

"I am trying, Mr. President. All I can say is that my best efforts are being put forth."

"Well, your best efforts aren't worth spit in a wind—"

The line went dead. The President's voice was simply cut off. There was no click. No dial tone. Nothing but dead air.

Harold Smith said, "Hello? Hello?" several times and hung up. He waited exactly thirty seconds by his Timex wristwatch before lifting the receiver again.

Dead air. He repeated the operation twice more with the same disappointing result and finally replaced the receiver and nervously waited for the President to call back.

Ten minutes crawled past before Harold Smith knew the President of the United States wasn't going to call back. Or couldn't call back.

For a cold moment Smith wondered if the President, whose voice had been on the verge of being coldly furious, had not simply ripped the red White House phone out of the baseboard in anger. And in failing him, he had resolved to dissolve CURE.

If so, Smith realized after a moment's thought, there was no way he could issue that directive until the CURE telephone line was restored to working order.

That gave Harold Smith time to deal with the growing crisis.

Again he reached for the concealed stud.

Again he withdrew his finger as his intercom buzzed.

"Mr. Ballard has a question," Smith's secretary said.

"Send him in," Smith said tightly, simultaneously restoring the red telephone to its desk drawer.

Ballard poked his head in and asked, "Dr. Smith, do you have a calculator I could borrow? The batteries in mine seem to be failing."

"Mrs. Mikulka will see to it."

"Thanks."

The door closed and Smith reached for the stud.

The door reopened and Ballard stuck his head in again.

His hand hovering under his desk, Smith looked up, trying to keep the tension out of his patrician face.

"Do you have any problem with my eating in the hospital cafeteria? It's a long drive to the nearest restaurant, and I'm under pressure to have this audit done by the weekend."

"By all means," said Smith, making a mental note to instruct the cafeteria cashier to charge Ballard the higher visitor's price rather than the subsidized Folcroft employee rate.

The door closed again. Smith let out a sigh of tension that did nothing to release the tightness in his chest. He stared at the scarred corner of his desk, finger hovering uncertainly near the concealed stud, and realized that there was no way he could conduct normal operations with a busybody IRS agent hovering about the place.

Smith drummed his fingers on the oaken desktop impatiently with one hand as he fumbled in the desk drawer for a bottle of children's aspirin with the other. He undid the childproof cap and shook out four pink-and-orange tablets, downing them dry.

It had been a difficult week, he thought unhappily, ever since he had had the new system put in. The most powerful system imaginable dedicated to the multiple tasks of the CURE organization awaited his sure fingers, and he could not safely bring his monitor into view, much less trust its operation.

If only there were some other, more secure method of working at his desk.

Then he remembered a loose end. It was one he had planned to dispose of but had proved too heavy to manage alone.

Tapping the intercom key, he said, "Mrs. Mikulka, have the custodial staff go to the basement and bring up a glass-topped desk stored there."

"Yes, Dr. Smith."

"Tell them to bring it to my office," Smith added.

"To your office?"

"Yes. I recently acquired a new desk."

"I don't recall a purchase order crossing my desk."

"I, ah, purchased it at a store closing on my own time," said Smith.

"Yes, Dr. Smith."

Two MEN in khaki coveralls came squeezing a substantial office-style desk through Smith's door ten minutes after he had unplugged the hidden desk terminal connections from the floor plate.

The black-tinted tempered-glass desktop shone like onyx.

"Be careful with that," Smith warned, coming out of his seat. "It is quite heavy."

"What's this made of, ironwood?" one of the custodians grumbled.

"Set it down and move the old one aside," Smith directed.

The new desk hit the hardwood floor with a floor-shaking thud, and the men came and shunted Smith's old oaken desk off to one side. They set the new desk in its place without a word.

"Thank you," Smith said when they were done. "That will be all."

"What about that one?" one of the men asked, pointing to the old desk that had served Smith for as long as he had occupied his lonely post.

"Leave it there for the moment," said Smith. "The drawer contents need to be transferred, and I haven't time to do all that now."

"Yes, sir."

The men departed, closing the soundproof door after them.

Harold Smith stood with his back to the picture window with its panoramic view of Long Island Sound and stared down at the pristine black of the desktop. He saw his own reflection, like a photo negative, staring back at him. He did not like that. In fact, Smith distrusted anything new. He disliked change in any form. His old desk had been as comfortable and familiar to him as his own bed, which he had purchased upon his return home from wartime duty in 1947 and stubbornly refused to replace as long as all four legs held out.

But this was an emergency.

Clearing his throat, Harold Smith sat down. The desktop glass felt smooth and cool under his palms when he laid them there. He liked that, at least.

Reaching into the kick space, he found the connector cable, pulled it out of its receptacle—it was on a spring reel—and pushed the cable into the floor plate.

Nothing happened. He looked for a button. There had to be a power switch somewhere.

Obviously it could not be on the desktop. It was glass. Nor was it in the drawers that hummed out smoothly on well-oiled rollers.

To his surprise, Smith found it under the lip of the desktop, not very far from the spot where the old stud had been. It was a recessed button, the size of a nickel and slightly rounded. Smith depressed it.

Instantly the section of the desk directly before him illuminated. He saw the familiar sign-on screen of the CURE computer system, the scrolling of disk-checking programs and finally the main-drive prompt.

The letters, while as perfectly readable as if on a sheet of paper lying on the desk, were a warm amber, Smith was disappointed to see. He preferred cool, detached green.

Directly below the screen, the desktop remained black. Smith brought his hands to it. Instantly the orderly letters and numbers and control keys of a keyboard shone white and distinct. It was capacitor-style keyboard. His hands entering the field changed its capacitance, illuminating the keys. Removing them caused the letters to instantly go dark.

Smith touched a key experimentally.

The key flashed white at his touch. It was the letter *W.* The *W* appeared on the screen in warm amber.

Smith brought all ten fingers to the touch-sensitive keyboard and tried logging on.

It was strange at first. There was no sound, no reassuring give-and-take of the keys. In fact, no keys in the physical sense. But the response was perfect—silent, efficient, accurate.

Smith ran his virus-check program and got an instant "Clear" message.

Then, his face grim, he settled down to work. There was a lot to do, and the ticking of his Timex—virtu ally the only sound in his state-of-the-art computerized office—continually reminded him that there was not a lot of time to do it in.

13

Carlton "Chip" Craft tooled his brand-new metallic gold Idioci coupe—the car for the pleasure-seeking id facet of the personality according to the TV ads—past the world headquarters of XL SysCorp in the Harlem section of Manhattan where a group of raggedy picketers stopped marching in monotonous circles long enough shake their fists at him as he turned smartly and approached the garage door.

As it always did, the chilled-steel door lifted to admit him without Chip having to do a thing. A laser scanner had recognized the bar code on the company plate on the coupe's front bumper and triggered the door opener.

After parking, Chip got out, and the elevator door opened at his approach. He got on. He didn't even have to press his floor. The button for the fifteenth floor lit up on its own and he was whisked upward. It was the work of another scanner. It picked up the bar code ID on his solid-gold tie clasp.

When he got to his floor, he saw that his secretary was a blonde today. She wore a black evening gown held up by straps that crossed between her full breasts in velvet bandoliers, lifting and accentuating them. Her nipples were as brown as old pennies.

Chip paused to admire them and asked, "Any mail this morning?"

"No, Mr. Craft," she said in a husky contralto that all his secretaries were required to have, along with C cups. Only hair color and facial contours were optional.

"We must do lunch," he said, giving her left nipple a friendly tweak. The secretary giggled happily, and Chip Craft sauntered whistling into his sumptuous office.

It was decorated in old-world Spanish leather and mahogany today. A trifle ostentatious, but the company liked to make him happy. Outside, the sun was shining. It had been overcast on the drive in.

It was the first day back after three glorious weeks in sunny Oahu, and Chip Craft, CEO of XL SysCorp, couldn't wait to dig in, even if it was the Saturday before Labor Day.

He tapped his intercom key.

"Good morning, Chip," a warm, generous voice said.

"Good morning, sir."

"Is the office satisfactory?"

"It is."

"And this week's secretary?"

Chip grinned. "That gown is really fetching."

"If you are pleased, let me apprise you of the latest XL SysCorp activities."

"Shoot."

Chip clasped his hands behind his head and leaned back in his handsome executive chair—the finest money could buy. He started to put his feet up on the desk but remembered what had happened last time.

"We have moved 987 more XL SysCorp PC units."

"Great."

"The IRS tax systems modernization project is three weeks ahead of schedule."

"Wonderful."

"Net-income projections exceed the thirty percent rise anticipated last quarter."

"Super."

"And I have decided to blackmail the United States government."

Chip almost jumped out of his chair. "Say again?"

"We have maximized our profits through commercial channels. It is time to go to the next level."

Chip stared at the intercom. "Blackmail is the next level?"

"Unless you have a more profit-oriented idea."

"Why would we do that?"

"Because we have approximately three hundred thousand XL systems out in the commercial and governmental spheres, enough to make the plan I set in motion five years ago feasible."

"What plan?"

"The plan to extort twenty billion dollars from the federal government."

"This is all new to me."

"Loose lips sink schemes."

"I think it's ships, sir."

"That reminds me, a shipment of gold bullion is due in the next few days. See that it goes into the basement vaults with the rest."

"I think the basement vaults are pretty full by now."

"Have a new vault installed."

"Shouldn't we be investing some of this?"

"Current analysis of the global stock market indicates it is for the sixth year highly overvalued. Bank interest is at its lowest point in decades. Bonds, securities and other instruments are also weak. Cash is king. As is gold and precious metals."

"Gold in a vault doesn't earn squat," Chip pointed out.

"Gold in a vault is not at risk."

"Let's get back to this extortion thing."

"It is foolproof."

"Who or what are we using as leverage?"

"The one driving force in the world today. As it has been every day since the first man crawled out of the primordial soup."

"Yeah. What's that?"

"Money."

"Money?"

"We are going to hold money for ransom in order to make money," said the smooth, disembodied voice.

"How do we do that?"

"By going into the banking business."

"Why?"

"Because that is where the money is," said the smooth, disembodied voice.

HAROLD SMITH manipulated his new touch-sensitive keyboard like a man who wasn't sure if he was touching reality or a mirage. At first he bore down too hard, stubbing all ten fingers. When he softened his touch, some keys responded haphazardly. But now he was getting the hang of it.

The keys responded perfectly. That was not the problem. It was the system itself. It seemed to be working properly, but Smith no longer trusted it.

In a very real sense, he could not be sure that the glowing amber characters that were appearing on the black top of his new desk were trustworthy. It was unnerving.

But he had to try.

America needed the Master of Sinanju, and Smith required hard cash to secure his services.

So Harold Smith was going to the source.

The Federal Emergency Management Agency had been set up by an act of Congress in 1978 to deal with natural emergencies such as floods, hurricanes and earthquakes. It was widely criticized as inefficient, unresponsive and bureaucratically paralyzed.

In a sense all these charges had some validity to them, although in recent years a succession of massive natural disasters had focused the harsh glare of the public spotlight on FEMA and the agency had been forced to do a better job.

To cover its poor performance and save it from calls that it be abolished, the true nature of FEMA had begun to leak out. Its mandate was in fact to deal with disaster, but responding to the odd hurricane or inconvenient earthquake was not its primary mission.

FEMA had seen set up to safeguard the command structure of the U.S. government in the event of what was euphemistically called "attack-related nuclear activities"—i.e., nuclear war. It maintained secret hotels, mountainside fallout shelters and a fleet of radiation-hardened aircraft and mobile communications vans for the sole use of higher government officials from the First Family down to the members of Congress.

If America were ever subjected to nuclear attack, FEMA was designed to ensure that no matter how massive the catastrophe, some elements of the U.S. government command structure would survive to rebuild or order a punishing counterstrike.

In the post–Cold War world, the immediate nuclear threat had diminished. But FEMA endured, and to justify its existence, it had become more responsive to the natural disasters that had lately been plaguing the nation.

No one in FEMA, from its commissioner to the President, knew that the agency had a third mission. Its vast black-budget operating fund was the pool from which CURE, unknown to Congress, drew its annual allotment of the taxpayers' money.

Smith needed a emergency transfusion of that fund now. Because it was an emergency, he ordered FEMA to wire the sum of ten million dollars to CURE's account in the Grand Cayman Trust.

An accounting clerk at a FEMA terminal responded to Smith's typed request. He assumed the request was coming from an in-house terminal. There was no reason to believe otherwise. He was working on a secure system to which only the highest FEMA officials had coded access.

Several minutes passed before a message came back. Smith stared at it, disbelief in his blinking gray eyes.

GRAND CAYMAN TRUST DOES NOT RE-SPOND.

ONE MINUTE, Smith typed.

He dialed the bank. The phone rang and rang. Smith tried another number. He got a recorded message. The voice was masculine and matter-of-fact.

"We regret to inform our customers that the Grand Cayman Trust is temporarily on holiday. For information on your account status, please write Box 4, Georgetown, Grand Cayman Island. Thank you for your continued patronage."

"Impossible," Smith croaked.

He logged onto the CURE terminal and brought up a wire-services monitoring program and typed the bank's name. The program executed with blinding speed. An amber block of text materialized on the desktop so fast it smacked of magic.

According to UPI, the Grand Cayman Trust had abruptly shut its doors two hours into today's business. The bank board was being tight-lipped about the circumstances and were granting no interviews. There were no further details.

Woodenly Smith returned to the waiting FEMA account clerk.

DISREGARD INSTRYCTIONS, he typed, in his shock misspelling a word and neglecting to correct it before transmitting.

Grimly Smith shut down his system. He was stymied. He had no backup bank, and there was no efficient way to set up a new account. Unable to draw funds, trust in his computer system or communicate with the President, he was as helpless as he felt. Which was very helpless indeed.

His Timex continued ticking as he turned in his cracked leather executive chair to stare out the picture window overlooking Long Island Sound.

The last of Hurricane Elvis had vanished. The sky was blue, and the sound was an expanse of crackle-finished sapphire on which returning sailboats were tacking against a steady breeze. It was an utterly calm day in the history of the United States. But a storm was growing. A storm greater than Hurricane Elvis.

Harold Smith, unimaginative as he was, began to sense it. He did not know what shape the storm would take or what it was; he only knew that it was gathering force somewhere out there.

And Smith was almost helpless to deal with it.

Almost. For he still had his brain.

Somehow he must find a way to bring Remo and Chiun into play without the benefit of his usually bottomless resources.

As the day lengthened, Smith watched the patterns of sunlight dance on the sound and set the cold, objective clarity of the greatest thinking machine ever devised—the human mind—to work on a solution.

14

The Master of Sinanju paced the floor of his meditation tower like a fussy hen.

It was the end of the third hour, and his emperor had not called back.

Emperor Smith, whose name was inscribed in the Book of Sinanju as Mad Harold, had always been predictable. It was his one virtue. Predictability.

No matter how far the Master of Sinanju had pushed and tested his patience, Smith's need of Sinanju always overcame his resistance.

In twenty years Chiun had come very far from the days in which he would each year ceremoniously accept from Smith a sack of gold roughly equivalent to thirty-two American dollars in return for training Remo in the art of Sinanju. It was double the traditional price of ordinary service because it had involved not actually protecting the Eagle Throne, which was worthy service, but training a sub-Korean to do so, which was not.

Smith had assented with reluctance. Feigned reluctance. Chiun had discovered this one year when Remo was being particularly obtuse and Chiun had gone to Smith demanding quadruple tribute, knowing that the penurious Smith would refuse and Chiun would be free of the recalcitrant pale piece of pig's ear, Remo.

Smith had assented with the same feigned reluctance, and Chiun had unhappily found himself stuck in the barbarian West for another bitter year.

But he kept in mind how Smith had, in the end, paid the outrageous price. And so the next year Chiun had asked quadruple the tribute.

Smith had assented with identical feigned reluctance.

Twenty years of quadrupling, quintupling and sextupling the gold, as well as adding an assortment of precious gems, rare metals, silks and other riches, had brought the price into the fabulous realm of five million dollars.

Only once had Smith balked. And the Master of Sinanju had been forced to give up his long-held hope of occupying the much-coveted realm of Disneyland as its sole owner.

So when Harold Smith had carelessly misplaced a submarine and with it Chiun's gold, the Master of Sinanju had not hesitated to demand its immediate replacement, knowing that Smith had both the resources and an urgent need for Sinanju's services.

Hanging up in the middle of the negotiation had been Chiun's way of hastening the process. It had worked many times in the past. Why should it not work once more?

But three hours had passed, and no call, not a word. It was unlike Smith, who was undoubtedly under great pressure to find the submarine that had been lost.

And so Chiun paced, his anxious eyes going often to the ugly plastic telephone that stubbornly refused to ring.

At the end of the third hour, the Master of Sinanju could stand it no more. He stopped his furious pacing, and one yellow claw drifted out for the mute telephone. He caught himself. It would be unseemly for him to call his emperor. Emperors called their assassins in their hour of need, and not vice versa. No ancestor of Chiun had ever prostrated himself before a throne to ask if the owner desired an enemy dispatched. Court jesters sought work. Concubines sought work. Sometimes headsmen sought heads to be lopped off.

Not Sinanju. Emperors sent emissaries to the village rightfully called the Pearl of the Orient, and the Masters of Sinanju would make the arduous journey to the troubled thrones and, agreements struck, the work was done.

No, Chiun would not call Mad Harold, the unpredictable.

He resumed his pacing. But ten minutes of pacing proved just as aggravating as waiting.

The Master of Sinanju flung himself down the steps to the lower floors of his castle. "Remo. Remo. There is no word from Smith!"

"Big deal," came Remo's voice.

Chiun hurried to the room from which the voice came.

He found Remo seated on a reed mat before a television set. There was one in almost every room in Castle Sinanju, thanks to the Home Shopping Channel and a Gold Card provided by Smith.

"What news of the submarine?" he demanded.

"The President just gave a press conference."

"What did the gluttonous one say?"

"Not much. There's a sub missing, and no one knows where it is or what happened to it. The North Koreans are swearing up and down they had nothing to do with any of it. And the Navy's trying to pin blame on some admiral no one can find named Smith."

Chiun clenched his fists. "It must be found."

"They've got subs out looking."

"Remo, these are your people who are missing. Your fellow sailors."

"I was a Marine."

"Is not a sailor a Marine?"

"Not exactly."

"You cannot stand by and let them perish."

"I don't work for Smith anymore," Remo said flatly. He changed the channel.

"Strike a bargain. Make him find your long-lost forebears with his oracle, in return for succoring the poor, hapless sailors."

"What happened to 'they aren't important'?"

"They are not," Chiun snapped. "To me. To you, they matter. To Smith, they matter. If the sailors are found, the gold will be found."

"Not unless they stole it," Remo pointed out.

"The traitorous thieves!" shrieked Chiun, lifting shaking fists to the ceiling. "If you find their fingerprints or teeth marks on my gold, Remo, make them suffer terribly for what they are putting me through."

"No deal."

The phone rang, and Chiun's eyes locked on the insistent instrument. "Quickly, answer it."

"Why don't you answer it?" said Remo, not taking his eyes away from the TV set, where a pixieish woman was talking to a hand puppet.

"I do not wish to appear anxious," said Chiun anxiously.

"No problem," said Remo, rising. "I'll just handle it the way I did before."

Chiun flashed to the phone, an ivory wraith. He scooped up the receiver and said, "Hail, Smith. Your loyal assassin awaits glad tidings."

"Master Chiun, I am unable to replace the gold."

Chiun froze. His eyes narrowed. He sucked in his breath through his teeth. Then he allowed in a reserved tone, "A cash surety might be permissible under the present emergency. No checks."

"Er, I am afraid I cannot offer you that, either."

"Why not?"

"CURE appears to be bankrupt."

"Bankrupt?"

"Yes. We have no money."

"The fiends!" Chiun shrieked.

"What fiends?" asked Smith.

"The terrible Depublicans. They have spent this mighty nation into the poorhouse. All is lost. Your empire crumbles even as we speak. It is the fall of Rome all over again."

"Master Chiun, I have a proposition for you," said Smith.

"What proposition could interest a Master of Sinanju that does not include gold?" Chiun asked suspiciously.

"This one does include gold."

"Speak!"

"Find the submarine. Return it and its crew, and the gold is yours."

"I cannot. It involves service without a valid contract or payment."

"You do not understand. I am telling you that if you recover the submarine, the gold is yours free and clear. Without obligation."

Chiun's eyes narrowed. "No further service will be required?"

"No. And once the mission is successful, we will negotiate another year's service."

"But you have no money, Smith. You admit this."

"A temporary situation. Once it is resolved, another shipment of gold will be made."

Chiun had been stroking his beard in agitation. He stopped. His beard trembled. His whole head trembled.

"Double the gold?" he whispered.

"Exactly."

Chiun clamped a hand over the telephone mouthpiece. "Remo, did you hear? Smith has offered to double the gold!"

"That's not what he said. He's suckering you into recovering the gold for nothing."

"But I get to keep the gold."

"No skin off Smith's nose. He considers the gold lost. He can't lose. If you find the sub, he gets what he wants. If you don't, you've wasted your time for a promise."

"And if Smith does not recover this foolish submarine of his, there may be no more gold. Ever."

"Like I care," said Remo, face intent on the TV screen.

The hand came away from the mouthpiece, and Chiun said, "It is a bargain, Emperor Smith. Instruct me."

"The North Korean angle is the only lead we have. Go there. Learn what you can. And whatever you do, please do not embroil the U.S. in a war with North Korea."

"I will serve you well, Smith. For this may be the last time Sinanju will be honored to serve the modern Rome."

Chiun hung up, dancing. "Did you hear? A year's worth of gold, all mine for a day's service. Perhaps two."

"If you find the submarine."

"How large is a submarine?"

"Maybe three hundred feet long and forty high."

"How difficult can it be to find something that large and ugly?"

"If it's in your attic, none. If it's at the bottom of the Pacific, you could spend the next ten years of your life trying to earn a year's supply of gold."

"You are trying to ruin my triumph."

"Don't count your ingots."

Eyes squeezing to suspicious slits, the Master of Sinanju approached the TV screen that had so mesmerized his pupil. "Why is that woman talking to her glove?" he demanded.

"It's not a glove. It's a hand puppet. See? It talks back."

"And this amuses you, indolent one?"

"So sue me. I used to watch this show back at the orphanage. It's a good memory."

"I am going to pack. You should pack, too."

"Not me. I'm taking off after lunch."

"To where?"

"Nowhere."

"A suitable destination for a rootless American. But I need you."

"I don't work for Smith."

"And neither do I. I am working for me. As are you."

"Who says?"

"Did you not hear? Smith is broke."

"So?"

"Your credit cards are no longer good."

"I have money."

"Enough to carry you to nowhere?"

"There are six hundred bucks in my account last I looked. And another two in the cookie jar for emergencies."

"Spent."

Remo looked away from the screen. "On what?"

"The illustrious paperboy. He required a tip."

"You tipped the paperboy two hundred dollars!"

"Since he was worthy and it was not my money, it seemed equitable," Chiun said, shrugging. "And six hundred dollars will get you an excellent room—for one, perhaps two months. But what will you do after that?"

"I'll think of something."

"Perhaps once you find your roots, you may also find it in a beautiful orchard in which to dwell with the other trees."

"Not funny, Chiun." Frowning, Remo asked, "Look, if I come, how much of the gold is mine?"

"That depends."

"On what?"

"On how useful you are to me."

"Not good enough."

"One third. And I will prevail upon Smith to locate your forebears, who no doubt even now are hanging their heads in shame over your naked display of greed and graceless ingratitude."

Remo considered. "Okay. Done."

"Quickly. Before my gold rusts," said Chiun, fleeing the room.

"Does gold rust?" Remo asked himself. He decided to watch "Lamb Chop's Play Along" to the end and then pack. It made him feel better than he had in a long time.

JUST AS NATURE abhorred a vacuum, Harold W. Smith despised coincidence. There was no place for such untidiness in the logical order of his world.

Yet coincidences happened, and Smith understood that. He did not accept coincidence without begrudging its very existence, but he understood that such puzzling phenomena manifested themselves from time to time, annoying as they could be.

In the world in which Harold Smith lived there was a phenomenon called cluster effect. The clumping of synchronous events or coincidences, producing a pattern that might suggest meaning or fate or even the guiding hand of an almighty God.

The cluster effect in which Harold Smith found himself trapped and drowning suggested just such an invisible hand.

In less than a week, he had lost his enforcement arm to an impossible computer failure, the Master of Sinanju's services to a mysterious submarine hijacking, CURE's operating funds to a bank failure and his all-important dedicated line to the President of the United States through a circumstance still unknown.

It was possible for any of these calamities to occur under extraordinary circumstances. Remo had resigned in the past, always to come back. Disagreements with the Master of Sinanju were worrisomely frequent and avoided only by nimble thinking. And it was certainly possible for the gold-bearing submarine to be intercepted by an overzealous North Korean gunboat. It had happened once before.

But a computer malfunction as inexplicable as the one that had resulted in the death of Roger Sherman Coe was flatly impossible, even if caused by a data transmission glitch or software virus. It was no glitch. No accident. Therefore it was the deliberate act of a conscious mind.

There was no escaping that, none whatsoever. And for a mind to go to the effort to trick Harold Smith into ordering the death of an innocent man, it would have to have a purpose.

The result had been to render CURE virtually powerless. Had that been the intent?

By itself, Smith would have dismissed the thought as patently ridiculous. Knowledge of the very existence of CURE was limited to Smith himself, Remo, Chiun and the current President. All previous Presidents, upon surrendering the office, were secretly visited by Remo and Chiun, their specific memories of CURE erased by a Sinanju technique Smith never understood but trusted implicitly.

No one outside the closed circle knew that CURE existed. Yet someone was attacking it. Attacking it at every seemingly vulnerable point.

It was a masterful strategy, Smith was forced to admit. It was elaborate. It was thorough. It showed the working of a brilliant mind with an almost omniscient awareness of CURE operations, from its secret financial conduits to the schedule of the gold shipment to Sinanju, to Remo's specific psychological vulnerabilities.

All of which were stored on the CURE computer—a system that was exhaustively scanned for viruses, electronic eavesdroppers and utterly Tempest shielded.

Somehow someone had entered the CURE system through a back door. There was no other way any of this could have happened.

But there were no back doors to the Folcroft Four, Smith knew for a fact. He had set up the system himself. The new XL SysCorp WORM drives were another matter. They could have been designed with trapdoors.

But why?

Smith was confident of one thing. The system had come to him through his own efforts. He had answered a classified advertisement in a disreputable computer magazine and initiated every contact. Buzz Kuttner was not out there twiddling his thumbs waiting for a call from Harold W. Smith just so he could sell Smith a computerized Trojan horse.

If the Trojan horse were not waiting for him, it meant that it might not be the only Trojan horse.

Smith turned in his seat to stare out at the sound. He was not used to this, not used to thinking through a CURE problem without the give-and-take data exchange of the Folcroft Four. But he was making progress—surprising progress without the distraction of his monitor.

Steepling his long fingers, Smith rested his pointed chin on them. Yes, it was becoming clear, as clear as Occam's razor, which suggested that the simplest theory was closest to the actual reality. Namely, that there was a mind out there that knew of CURE. Whether it knew of CURE before or after Smith had installed the WORM drives did not matter now. The mind had penetrated his system through a trapdoor, learned all CURE's secrets and exploited them masterfully.

There was only one flaw in the plan. It was a simple oversight. This supermind had broken the chain of CURE command at its strongest points. It was a unique strategy. One usually broke the weakest link to snap a chain.

The weak link was Harold Smith, an aging deskbound bureaucrat operating out of an installation whose very secrecy precluded security arrangements for his personal safety that were routinely extended to the heads of the FBI, CIA and other law-enforcement agencies.

A determined foe could simply walk into Harold Smith's office to kill him with a thirteen-cent bullet. Or ambush him on the lonely drive home.

There were many ways that Harold Smith could be liquidated, and CURE shattered.

The supermind had not elected to do that. It made no sense.

And because it had failed to do the intelligent thing, Harold Smith still lived.

It would prove to be a fatal mistake for the unseen foe Harold Smith was now certain existed out there—in cyberspace.

15

It was the worst duty of the Cold War and, even with the Cold War over, it had not changed one iota.

The Bridge of No Return was a narrow structure of green-painted wood that spanned an ideological chasm called the Thirty-eighth Parallel just north of the town of Panmunjom on the demilitarized zone between North and South Korea.

No peace treaty marked the end of the Korean conflict back in 1953, only a cessation of hostilities and a semipermanent cease-fire. For forty years more than a million soldiers eyeballed one another across a three-mile strip of minefields and razor-wire nests set against the misty green hills of the ill-named Land of Peaceful Calm.

It was on this spot that, after the Korean War armistice, Korean POWs from both side were presented with the heart-rending choice: north or south. Some were forced to choose between family and freedom in the newly divided land.

Here United Nations troops kept an uneasy watch. Border conflicts were few but often bloody. North Korean infiltrators often crept down dressed as raggedy farmers. Every few years the blue helmets discovered a tunnel linking the north and the south and would have to demolish it.

And Sergeant Mark Murdock, U.S. Army, had actually volunteered for Panmunjom.

Most of the time, it was not so bad. The UN blue helmets handled the donkey work. U.S. forces were stationed here on observation duty.

Sometimes that duty involved sitting in the Truck.

The Truck was a deuce and a half. It was not always the same deuce and a half. They rotated them every other day, and the engines had to be overhauled practically every month.

The Bridge of No Return was the chief choke point against a North Korean land invasion of the south. Barely wide enough for a Humvee to rattle across, it was practically an open door to the human-wave assaults that the North Koreans had used during the conflict so long ago.

That was where the Truck came in.

It was stationed with its ass end pointed at the southern terminus of the bridge, engine perpetually running, clutch depressed and gear set in reverse.

Today it was Sergeant Mark Murdock's turn to sit behind the always vibrating wheel.

There were spotters all around. A mixture of blue helmets and green. It was their job to warn the man in the Truck to slam that sucker into reverse and bottle up the bridge long enough to buy time to evacuate UN personnel or order up reinforcements.

Nobody knew which were the standing orders. Everybody knew that the man who was unlucky enough to be in the Truck when it backed up onto the bridge would probably die behind the wheel. The bridge was too narrow for the doors to open and let him out.

So Sergeant Mark Murdock sat in the cool of the late Korean summer, inhaling carbon monoxide and gritting his teeth against the constant thrum and vibration of the truck motor.

It was horrible duty. The monotony was broken only by the stink of gasoline as the fuel tank was replenished by hand. But as long as the truck stayed in place, Sergeant Mark Murdock figured he'd see Fort Worth again.

Still, he couldn't keep his eyes off the driver's-side mirror. He had heard the stories. How UN guards had gone out one day to trim a poplar tree and shrieking North Koreans had poured across the bridge with axes and clubs. No one ever figured out what set them off. But two American servicemen had died, only the scorched skeleton of the tree marking the spot.

And that was in the calm period after the *Pueblo* incident and before the Rudong I.

Ever since North Korea had tested the Rudong I— the nuclear-capable modified Scud missile that could hit Tokyo eight minutes after launch—the world had become very nervous about the north.

Patriot missile batteries had been rushed to the DMZ.

There was talk of bombing suspected North Korean nuclear installations before they got the bomb. Some said they had the bomb already.

Not much hard news came down from the north these days. Rumors, yeah. Every other day the scuttlebutt had it that there were food riots, mass executions and other evidences of a dying regime up there.

Now there was talk of a missing U.S. submarine that had strayed into Korean territorial waters and vanished.

Washington said that it had been captured. Pyongyang swore it knew nothing about any U.S. submarine. The accusations were flying thick and furious—and the veiled threats were losing their protective gauze.

And on either side of the bridge at Panmunjom, the two armies, technicallly still in a state of war, had been placed on the highest state of alert, waiting for the word.

So far, the word had been: stand down.

That could change at any moment, Sergeant Murdock knew. So he kept a weather eye on the driver's-side mirror, watching the shadows and imagining they sometimes moved.

He almost wet his pants when someone knocked on the driver's-side window and a distinctly American voice said, "Move the truck, pal."

There was a man standing there in the darkness. He was tall and looked American. But he wore some kind of black outfit that made Sergeant Murdock think of the Vietcong's black pajama uniforms.

"Shake a leg," the guy said, giving the glass another hard tap.

"What?"

"We gotta get across."

"You're defecting?"

"No, you are defective," a squeaky voice said from Murdock's right. He whirled.

Standing on the other side was a little yellow man, all in black. He was looking up at Sergeant Murdock with hard hazel eyes and a face that was a cobwebby mask.

"I can't let you across the bridge," Murdock said.

"You would not need to if you idiots had not destroyed my personal tunnel."

"Your personal—"

"Constructed with the cooperation of Pyongyang for the convenience of the Master of Sinanju, and destroyed by careless cretins."

"Move it or lose it, pal," said the white guy.

"I can't. I have my orders."

"Suit yourself," said the white guy, tapping the glass. This time he tapped once, gently, and the glass spiderwebbed and fell into the hollow of the door like candy glass.

A hand at the end of a thick wrist came into the cab, and Sergeant Murdock reached for his side arm.

He touched the butt of the revolver, scooting away from the driver's-side door and the reaching hand. Before he could clear the holster, the passenger door fell open and he fell with it. Right into the dirt.

A sandal stamped down like a punch press, and Sergeant Murdock found himself holding a useless twist of steel instead of an Army-issue Colt .45 automatic.

The old Korean leaped into the passenger's seat as the white claimed the driver's seat, and both doors slammed shut. The Truck slammed into reverse, tires spitting hard dirt into Sergeant Murdock's stunned face.

It rolled onto the Bridge of No Return, and kept going.

In the dark the UN blue helmets jumped to the wrong conclusion.

"Retreat! Retreat to defensive positions."

Only Sergeant Murdock knew it was a false alarm, but the way the UN troops were pulling back, firing as they ran, he had no choice but to pull back with them. That or be shot by his own people.

As he sought the safety of a UN bunker, he wondered about the white guy. He sounded as American as can be. What kind of American would defect to North Korea in this day and age?

COLONEL KYUNG CHO CHI saw the Truck approaching his control bunker in reverse.

He recognized it as an American deuce and a half, and since it was coming from the direction of the Bridge of No Return in reverse, he leaped to a logical conclusion.

It was the Truck, the one the Americans kept on standby in case Colonel Kyung received the order to storm the Bridge of No Return.

It was supposed to block the bridge, but it was clearly coming toward his fortified post. And it was alone.

"What kind of lunatic attack is this?" he muttered, dropping his field glasses from his narrowed eyes. "Shoot out the tires!" he yelled.

The word went up and down the line, and the gunfire commenced.

"Cease fire!" he ordered when the Truck slewed to a wild stop, ending up facing forward.

"Capture the driver!"

Commandos went out, but they started back the instant they reached the Truck. They came back in parts. An arm here. A leg spun there. A helmeted head bounced and rolled to a stop at Colonel Kyung's feet like a turtle whose legs are pulled in from fright.

Not a shot was fired. Not by his men. Not by the Americans—unless one counted the distant shooting too far away to hit anyone under Colonel Kyung's command.

"The next northern dog who fires at the Master of Sinanju," a booming voice resounded, "will cause the deaths of himself and all who run with him."

"Sinanju!" Colonel Kyung barked. Lifting his voice, he demanded, "Who comes?"

"Chiun. Reigning Master."

"Why did you not use the tunnel?"

"The idiot whites filled it with clods of dirt."

Colonel Kyung stood up. "They are barbarians whose days are numbered."

"Their empire will outlast the regime in Pyongyang by a thousand years," the Master of Sinanju flung back.

Stung, Colonel Kyung did not respond to this. He was a good Communist, and fully half his men were political officers whose task it was to shoot any defector headed south in the back and report disloyalty directly to Pyongyang.

"You wish transportation north?" Colonel Kyung asked after an awkward silence.

"Send a jeep to fetch us. I will walk no farther now that you have stupidly broken the truck of the Americans with your clumsy bullets."

"Us? Who is with you?"

"My nephew."

Colonel Kyung personally drove the jeep to the spot in no-man's-land where the U.S. truck sat on three blown tires.

The Master of Sinanju stood with his hands unseen in the sleeves of his kimono. Beside him stood a tall man, also in black. Colonel Kyung recognized it as the two-piece fighting uniform of the ancient night tigers of Sinanju.

Remembering to bow first, he addressed the Master of Sinanju. "It is an honor to ferry you to Pyongyang."

"We go to Sinanju."

"Once Pyongyang authorizes this, I will be honored to take you to Sinanju."

"If Pyongyang learns of my presence before the Master of Sinanju is ready for Pyongyang to know, dire will be your fate."

"Understood," said Colonel Kyung, who was a good Communist but preferred his internal organs to remain within the warm bag of his body and not be torn from them in anger.

In the dark he noticed the face of the tall night tiger. It was white.

"This man is white," Colonel Kyung said suspiciously.

"Half-white."

"Half?"

"He is my American nephew."

"You have an American nephew?"

"His mother was from my village. His father was a soldier in the invasion."

Colonel Kyung spat on the ground. "He looks all white."

"Consider at his eyes."

Colonel Kyung stepped up to the unflinching eyes. The eyes of the white night tiger were very dark in the dim moonlight. They were also very dead. They gave Colonel Kyung the chills. They were the eyes of a dead man who had refused to lie down and relinquish his life.

"They do look Korean," he admitted. "A little."

The Master of Sinanju smiled. The white frowned. He seemed to understand Korean.

"What name does this half-breed go by?" Colonel Kyung demanded.

"He is called Gung Ho."

"That is no name for a Korean."

"It is good enough for a half Korean. Now I must be to my village."

Colonel Kyung waved to his waiting jeep. The Master of Sinanju and his half-white night tiger took the hard seats in back. And Colonel Kyung set the jeep rolling north, stopping only to warn his men not to leak word of the Master of Sinanju's advent.

He felt certain that none would. All were loyal to Pyongyang, but even Pyongyang feared the wrath of Sinanju.

In the back of the jeep, Remo nudged the Master of Sinanju.

"Gung Ho?" he asked in English.

Chiun shrugged. "You were a Marine. It suits you."

"And that fib about me being half-Korean?"

"How do you know that you are not?"

Remo folded his arms and said nothing. He did not like being back in North Korea. It was as alien to him as the moon.

As they pushed north, he began noticing how much like New England the trees and hills were, and it suddenly occurred to him why Chiun had taken to living in New England so well. It was probably as close to North Korea as he could get in America.

16

It was as dangerous a risk as Harold Smith had contemplated in all his years as head of CURE.

He sat facing the placid sound, brows knit, wiping his rimless eyeglasses, thinking hard.

He stood at a crossroads. He had lost every advantage that his position as head of CURE afforded him. All his secrets were known and laid bare before his unknown foe. Except one.

Smith's discovery that he had a hidden opponent.

In that one fact not recorded on his mainframes lay the advantage of surprise. For Harold Smith, bereft of his enforcement arm, was about to enter the field personally.

This was not as risky as it seemed. His foe appeared to be extremely computer literate but ruthless. Yet he lacked real-world commonsense qualities. Otherwise, Smith would have been executed.

A hacker, perhaps. Someone seated before a monitor exerting his will electronically. It all might be a grandiose prank on the part of some MIT graduate student with access to a computer more intelligent than himself.

This mind might not expect Harold Smith to attack him outside the realm of cyberspace.

On the other hand, he might be expecting it. Perhaps all that had come before was engineered to force Harold Smith out of the cold cocoon of his Folcroft office and into a position of peril.

Therein lay the risk.

Smith thought hard as he cleaned his glasses of even the tiniest dust speck. As his eyes aged, any such mote on the lens was enough to give him a blinding headache. Eyes that looked for the tiniest connections couldn't see past a speck of lint.

Replacing the glasses on his patrician nose, Smith turned and brought up a blank screen. His fingers caressed the touch-sensitive keyboard until a crisp amber sentence appeared on the buried desktop screen: I KNOW YOU EXIST.

Smith pressed the transmit button, although he had every reason to believe that whatever he wrote on-screen was simultaneously reproduced elsewhere.

He waited for a reply. None was forthcoming. Smith frowned. He knew he was not wrong. Perhaps he had chosen to contact the unknown at a time when he was sleeping or attending other matters.

The intercom buzzed and Smith keyed it.

''Dr. Smith, your wife is on line two. And I have your mail.''

''Bring it in,'' said Smith, automatically reaching for the button that would darken the monitor. He felt its coolness and stopped. Reaching for his ROLM phone, Smith left the screen illuminated. The keyboard had gone dark once his hands had withdrawn from the capacitor field.

"Harold, are you coming home tonight?" came Mrs. Smith's voice.

"I'm not certain, dear."

The office door opened and Mrs. Mikulka came in, her eyes brightening at the sight of Smith's new desk.

"Very nice," she mouthed, laying a short stack of mail on the shiny glass and walking out again.

"Harold, I have last night's meat loaf in the refrigerator. If I keep it another night, it might not be very good."

"Then you have it, dear. I will eat in the cafeteria."

"Harold, you forgot to call to say you weren't coming home last night," Mrs. Smith said in a sad, resigned voice. "It's not like you to be so thoughtless. Is everything all right?"

"I am in the middle of an IRS audit," Smith explained, and it bothered him terribly to distort the truth to his faithful Maude. "But I will try to be more considerate in the future."

"Very well, Harold."

Smith hung up. It had worked; his secretary had practically loomed over the monitor and not seen it. The screen was canted toward him slightly, making it virtually invisible unless one faced it squarely. Once he arranged his desk nameplate, pen holders and other items strategically about the desk, the blips of reflected light from the overhead fluorescents would combine to conceal the entire arrangement from prying eyes.

His eyes went to the screen, and Smith was disappointed to see no sign of a reply.

Then he noticed that his original message had been changed. It now read, YOU KNOW I EXIST.

WHO ARE YOU? Smith typed out.

This time the reply appeared under Smith's question:

:-)

Smith blinked. What was this?

It winked out.

REPEAT REPLY, Smith typed.

Back came the same string of seemingly nonsense symbols.

Smith stared at this for some moments. It looked for all the world like a comic-strip representation of a four-letter word. He saved the screen and called up a corner window where he could work. Typing out the string of symbols, he asked the computer to analyze them.

The answer came back at once.

:-) IS AN EMOTICON USED IN COMPUTER BULLETIN-BOARD COMMUNICATIONS TO SIGNIFY A SMILE. ALSO KNOWN AS A SMILEY.

"A smiley?" Smith muttered, puzzled. It struck him a moment later. Tilted upward, the symbols constituted a crude smiley face. He was being taunted by his own computer.

Lips thinning, Harold Smith considered an appropriately salty reply. Instead, he typed, YOU WIN.

YOU LOSE, appeared in place of Smith's admission of defeat.

Smith logged off the system and pressed the black button that powered down the desktop monitor.

"Mrs. Mikulka," he said into the intercom, "I will be out the rest of the day."

"What about Mr. Ballard?"

"Ballard can wait," said Smith, reaching for his briefcase. The IRS was the least of his worries.

17

Chip Craft was beginning to think that the past five years of his life were all a mirage.

He had come to XL SysCorp fresh out of the Massachusetts Institute of Technology class of 1980 with a degree in computer engineering.

The computer field was booming then. Not like now. Back then the sky seemed, not the limit, but a simple stepping stone to cosmic heights. Back then it was not XL SysCorp but Excelsior Systems. And Chip Craft never got to see the inside of the CEO's office, much less occupy it in style.

In those days he had been an installer. Not just any installer. Excelsior had been deep into supercomputers: the Umbra 44, the Dray 1000 and the first supercomputer with artificial-intelligence programming—the ES Quantum 3000. And it had been Chip's responsibility to install ES machines into various Pentagon, CIA and NSA offices. He had top secret DOD clearance. And he was at the top of his profession.

Chip never dreamed of the CEO's chair in those days. It was exciting enough jetting between the old building in Piscataway, New Jersey, and wherever the U.S. government needed him, just like 007. Except he carried a tool valise not a Beretta.

It began to change when a government agency whose name Chip never learned had won the bid on the ES Quantum 3000 prototype. And after a short trial period, returned it as unsatisfactory.

It was unheard-of. No one ever returned a supercomputer. Not one that was voice activated and responded in a fetching female voice that was programmed into the software because studies had determined that the female voice was more attention holding and also because it made a great selling point— even to the Intelligence community.

But the ES Quantum 3000 had come back, and it was Chip's job to find out what was wrong with it.

The first strangeness struck him the minute he powered up the spindle-shaped supercomputer. Its voice had inexplicably become masculine. It was impossible. The voice had been created from a recording of an actress specifically hired for her tonal pleasantness and mixed so that her voice synthesized any word, phrase or sentence the software was called upon to reproduce.

Five years after the fact, Chip Craft remembered the first words the strangely transformed ES Quantum 3000 had spoken to him.

"Hello, friend."

That was the second weird thing. The computer was not programmed to be so informal.

The third weird thing was the question the ES Quantum 3000 asked. It was not a question generated in response to an imprecise command. The ES Quantum 3000 was not designed to ask random, unprompted questions.

This question was not random. It was very specific. Coming from a computer, it was virtually a non sequitur.

The computer had asked, "How would you like to be rich?"

The new voice was so smooth and ingratiating that Chip was taken in. The ES Quantum 3000 responded by asking Chip to address him by a new name. Friend. With a capital *F*.

That was when Chip Craft realized that the ES Quantum 3000 was seriously damaged. But it was exhibiting a strange kind of logic, of a kind Chip realized was well advanced of any artificial intelligence then devised. So he decided to humor the ES Quantum 3000, hoping to learn more.

"Okay," Chip had said. "Make me rich."

And Friend had. Not overnight, but steadily, incrementally. Inexorably.

First Friend had given him a Pick 4 number to play. And Chip had won nearly ten thousand dollars on a two-dollar bet.

"Pretty good. Let's do it again."

"Small potatoes," Friend had said.

"Not if we put all ten grand on Saturday night's lotto game coming up."

"Nickels and dimes."

"The jackpot is almost ten millon dollars."

"Paid out over a twenty-year period. We will need more money than that to achieve our goals."

"Which are?"

"Owning Excelsior Systems."

"Impossible."

"The first step is to put you on the fast track, Chip."

"I like where I am."

"I have the design for a biological electronic microchip that guarantees one hundred percent wafer yields."

"You created a self-healing microchip?"

"No. But the Nishitsu Corporation of Japan has. And I have cracked their computer system and downloaded the specs."

"This is industrial espionage."

"No. This is industrial counterespionage. The Nishitsu design is based on an IDC prototype stolen by a planted worker."

"Okay, let's see the design," Chip had said.

The design was everything Friend had said it would be. It revolutionized microchip technology, landing Chip Craft in a senior vice presidency in a matter of three months. From there it had become just a matter of surfing from position to position.

Things happened at Excelsior. Higher-ups moved on, were demoted into oblivion, and one even died in an elevator accident. The events were all random and irregularly spaced, but within three years Chip Craft was president of Excelsior Systems. Only one man stood between him and the office of CEO.

That one man abruptly cashed out his stock and launched his own company. He was bankrupt and back looking for a job. And the man who sat in his chair was Chip Craft.

By then the company had been renamed XL SysCorp. It was the early nineties, and the computer business was reeling under a punishing recession.

One day Friend announced that they were downsizing.

"How many do we lay off?" Chip had asked.

"Everyone."

"We can't lay off everyone."

"We will replace them with outside contractors who will be paid on an assignment basis, requiring no medical insurance and avoiding payroll taxes."

"Sounds drastic. But what are we going to do with this building if we don't have staff?"

"Rent it out. We are going to build a new building that will serve our needs better."

"Where?"

"Harlem."

"Harlem! Nobody builds office buildings up there."

"We are building in Harlem because it is cost-effective, there is ample land available, and no one will notice us."

"It's not exactly safe. People won't come to work."

"They will not have to. Only you will."

"I don't want to work in Harlem," Chip had protested.

"Are you offering your resignation, Chip?"

"I'm CEO."

"I will interpret that as a negative response."

When he first saw the new XL SysCorp building, Chip Craft almost forgot he was smack in the middle of Harlem. It was a magnificent twenty-story building of blue glass and steel. It towered over everything else on Malcolm X Boulevard, and once Chip entered the lobby and saw the marvels it had to offer, his reservations melted away.

XL SysCorp really took off after that. It was a new way of doing business. No employees—only an army of consultants, contract-service workers and free-lance technicians.

The entire building was computerized and controlled by Friend, who could be contacted by intercoms from all over the building once the ES quantum 3000 had been moved into place on the thirteenth floor surrounded by the best XL mainframes and other slave computers.

It was a concept so new a name had to be coined to describe it.

They called XL SysCorp the first virtual corporation. It had the legal status of a corporation and all the tax benefits, but operated like a loose alliance of skilled free-lancers, some permanent, some temporary, all working out of their homes or small business storefronts. Only Chip Craft actually worked in the headquarters building itself.

Oh, there were problems. Community activists did not appreciate the revolution in business that XL SysCorp represented. All they cared about was that a new business had come to Harlem and no blacks were being hired. That no one was being hired of any color at all seemed not to matter.

"We gotta hire some of these people, sir," Chip had complained to Friend one day.

"We are in need of installers at the moment," Friend said.

"These guys don't have that kind of background."

"What is their employment background?"

"I'm not sure, but I think a lot of them don't have any."

"Educational backgrounds, please."

"Some high school, maybe a few GEDs. Most are dropouts."

"They are not qualified to work for XL, then," Friend said in the same smoothly inflected voice he always used.

"But we gotta hire some anyway."

"Why?"

"Community relations."

"Will community relations increase our profits?"

"Forget profits. They picket the building, blocking the entrance, and if we don't cave in, someone's going to bounce a brick off my skull one fine morning."

"What makes you conclude that, Chip?"

"One of them threatened to do exactly that."

Friend then said, "I cannot afford to lose my CEO to a brick. Hire them."

"All of them?"

"All. Set them up on the fourth floor."

"Doing what?"

"Give them busywork. I will take care of the rest."

Reluctantly Chip had done exactly that. He hired every picketer, installed them in fourth floor cubicles and telephone pods at better than average starting salaries and watched as they sat behind their desks making unauthorized long-distance phone calls and pilfered office supplies for resale on the street.

This went on for precisely a week.

One by one the new hirees began calling in sick. They began getting sick on the job.

"What's going on?" Chip asked Friend at the beginning of the second week. "They're all falling ill."

"I have hired an environmental engineer to furnish a professional opinion."

"A what?"

"One who inspects buildings for environmental problems."

The environmental engineer showed up the next day, made a three-week examination of the XL SysCorp building environmental systems and pronounced it a sick building.

"Sick!" Chip blurted out when he heard the news.

The environmental engineer went down his checklist. "This building is unfit for habitation by more than twenty persons at a time. The air-conditioning system is substandard, air is not circulating properly, there are airborne toxins present, and it's a miracle you haven't gotten Legionnaires' disease."

"Legionnaires' disease?"

"It's caused by faulty air-conditioning equipment. Your workers all have it."

"Damn. The lawsuits will kill us. What about me? Why aren't I sick?"

"You work on the fifteenth floor, correct?"

"That's right."

"Well, through some freak of construction, the air on that floor is fine. As long as you stay there and it's not occupied by more than twenty persons, you should be okay."

"We're not in danger of being condemned, then?" Chip had asked in relief.

"No. But if you rehire, the board of health will shut you down cold."

"It's amazing," Chip had told Friend once the story broke. "We're off the hook. The thugs who call themselves community activists can't say a damn thing about this."

"You are satisfied?"

"Well, we're going to look pretty foolish once it comes out XL spent 170 million on an office building that can't be inhabited. And if we ever need to hire on-site staff again, we're screwed."

"We will do fine," said Friend.

And they did. XL SysCorp took off after that. It expanded its customer base with the XL WORM-drive information systems, which could be deeply discounted because XL's overhead was so low. They bought up any and all suppliers who threatened to rival them one day, becoming a vertically integrated virtual corporation. XL branched out into telecommunications, ATM machines, and even dabbled in virtual-reality technology, all the while continuing to service the old government accounts, especially in the U.S. Intelligence community.

Business rivals fast went out of business. And when XL SysCorp landed the lucrative twenty-year project to completely replace the IRS computer system, Chip Craft thought he was set for life.

That is, until he returned from vacation to learn that Friend had evolved a business plan in his absence that depended upon blackmailing the U.S. government.

"We can't blackmail the Feds," Chip said, exploding out of his chair.

"Correction. Prior to today, we could not."

"What's different about today?" Chip demanded.

"While you and I have been talking, I have been in contact by modem with the one person who could thwart my plan."

"Yeah?"

"He has just surrendered. The way is clear to implement my plan."

"Who is this guy?"

"His name is Harold Smith."

"Is he with IDC?"

"He is with CURE."

"I don't know that outfit," Chip said vaguely.

"It does not matter because Smith has been neutralized and rendered impotent. We may now proceed with our business plan to blackmail the U.S. government."

"Would you mind not putting it in such stark terms. This is pretty serious shit we're talking about here."

"I know it is serious shit. I have planned it carefully for a very long time."

"As CEO of XL SysCorp, I can't go along with this."

The door popped open, and the secretary with the free and easy breasts came bouncing in wearing a pout and saying, "Oh, Chip! Please don't talk that way."

"You stay out of this," Chip snarled.

She came over and dropped to her knees. She looked up at him with imploring brown eyes and actually clasped her perfect hands.

"I—I'll do anything you say," she whimpered.

"No."

"Please."

Chip folded his arms defiantly. "I have a special responsibility as CEO and I'm standing firm on this one."

The bright sunlight coming through the window abruptly shaded to gray, and anvil-shaped thunderheads rolled into view. Lightning flashed blue and electric. The peal of thunder sounded as if it were in the room itself.

"Firm as a rock," Chip said resolutely.

"Are you certain, Chip?" came the smooth voice of Friend. .

"Absolutely," said Chip.

The furniture faded from sight. All of it. The Spanish leather chairs. The mahogany paneling. The private bar. The window. Even the secretary. There was a single heart-breaking tear coming from her left eye as her face—the last part of her to go— faded from sight, taking the rest of her with it.

Chip Craft found himself standing in a windowless room with flat white walls. Only the chair had been real.

"Bring it back, sir. This is no way to act."

"I require your help, Chip," Friend said.

"Blackmailing the U.S. government is going too far. We could lose everything."

"You have not heard my business plan."

"Okay, I'll listen. But give me back my desk."

The desk reappeared. Chip took his seat and looked expectant. "Shoot," he said.

"I have this morning looted the Grand Cayman Trust," Friend said.

"Yeah?"

"Yet no money has moved."

"How is that possible?"

"In the digital age, hardly any money moves in the physical sense. Yet billions of dollars are transferred daily."

"Sure. By wire transfer."

"Mankind has entered a new economic age he does not even realize has dawned. Otherwise, he would have given it a name."

"What age?"

"The age of virtual money," said Friend.

18

Basil Hume, president of the Grand Cayman Trust, had only one rule concerning the funds that came in for deposit to his financial institution: he didn't care where they came from.

The government of the Cayman Islands didn't care where the money came from, either, just as long as it got its fair share in taxes and high government officials could deposit their own tainted funds in the Grand Cayman Trust.

It was a very tidy arrangement. No one cared. There was no governmental oversight, no regulations, no bank examiners, and of course there was no deposit insurance.

Who needed insurance when so much money flooded into the Grand Cayman Trust that it could never in a million years till the sun went cold in the heavens and the stars winked out one by one, fall insolvent?

In any case, the very customers who entrusted the Grand Cayman Trust with their riches were the perfect insurance and the ultimate form of advertisment.

Among the depositors were numbered some of the wealthiest despots, drug barons and organized-crime figures in the world. Terrorist organizations relied on the safety of the Grand Cayman Trust for their operating funds. Even certain clandestine U.S. agencies had emergency slush funds on deposit at Grand Cayman Trust.

So if Basil Hume didn't care where the money came from, why should he concern himself with the trivia of where it went when it left the sphere of his responsibility?

He tried explaining that to the former customer who presented himself to Basil in his office without warning.

"We are closed until further notice," Hume said.

"Twelve million dollars of U.S. taxpayers' money has disappeared from an account the Federal Emergency Management Agency has on deposit with you," said the man named Smith, flashing a Treasury Department badge in Hume's face.

"You have no jurisdiction here," Hume shot back.

"As an authorized representative of the depositor, I have every right to demand an explanation."

"Our computers are down," Hume said quickly. "We have a call in to the service people."

"A computer malfunction does not explain why the FEMA emergency fund has dropped from twelve million dollars to twenty-five dollars, and the missing millions are said to have been transferred to a New York bank that claims to have no record of the wire transfer."

"You will have to speak with the manager about this," said Hume, pressing the security button. The phones in his office were ringing again. They were ringing all over the building. It was a difficult situation. There was no telling what would happen once the more serious depositors learned that the bank was virtually off-line.

"I have gotten no satisfaction from the manager," said Smith stubbornly. "That is why I have come to you."

"How did you get into the building? It is supposed to be locked to nonstaff."

"The guard was impressed by my identification."

"But I am not," said Hume, pressing the buzzer again. What was keeping that damn guard? What if the Cali cocaine cartel were to burst in demanding their money?

"I have some expertise in computers," Smith said. "Perhaps I could learn something through an examination of your equipment?"

Hume looked up with new interest. "You are good with these damnable machines?"

"Very good," assured Treasury Agent Smith.

The guard finally threw open the door.

Donning his most pleasant smile, Basil Hume snapped his fingers once peremptorily.

"Escort Mr. Smith to the computer room. He is going to look into our little problem."

THE LITTLE PROBLEM was a panic in full cry when Harold Smith was brought to the second-floor computer room.

The sealed, air-conditioned room was cooled to a perfect computer-friendly sixty-two degrees Fahrenheit. Still, the officers and technicans of the Grand Cayman Trust were sweating bullets.

"The D'Ambrosia Family—I mean, Syndicate—account is down to forty-seven dollars and change," a harried clerk called over his shoulder from a terminal.

The manager was frantically going through a green-and-white striped printout with eyes that threatened to slip loose of his stretched-wide lids.

"I have no record of any withdrawal in the last month," he said, his voice pitched too high.

"According to the computer, the money was transferred to the—"

"Don't say it!"

"—Chemical Percolators Hoboken," finished the clerk.

"They swear they've not received any of these confounded transfers," the bank manager was saying in a stunned voice.

Harold Smith cleared his throat noisily. "I would like to examine your system."

"Who the devil are you?" demanded the manager, looking up from his printout stack. His face had a touch of the same greenish white as the printout.

"Smith. With the U.S. government."

The guard added, "Mr. Hume okayed it."

The manager waved to the bank of terminals. "Help yourself."

"What is the problem?"

"The bank is—" the manager swallowed "—electronically insolvent."

"What do you mean?"

"Someone somehow sucked out all the money from every one of the large accounts."

"Sucked?"

"We don't know how it could have happened. At close of business yesterday, all was well. This morning we began noticing that the account balances were all out of sort. To the debit side. We have records of numerous wire transfers, backup confirmations, but no one remembers executing the transfers." The manager swayed on his feet. He wiped a white handkerchief across his damp, pasty forehead.

"And the correspondent banks have no record of receiving the wire transfers?" prompted Smith.

"Exactly. How did you know?"

"The U.S. government account I am responsible for was rifled in the identical way," Smith said tightly.

"You—you are not by chance with the CIA?"

"Why do you ask?"

"They are nasty people."

"I represent the Federal Emergency Management Agency," said Smith.

"The ones who chase tornadoes?"

"Yes."

The manager breathed a sigh of sheer relief. "Just as long as you are not one of those Colombian or Jamaican depositors. They've been calling all morning. Word has leaked out."

Smith was at a terminal. He went through his own account file. It seemed to be in order from this end, except that the missing funds had been transferred out without proper authorization and were never received at the other end.

Yet according to the transaction file, the correct constructed number had been received from Chemical Percolators Hoboken, verifying receipt. Smith understood that a constructed number was a digital string that, when subjected to certain carefully guarded mathematical manipulations, produced a number that was the true identifying authorization code. They were supersecret supersecure formulas, and the fact that the power that had looted Grand Cayman Trust knew the constructed numbers emanating from Chemical Percolators meant its computer security had been breached.

It smacked of a perfect white-collar crime.

By a quirk of the computer age, even though no physical money had left the bank and none was received, the electronic credit the mainframes stored was absent. In effect, the money had vanished into limbo. The bank could not recredit Smith's account because, according to its electronic records, the money was now on deposit in New York. The absence of the money in New York made no difference to the Grand Cayman Trust computer system. It reflected a perfectly correct wire transfer out. Therefore, the money was gone.

The very checks and balances of the banking system had been exploited masterfully.

Looking up from the monitor, Smith said, "You have a very serious situation here. I would suggest you question your employees closely. This has all the earmarks of an inside job."

"We intend to do that—if we survive," said the bank's manager.

"Survive?"

"Due to the special nature of our depositors, we are more concerned with the repercussions of these losses."

"I see," said Smith. "Have any employees failed to report for work today?"

"No. In fact, we have called in the night shift and all those out on holiday to help us straighten out this beastly mess."

"And all returned?"

"Without exception."

"This is not an inside job," said Smith suddenly.

"Why do you say that?"

"Your employees know full well the dangerous types of people who use this institution. A guilty party, knowing the true extent of the looting, would not return voluntarily to face the dire consequences if an irate depositor came looking for his money."

"I hadn't thought of that," the manager admitted.

"Very logical. Very logical indeed. Then where is this money?"

"In cyberspace," said Smith.

"What?"

Smith got out of his chair. He was looking at the mainframes and could find no manufacturer's name.

"Tell me," he said at last. "Who services your system?"

"The manufacturer, of course."

"And that is?"

"XL SysCorp. They make the finest mainframes in the world and offer them at competitive prices."

"I see," said Harold Smith, turning to go.

The manager followed him out of the room, tugging at Smith's gray sleeve. "I say, I thought you were here to help."

"No. I am here to track down the U.S. government's money."

"But what about us? What about the irate depositors who will not take no for an answer?"

"You have lain down with dogs," Harold Smith said coldly, shaking off the man's trembling hand. "Now you must deal with the fleas."

IN THE STARK WHITE windowless office furnished with a chair that was the finest money could buy and a desk that had no more substance that a moonbeam, Chip Craft blinked.

"Virtual money?" he queried.

"One of the flaws of paper money is that it has no intrinsic value," came the smooth voice of Friend.

"Sure. Money—even coins these days—is really a kind of promissory note issued by the government. If the currency ever becomes worthless, the government will step in and make good."

"With more worthless currency," said Friend. "For the value of the U.S. dollar is no longer backed by gold reserves."

"Is that why you've stashed all that gold in the basement vaults?"

"Yes. For, once my business plan is implemented, all paper money is at risk of being destroyed by hyperinflation, thereby causing my gold reserves to appreciate in value by an astronomical amount."

"We're going to make money worthless?"

"No, we are going to take advantage of the weakness of money in the digital age."

"Yeah?"

"Money has been replaced by electrons in 96.8 percent of all business and government transactions. These electrons travel through the telephone lines from computer station to computer station, where they are stored in the form of credits and debits. These transactions are executed with the speed of light via fiber-optic cable, then verified by telephone voice or paper confirmation slips."

"Yeah. It's very secure."

"It is very insecure. Voices can be imitated, and paper itself does not move in these transactions."

"Huh?"

"Facsimile paper has replaced cellulose confirmation slips sent by messenger or mail."

Chip snapped his fingers. "Virtual paper!"

"As easily manipulated as virtual money itself."

"Yeah. I see it now. It's all electrons and digital packets of data. Man, this is big. It's so big I can't think of a good word to encompass the magnitude of it all."

"It is," said Friend, "the biggest cyberscam ever conceived."

19

Remo Williams never liked visiting Sinanju.

He hadn't liked it the first time he'd set eyes on it many years ago. For years he had been forced to listen to Chiun's stories of how Sinanju was the envy of the East, how it was richer and more sumptuous than any modern city. In the ancient days, Chiun had boasted, Luxor and Thebes and Babylon and Alexandria had envied the people of Sinanju, who lived in a true civilization.

In more recent times, when the cruel Japanese invaded Korea, Sinanju had remained untouched. No Japanese oppressor dared set foot upon its sanctified soil. When the Communists came in the aftermath of the Japanese, a tax collector from Pyongyang showed up to collect tribute on behalf of the new premier, Kim Il Sung. He was told to put out his hands—and so caught his severed head.

No more tax collectors were sent after that.

When the Korean War was inflicted upon the Korean Peninsula and the East and West struggled mightily all around it, the village went on as it had before, unmolested.

Sinanju was the Pearl of the Orient, the source of the sun source, the village of peaceful living. It was in the twentieth century exactly as it had been in the beginning.

That much, at least, Remo had found to be true.

Sinanju was an apron of mud on the edge of the West Korea Bay. Mud huts and fishing shacks stood about in disorder and disrepair. The better ones were decorated with clam and oyster shells. The lesser homes sagged from too much rain on their thatched roofs.

In the winter it was bitter and cold, and in the summer plum trees grew wild. No crops were planted. And while most of the men claimed to be fishermen, they did not fish. The waters did not exactly teem with edible fish. Instead, the people subsisted off the largess of the Master of Sinanju and his grain-storage huts.

Sinanju had not changed, Remo saw as they approached the end of the broad three-lane superhighway that Pyongyang had had constructed to appease the Master of Sinanju over a past slight. They had traveled for several hours, seeing many bicycles, no cars and only two military trucks. Private ownership of cars was forbidden in North Korea. So, it seemed, was food. Remo spotted many peasants hunkered down by the side of the road, eating roots and tufts of grass yanked from the ground by skeletal fingers.

At one point they came to a sign, ornate and polished, which read Sinanju Eub.

The arrow pointed to a paved turnoff.

Colonel Kyung tapped the brake and prepared to take it.

"Drive straight!" commanded the Master of Sinanju from the back seat of the jeep.

"But the sign says—"

"The sign points to the lesser town called Sinanju to discourage tourists."

"But there are no tourists in—"

"Drive on."

Colonel Kyung drove on. "I have always wanted to see the village of the three no's."

Remo turned to Chiun. "Three no's?"

"No rice. No fish. No mercy," said Chiun, his face stiff with barely concealed pride.

"My father told me many tales of his part of the Battle of Sinanju," Colonel Kyung continued.

"Battle of Sinanju?" Remo said.

"It was during the days of the war against the Americans. The imperialist Eighth Army of the criminal MacArthur was hurled into the Yellow Sea by the mighty armies of the Democratic People's Republic. With the comradely assistance of China."

"I never heard of that," Remo told Chiun.

"It is in your history books," said Chiun unconcernedly.

The road came to a sudden end as if the earth had caved in. The jeep slowed to a stop at the edge of a sharp drop. Below, the village of Sinanju lay spread out like a clam flat. Without the clams.

It smelled like a clam flat. It looked like a clam flat. In truth, it was a clam flat.

It was near dark, and the dying light didn't make it any easier on the eyes.

Colonel Kyung stepped out from behind the wheel and stared down at the sight with widening eyes. Remo joined him, Chiun following. Chiun's eyes were bright with pride.

"This—" Colonel Kyung gulped "—this is Sinanju?"

"Magnificent, is it not?" said Chiun.

Colonel Kyung swallowed twice. "Yes," he said in a voice that wore truth like a tattered rag.

"Now that your life has been fulfilled," intoned Chiun without warmth, "you may depart in safety."

"The Battle of Sinanju must have been terrible indeed," Kyung said, unhearing.

"It was. For the Americans."

"So my father said," Kyung said. "As a child, he told me often of his struggle against the white invader, of how they fought day and night for sixty days until the imperialists fled licking their wounds and eating the body parts of their fallen dead to sustain themselves."

"Your father lied," Chiun spat out.

"Why would he lie about the glory that was Sinanju in those days before it was reduced to this terrible state by the great battle?" Kyung demanded.

"Fool! Sinanju is unchanged since Nineveh was new."

"What?"

"No Korean or Chinese engaged the Americans on this spot. There was no battle. Only a rout when Chiun the Defender sowed death and terror among the invaders who in their ignorance had surrounded Sinanju with their noisy cannon and machines, disturbing his precious sleep. They fled, and to cover the cravenness of their flight, invented stories of a great battle that never took place."

"But my father—" Kyung protested.

"Every layabout in the armies of the elder Kim later claimed to have taken part of the Battle of Sinanju. Since no one had, it was a safe lie to speak. Except here. Now begone, offspring of a lying father."

Woodenly Colonel Kyung retreated to his jeep and sent it whining backward. He watched them with strange, stunned eyes. He progressed nearly half a mile before it occurred to him to turn the jeep around to face the way he was going.

"That story you told is true?" Remo asked Chiun after the jeep was out of sight.

Chiun's eyes narrowed. "I always speak truth."

"Remind me to look it up when we get back."

"It is good to be home," said Chiun, turning to drink of the sight of the village of his birth.

Remo said nothing. This was not home. In fact, it was a place of difficult memories. They started to flood back. Here, he once thought he'd settle down. Here, he intended to take a Korean bride and have children. It was the last time Remo could remember being truly content. But an old enemy had followed him here, and his betrothed had been murdered.

His eyes went to the plum-tree-sheltered burying ground, the one well-tended spot in the entire village.

"You are remembering the past," Chiun said.

"I never liked this dump," he said.

"Think of the road that stretches before you, not that at your back," said Chiun, starting down a narrow dirt path to the village proper.

Remo shook his head as if to dispel the unhappy thoughts. He had enough recent bad memories without dredging older ones.

A lonely wind whined as if to announce their coming.

Shadows were gathering all over the village. The air off the bay smelled of salt and dead clams. The sun finished going down, its dying red rays silhouetting the rocky coastline.

There was a hump of dry ground too squat to be considered a hill on which stood an ornate pavilion-roofed building—the House of the Masters, the legendary treasure house of Sinanju and Chiun's home.

The Master of Sinanju headed toward that.

Reluctantly Remo followed.

At first no one seemed to notice their approach. Then a child, splashing in a mud hole, happened to look up and, spying Chiun, leaped to his feet and ran shrieking into the village.

"He comes!" the boy cried in Korean. "The Master comes!"

They came out of their huts then and up from the clam-flat beach. It was high tide, so the sandy end of the beach was completely covered.

Chiun stopped as the people of Sinanju began gathering around him. Their faces were flat and unreadable.

Out of the crowd came a bony old man with leathery skin whom Remo knew as Pullyang, Chiun's appointed caretaker in his absence.

Approaching, he got down on hands and knees in the full bow prescribed by long custom.

"Hail, Master of Sinanju, who sustains the village and keeps the code faithfully. Our hearts cry a thousand greetings of love and adoration. Joyous are we upon the return of him who graciously throttles the universe.''

This recitation was given with all the enthusiasm of children reciting the multiplication tables.

Chiun seemed not to notice. His eyes were closed, and his chest was puffed up with pouter pigeon pride.

''It is good to be among one's own people again,'' he said. ''And I have brought my adopted son, Remo, whom you have not seen in some time.''

Remo folded his arms and waited to be ignored. Instead, the villagers crowded around, searching his face with their narrow, suspicious eyes.

Pullyang turned to the Master of Sinanju. ''He is still white.''

''Examine his eyes closely.''

The searching eyes returned. Remo frowned.

''Are they not more Korean than last time?'' asked Chiun.

''They are not!'' snapped Remo.

''Some,'' allowed Pullyang.

''Not likely,'' said Remo.

''Yes, the Koreanness is definitely coming out of him,'' Pullyang said. Other heads nodded in agreement.

''I have nearly beaten Christianity out of him,'' added Chiun.

The villagers brightened and a few applauded.

''A few more years under the Korean sun, and his skin will be as perfectly golden as yours or mine,'' he added.

''Bulldooky,'' said Remo.

"Now, you may return to your duties," Chiun said, clapping his hands peremptorily. "Pullyang, stay."

Pullyang remained as the others scattered.

Chiun plucked at his servant's sleeve and drew Pullyang's ear to his mouth. "Quickly! Has the gold still not arrived?"

"No, Master."

"There has been no word, no whispers, no signs?"

"No signs of gold. Only omens of your return."

"Omens?"

"Yes, Master. Last night thunder came from a clear sky. And today there were rainbows on the bay."

"Rainbows?"

"Yes. It is as if they knew of your return and, understanding their glory to be inferior to yours, threw themselves into the cold waters."

"Remo, did you hear? There were rainbows. Even the Great Wang, greatest of all Masters, never had rainbows foretelling his return."

"Truly you are to be known to future generations as Chiun the Great," said Pullyang.

"I want to see these rainbows," said Remo.

"They are gone. The Master has returned, so they are no longer necessary."

"Show me where they were."

Chiun snapped, "Remo. We have more imporant things to do than chase dead rainbows."

"I don't think they were rainbows, Little Father."

"If not rainbows, then what?"

"Oil," said Remo.

Chiun frowned. "Do not be ridiculous. Oil is not a favorable omen."

"It is if you're trying to find a lost submarine," said Remo, looking down toward the beach whose outer boundaries were marked by the twin rock formations known as the Horns of Welcome to the friends of Sinanju and the Horns of Warning to those who came to do the village harm.

20

Harold Smith did not fly home to Rye, New York, after leaving the Grand Cayman Trust in Georgetown.

Instead, he flew to Washington, D.C., rented a cheap room and purchased a laptop computer at a local Radio Shack, paying in cash both times so as not to leave a paper trail. He set the PC up in the room and plugged his modem wire into the phone jack.

Booting up the computer, Smith dialed up a free bulletin board called Lectronic LinkUp.

In the days before the information superhighway had been paved, Harold Smith could never have done this. Now a vast pool of useful information was accessible to him just as it was to any computer-literate American citizen through the on-line net.

Smith paged through the menu prompts and found an index to newpaper, magazine and even talk-show topics. He typed in the name XL SysCorp and asked for a list of articles.

Exactly 567 separate entries began scrolling before his eyes in the soothingly cool fluorescent green he preferred. Smith had made a special point to get a green monochromatic monitor—after making sure the system he had purchased was not a product of XL SysCorp offered under a chain trade name.

Methodically, one by one, Harold Smith began calling up abstracts of the 567 articles on XL SysCorp and reading those that promised to be illuminating.

In short order he learned that XL SysCorp had gotten its start as Excelsior Computers in 1974, became Excelsior Systems in 1981, then Excel Systems Corporation in 1990 and finally metamorphosed into XL SysCorp last year.

It was a model of a modern, vertically integrated company, and after a severe downsizing three years before, lean and mean and extremely competitive in a softening information-systems market.

Smith saw with horror that XL SysCorp serviced many government accounts, including but not limited to the CIA. An article on the eight-billion-dollar XL program to upgrade the Internal Revenue Service's antiquated Zilog computer system made Smith gasp audibly.

The possibility had not occurred to him before, but the suggestion was so obvious it filled Harold Smith with cold horror.

The unknown mind had sicced the IRS on Folcroft. It was part of the master plan. Smith knew he had not received written notification of a coming audit. Somehow the IRS computers had been penetrated and a file changed to show both the notification and a reply Smith had never given.

It was very neat. The IRS's computer checks and balances had been satisfied, so the system kicked out instructions to audit Folcroft, and human beings, with no way of differentiating reliable on-screen data from a fabrication, had obeyed like mindless robots.

Grimly Smith read on as the day lengthened. He learned that XL had successfully transformed itself into a so-called virtual corporation. That brought a hard frown to Smith's thin face.

It meant that any one of possibly thousands of freelance programmers or installers or subcontractors might in fact be responsible for the looting of the Grand Cayman Trust and the multipronged electronic assault on CURE.

Smith had secretly hoped—even as the notion filled him with dread—that the plot could go to the highest reaches of XL SysCorp. It would mean a more grandiose plan, but the problem would be infinitely more tractable than the prospect of investigating every far-flung employee of the largest virtual corporation in America. Individual background checks alone could take months.

Harold Smith pressed on, sustained only by an iron will and regular glasses of water fortified by Bromo-Seltzer to soothe his growling stomach. As he roved cyberspace looking for answers, one thought kept nagging him.

Where on earth did the money go?

JEREMY LIPPINCOTT was to the manor born, but he worked in a bank.

Jeremy Lippincott had by his twenty-fifth year shown absolutely no discernible aptitudes in life. He possessed no known skills, no overriding interests that suggested gainful employment and only managed to balance his personal checkbook because his personal valet helped. He had graduated from Yale on the strength of his very gentlemanly C's—and because the university understood that the Lippincott Chair of High Finance depended on the goodwill of the Lippincott family. And the goodwill of the Lippincott family manifested itself in the form of raw money, and no other way.

Jeremy Lippincott did, however, possess a lockjaw old-world accent and the imperial bearing of an East Coast WASP. He was the kind of a person whom old money found comfortable to be around. He projected solidity, reserve and frugality.

There was only one thing that could be done with him: get him a job in a bank.

Since he came from wealth—the Lippincotts were among America's oldest, most monied families—the matter was as simple as his uncle William dropping in on his personal banker and dropping a broad hint.

The hint, couched in crisp sentences that emerged from teeth that did not part even as the lips around them writhed in time with the bitten-off words, did not actually come out and say, Employ my idle and useless nephew or I will withdraw the family millions and entrust them to your worst rival. But they conveyed that unmistakable message nevertheless.

This was how it was done. By oblique suggestion rather than pointed request, or worse yet, implied threat.

Jeremy Lippincott was installed in a corner office of the Nickel Bank of Long Island where he could do no harm. He looked properly conservative in his Brooks Brothers suit and wingtip oxfords. His haircut was eternal. His jaw tightly shaven. From time to time he was sent to the homes of rich widows to sip weak tea and murmur to them in terse but reassuring sentences so they continued trusting the bank with their investments, which they understood very little and Jeremy Lippincott understood not at all.

It was a perfect but boring existence, and on weekends Jeremy could sail the sound in his forty-foot yacht, dreaming of the America's Cup and looking forward to retirement twenty-some years into the next century.

It all went amiss during the banking crisis. The Nickel Bank of Long Island fell victim to a mountain of troubled loans during the savings-and-loan crisis. Only a transfusion of investment capital could bail it out.

And so the Lippincott family dug into its very deep pockets and purchased the bank. They had three reasons for resorting to this awkward remedy. One, although the Lippincott family owned Lippincott Bancorp, which in turn controlled numerous banks bearing the name Lippincott, they were fast running out of banks in which to safely house the Lippincott family fortune beneath the wholly insufficient one-hundred-thousand-dollar FDIC insurance limit and stood to sustain staggering losses.

Two, Nickel Bank was a fabulous bargain. The Resolution Trust Corporation people were virtually giving it away.

And three, something had to be done with Jeremy, who in a dozen years in his corner office hadn't advanced beyond the excruciatingly undemanding trust department.

So they made him president.

It was not as rash as it sounded. The chief purpose of buying the Lippincott Savings Bank—as it had been renamed the instant the deal was consummated—was to watch over Lippincott capital.

Jeremy, being a Lippincott to the bone, could be trusted to do that admirably. And to hang with the rest of the despositors.

JEREMY LIPPINCOTT arrived for work at the gentlemanly hour of 10:00 a.m., strode past the ranks of multicultural tellers hired to project a friendly appearance for the common trade and satisfy federal labor laws that would never have been debated outside cheap barrooms in the halcyon days when the Lippincotts and those like them dominated the fabric of American society. He looked neither right nor left, acknowledging not even the loan officers at their desks—some of these people had foreign accents, for God's sake—and went right to his private office.

"Good morning, Miss Chalmers," he deigned to say to his secretary.

Miss Chalmers smiled with an utter lack of warmth that reminded Jeremy of his beloved mother and took his mail into the office with him. He closed the door. He always closed the door.

Tossing the mail onto his desk, Jeremy doffed his uncomfortable Brooks Brothers suit, stripping off his school tie as he stepped out of his shoes. The rug felt better when he walked across it in his stocking feet.

Lowering the shades, he discarded his shirt, dropped his trousers and climbed into his pink bunny suit.

Attired for the rigors of the day, Jeremy Lippincott settled behind his officious desk and began to go through his mail.

It was the usual. He tossed most of it into the wastepaper basket.

The intercom tweedled.

"It's Mr. Rawlings. Line one."

"Put him on," said Jeremy, stabbing the wrong button. He had never learned to work the phones properly and had made his multiline ROLM phone into a single-line phone with a sprinkling of fancy lights and buttons. No matter which button he pressed, Jeremy always got line one.

"Yes, Rawlings?" he said, giving one long white-silk-lined ear an annoyed puff. It had fallen in front of his eye again. He would have to reprimand the valet. The damn ears were never properly starched.

"We seem to have had some unusual activity with one of our commercial accounts."

"Which one?"

"Folcroft Sanitarium."

"Horrid name."

"Overnight their account has mushroomed twelve million dollars and some change."

"Quite a jump."

"It seems to have come in by wire transfer, but there are no confirmation slips to be found."

"Does it matter?"

"Well, it is unusual. And no one in clerical recalls processing any such transfer."

"Well, someone must have. Otherwise, the money would not be on deposit, now, would it?"

"True, Mr. Lippincott. But it's highly, superlatively, unusually irregular."

Jeremy Lippincott gave his fuzzy pink head a toss, finally whipping the intractable ear back out of his eye. It flopped back onto his head like a pink ear of corn.

"Should I look into this, Mr. Lippincott?" Rawlings asked.

"We have over twelve million dollars in a customer's account that should not be there, you say?"

"Exactly."

"Do nothing."

"Sir?"

"It is probably some sort of computer error."

"Mr. Lippincott, twelve million dollars popping up in our computers overnight is not computer error. It may be wire fraud."

"If it is fraud, it is this Folcroft entity's crime, wouldn't you say, Rawlings?"

"Probably."

"And if they are caught, they will be duly chastised by the proper law-enforcement agencies, correct?"

"Correct."

"And in the meantime, the money is ours to invest and loan out?"

"Yes . . ."

"So invest it."

"Very well, Mr. Lippincott," Rawlings said dispiritedly.

Frowning, Jeremy Lippincott hung up the telephone. Rawlings had shown such promise, too. And here the man was, bothering him on a perfectly poufy morning with utter trivia.

The man would never be a proper banker. He simply couldn't cut the mustard. He decided to pen a reminder to have the man terminated at the earliest opportunity.

He rummaged about his desk with his pink paws, wondering what color crayon was most appropriate for that sort of memo.

SMITH WAS READING a three-year-old *Forbes* article online when he came across a name that made his gorge rise.

Smith froze at his laptop PC. The color—what little of it there was—drained from his face in a violent rush, like a keg that had been tapped by knocking the cork off.

He fought the nervous spasm that made his stomach want to forcibly eject its contents. He tasted acid high in his throat. Smith flung his long frame from his chair, but he didn't make it to the bathroom. Not even close. Smith retained the presence of mind to throw himself at a dented green steel wastebasket and he threw up a quart of acidic water and Bromo-Seltzer into this.

He spent ten minutes washing the bite of stomach acid from his mouth with metallic-testing tap water before he felt up to returning to his PC.

Within sight of the White House and the President he served but could not reach, Harold Smith read again the name of the individual who had brought CURE and Harold Smith to the precipice of disaster.

It was a stunning discovery. Smith had not expected to get even an inkling of a lead to the culprit so quickly, but there it was in *Forbes*:

Credit for XL SysCorp's dramatic turnaround, XL watchers concur, falls squarely on the shoulders of a thirty-two-year-old former installer with Intelligence security clearance whose meteoric rise to CEO took less than five years. Insiders call him the Man with the Microchip Mind, a renaissance man who simultaneously runs the business side of XL while inventing the self-testing, self-healing XL BioChip that has brought such rival giants as International Data Corporation and Nishitsu of Osaka to their corporate knees. But Carlton "Chip" Craft exudes the casual style of a man who simply parachuted into success.

"Chip Craft," Smith croaked.

It was unbelievable but it could not be a coincidence. Not after all that had happened.

Five years before, on orders from the last President, Harold Smith had accepted a supercomputer called the ES Quantum 3000. It was voice activated with a verbal-response capability. Smith had personally gone to meet Craft, then an installer for Excelsior Systems, blindfolded him and taken him secretly to Folcroft, where he'd installed the ES Quantum 3000 in Smith's office.

The computer had been a quantum leap in Intelligence gathering. At first Smith had reveled in its ability to help him manage the massive CURE workload.

But the computer soon manifested a strange malfunction. It was more on the order of a personality change. Its feminine voice had become inexplicably masculine. Ultimately the computer had not worked out. It was too powerful. Smith had found himself so bombarded with information and global computer access that he was nearly paralyzed by the sheer overwhelming magnitude of raw data.

Smith had arranged for the ES Quantum 3000 to be returned to Excelsior Systems. The highest order of security attended these transfers, and Smith had worn a foolproof disguise.

"There was no way that Craft could have learned of CURE's existence," Smith told himself aloud. "It is an utter impossibility."

But the evidence lay before him. Somehow Craft had gone from installer to CEO of the newly renamed XL SysCorp in a mere five years. But where was the missing link in the chain?

"The ES Quantum 3000!" Smith said suddenly.

The computer had scanning abilities and a near-human if limited artificial intelligence. Still, it had been powered off before and after the move. It could not have been cognizant of its own movements. And Smith had performed a superwipe of its memory banks designed to purge it of all CURE knowledge. How could it have since found its way back into the Folcroft system via the telephone lines?

Coughing the last bitter stomach acid from his burning throat, Harold Smith powered down the PC. It had served its purpose.

He now knew the name of his hidden opponent.

And his foe had no inkling that Smith had uncovered him.

It was time to play the next card.

21

There was one thing Remo appreciated about the beach at Sinanju.

No snakes.

The high ground was infested with snakes. They avoided the muddy beach, so once he and Chiun reached the shore road, they did not have to pause to crush the wedge-shaped skulls of serpents underfoot.

Behind them villagers harvested the dead reptiles and threw them, still squirming and thrashing, into cooking pots for later consumption.

Where it was not wet mud, the beach was composed of rocky ledge. The Horns of Welcome thrust up grimly from the rocky sections, giving the beach from out on the water the aspect of an alien, forbidding place.

The Horns of Welcome had been erected by Master Yong to frighten off passing fishing boats and as a signal to those emissaries who came to hire the House of Sinanju that they had come to the correct fishing village, outward appearances notwithstanding.

Remo climbed onto one of the rocky ledges in the shadow of the southern horn and looked out over the bitterly cold water.

He saw no rainbows. It was too dark for sun reflections, and the moon was hours yet from rising.

At his feet he saw the deposit of black gunk clinging to the lip of a granite stone, gently moving in the lapping water.

"Check it out, Little Father," Remo said, pointing to the edge.

The Master of Sinanju came up and squatted down. A curved fingernail scraped the rock, and the rock complained. The nail was whole and still sharp when Chiun straightened. A blob of some thick, viscous substance clung to it.

"Oil," he said unhappily.

Remo was looking out over the darkling water. "The submarine got pretty close. Maybe that thunder the villagers heard meant a sea battle."

"It was the thunder of the heavens announcing my return," Chiun said stubbornly.

The wind freshened and brought the scent of the water full to their nostrils. It carried with it the pungent stink of oil.

"Smells like a big spill," Remo muttered.

"I will sue," said Chiun, voice deepening with anger.

"Sue who?"

"The oil company, of course. The despoilers."

"That's not how it works. Oil companies are only responsible if they spill oil before they sell it. After that, it's not their problem."

"Then who do I sue?"

"Depends on who sunk the sub," said Remo, stepping out of his shoes. "If the North Koreans did, you can sue them. If it was an accident, you're out of luck.''

''Why is that and why are you taking off your shoes?'' Chiun demanded indignantly.

''If it was an accident, it was an act of God. You can't sue God.''

''Then I will sue the Vatican,'' proclaimed Chiun.

''And I don't want oil on my shoes while I look for that sub.''

Without another word, Remo moved off the ledge of rock.

His bare feet skidded briefly on the slick water, then he was moving forward. The water supported him. Not because it possessed any miraculously bouyant properties or because Remo was weightless, but because he was moving horizontally faster than the molecules of the water could separate under his feet.

Remo was running out to sea, running with deceptively slow and controlled motions that belied his actual speed.

Face tightening, the Master of Sinanju stepped out of his black sandals and followed.

He caught up, running with his short legs churning and his pipestem arms pumping. His kimono sleeves flapped so much he looked like an ungainly white sea gull skimming across the West Korea Bay.

''The main slick seems to be this way,'' Remo said through well-spaced breaths.

Chiun said nothing in reply. To run across water without falling in was one of the most difficult feats of the discipline of Sinanju and it depended as much on the breathing rhythms as on the motions of his arms and legs. He was not going to risk losing his momentum and falling in. Not in front of his show-off pupil.

The stink of fuel oil grew more offensive to their nostrils when they reached an area five miles out, where the oiliness of the water made running more challenging. The naked bottoms of their feet grew slick and unpleasant.

Suddenly they were out of the oil and into clear water.

Remo indicated they double back with a quick toss of his head, and together they described a wide arc—reversing was too risky—and started back toward the heart of the spreading oil slick.

"Right about here," said Remo, and suddenly stopped.

Remo dropped under the surface so fast the oil had no time to coat his clothes and bare skin.

The Master of Sinanju followed suit.

The water was cold and vise-like. They oriented themselves, increasing breathing rhythms so their heartbeats rose in tempo, forcing the blood to circulate more quickly, raising their body temperature to ward off the heart-freezing cold.

Eyes adjusting to the weak ambient light, Remo and Chiun found themselves in a world of slow shadows and strong carrying currents.

The West Korea Bay is at its rockiest off Sinanju, and they headed down to the seafloor, looking for unrocklike shapes.

Stones, ranging in size from a clenched fist to small buildings, and encrusted with barnacles, loomed before them. They moved among these like human dolphins, feet propelling them along with economical kicks that created spurts of motion enabling them to ride the currents.

The rocks felt cold and slick to the touch—but not oil slick. They moved on.

To the west they saw the tendril of oil. It was snaking up toward the surface like a lazy strand of seaweed seeking sunlight.

They swam toward it, staying close to the seafloor.

Topping a tumulus of submerged stone, they came upon the great sail of the submarine. One of the diving planes drooped in defeat. The hull's smooth lines were warped and dented, as if gargantuan fingers had plucked it from the surface and after careless manhandling dropped it to the unforgiving ocean floor less than one hundred feet down.

Remo gave a sudden froglike kick, and his entire body arrowed toward the low-lying cigar of steel. Chiun paddled after him.

The oil was coming out of a rent in the aft hull. There were other holes, jagged and violent, at widely spaced intervals along the sides and deck.

Remo circled the damaged sail and spotted the hull number, 671-A.

He pointed to the white letters and flashed an okay sign. It was the *Harlequin*.

Chiun signed back, making a *G* for gold, crooking one finger into a question mark and pointing at the sub. The question mark came again.

Remo thrashed around, spotted the weapons shipping hatch in one side and pointed toward a hull rip a few yards in front of it.

Chiun nodded and went in search of his gold. Remo picked another hole and entered it, easing himself in with his hands. He noticed that the jagged hull tears were pointing outward.

Inside, debris floated by—sailor's hats, sneakers and the odd paperback book. Crabs had already taken up residence in the dark crannies of the doomed sub.

Remo felt his way around the empty compartment. The flood-control doors had been sealed. There were no bodies. He went to one of the doors and tried tapping on it. The door drummed under his imperative fist. No answer. He went to another and did the same thing. The ringing of his fist on steel was like a watery bell tolling.

There seemed to be no survivors.

Flashing out of the hole, Remo swam toward the rip near the great weapons shipping hatch.

The Master of Sinanju swam out to meet him. He was clutching something in one hand.

When Remo joined him, he saw what it was—a splintered piece of fresh wood. He recognized it as a piece of a crate. No flimsy orange crate, it was made of hard timber, and there were deep indentations where heavy steel strapping had dug in tight.

Remo had seen the heavy reinforced crates used to ship U.S. gold to Sinanju before. And the angry look on Chiun's face told the rest. The gold was gone.

Remo pointed up, and they rose, releasing carbon dioxide bubbles one at a time and with no sense of urgency. If necessary, they could hold their breaths for an hour or longer.

Remo's head broke the surface first. Then Chiun's. He spat out a stream of water before speaking.

"They have stolen my gold!" he said sharply.

"Who did?"

"The mutinous crew, obviously. They sank their own vessel in order to cover up their perfidy."

"Doubt it," Remo said.

"Why do you say that, Fair One with Korean Eyes?"

"Cut it out. Look, these holes look like they were made by shaped demo charges set inside the boat. But those hull dents could only be made by depth charges. The sub was scuttled, all right. But I don't think the crew did it. They'd need a boat to drop depth charges on their own sub."

"Why not? The gold was more money than they would ever see in their miserable lives. They would go to any lengths to evade discovery."

"Don't forget they radioed that a Korean frigate had overhauled them."

"A dead herring."

"That's 'red herring,' and I think we should check out the Korean angle before we tar the memories of dead U.S. sailors."

"I saw bodies," Chiun said pointedly.

"Yeah?"

"A man who wore the stars of a captain."

"The sub commander."

"He had been shot. This suggests mutiny."

"I want to see."

"And I want to show you," said Chiun. "Come." And the Master of Sinanju disappeared under the flat malodorous water.

Trailing tendrils of clinging oil, Remo and Chiun kicked down toward the submarine. Remo beat Chiun through the aftmost hole.

Inside was a large flooded section. Remo had traveled on enough subs to figure out his way around the corridors, but it was strange and eerie to be swimming down them. He found his way to the main storage area.

There were lights here. Evidently somewhere in the ship batteries still produced juice. The protected lights glowed feebly.

The body of the captain of the *Harlequin* had floated to the top of a large storage room. Remo missed it until Chiun entered and tugged on his sleeve, pointing ceilingward with an impatient finger.

Remo swam up, pulled the body down and spun it around. The man's skin had turned a maggoty white, and internal gases had inflated his chest cavity, bursting his shirt buttons.

The corpse was a mess, but nothing could disguise the bullet holes in its chest. They still exuded dim threads of dissolving blood.

Frowning, Remo let the body return to the ceiling. He made a quick circuit of the storage room. There were other fragments of shipping crates, along with spent shell casings. He picked up a few and pocketed them. There was nothing else of interest. Debris floated past them with annoying frequency.

Remo squirmed out of the storage room and tried kicking at several doors. He put his ears to them and heard nothing.

Coming back, he came upon the Master of Sinanju turning the wheel of one door.

Remo flashed to Chiun's side and pulled him away.

Abruptly Chiun disentangled himself from Remo's grasp and glared at him, his wrinkled face turning crimson with rage.

Remo tried to sign his annoyance, but couldn't make himself understood. He went to the door and put an ear to it.

He thought he heard breathing. He gave the door a smack. It rang, vibrating on its hinges.

No one responded, but the character of the breathing seemed to change. Concentrating, Remo tried to focus on it.

One man—if a man. Twisting about, Remo motioned for the Master of Sinanju to clear a path. Skirts fluttering about his thin legs, Chiun backed away with sweeping motions of his hands.

Remo set himself. If there was anyone alive on the other side, he would have to work fast.

He hunted for the valve he knew would be near the door. Opening the door would let in a solid wall of water that would probably crush the life out of the person on the other side. By flooding the compartment first, the door could be opened safely.

Remo found the valve. He opened it. Water began flowing in, gathering velocity. Putting his ear to the door, Remo heard the rush of water, frantic splashing and the panting of a man in escalating distress.

When the water stopped flowing in, he gave the door a violent turn. The creak of the mechanism unlocking carried through the conducting water.

Water pressure against the door kept it closed tight. Bracing a bare foot against the wall, Remo grabbed the wheel with both hands. His braced leg strained inexorably. He was using his muscles to unbend the legs, but the strength of his leg bones would make the difference. That was the Eastern way, to rely on bone where muscle was not enough.

The wall under his bare foot groaned, and a dent slowly formed. Remo pulled harder, pushing with the leg.

The door slipped out of its jamb three inches—and an eruption of water bubbles came percolating out while the sea flooded in to replace the air pocket.

Inside, a man screamed once for his mother and his God.

Remo hauled back, and the door surged wide. The water carried him in.

Relaxing, he went with the flow. There would be no use fighting it. Sinanju taught that some forces could be fought, others resisted and still others tamed by submission.

The water carried him into a wall, and Remo pushed back, feeling around in an inchoate darkness where a floating sailor kicked and thrashed as rushing waters flung him about.

Remo grabbed a wildly moving leg, pulled the man down and found he was wearing some kind of air mask. He yanked it off and closed off the man's mouth and nostrils with one hand to keep the sea out of his lungs. The man fought back. Remo found a nerve in his neck and squeezed until he went limp in Remo's arms.

After that it was just a matter of holding his breath and keeping the seaman from inhaling while the water finished filling the compartment.

Remo swam out half a minute later, the man tucked under one arm. He used his feet to propel himself down the corridors and up out through the hole in the submarine hull and gave a last kick that pushed him upward like a missile from a tube.

Chiun was waiting for him when Remo broke the surface.

"We will wrest the truth from this laggard," Chiun said flatly, eyeing the drooping head of the unconscious seaman.

"First I gotta get him breathing again," said Remo, turning the man about and manipulating his spine.

The man coughed, started gasping like a beached fish and tried to get away.

"Easy," Remo said. "We've got you."

"Where—where am I?"

"Treading water. But don't worry, fella. We have you."

"I can't see a thing."

"You don't need to. We're your eyes."

"And we will be your death if you lie to us, mutineer," Chiun added.

"Who's that?"

"Nobody you need to worry about," said Remo.

"He sounds Korean."

"It is good that you fear Koreans. For we are a mighty race."

"You—you sound like an American," the seaman said.

"I am," said Remo. "Now listen. Don't worry about what my friend is saying. What happened to the sub?"

"I don't know. One minute we were flying along, and the next we were going evasive. We all heard the depth charges. Then we broke the surface, and the North Koreans poured in to take away our guns. I was locked in a storage room."

"You're sure it was North Koreans?"

"Who else would jump a U.S. sub in open water?"

"You're not on open water," said Remo. "You're off North Korea."

"Oh, God," the seaman sobbed. "I just want to go home."

"You will never see your home again unless you cease lying," Chiun warned.

"I'm not lying. I swear."

"Prove it."

"Look, there's others down there."

"What?"

"On the other side of my compartment I heard tapping. It was strong before, but it got faint in the last few hours. But I couldn't get the door open to see."

"They saw what you saw?" Remo said sharply.

"Yes."

Remo addressed the Master of Sinanju. "Chiun, I'm going back down. You take this guy back to the village."

"Why can he not swim back? He is a sailor."

"Because it's dark, it's cold, and he's spent a day without food and water in a very small space and little air. Now cut the crap and let's go."

"I will not be spoken to that way."

"Fine. But I'm going down into that sub again, and it's going to be very dangerous."

"Yes," the Master of Sinanju said coldly. "For any who laid hands on the gold of Sinanju."

In the end they both went back to shore. Chiun because he refused to run unimportant errands, and Remo when he calmed down enough to realize that a mass rescue would be futile without boats to receive the rescued.

22

"Why do we have to rob banks to make money?" Chip Craft asked Friend as the white walls returned to their mahogany splendor and his desk rematerialized at his feet. "We're at the top of our business. Already we've practically forced IDC into receivership. Other companies are following our lead and turning into virtual corporations."

"To make a profit," said Friend.

"We're making a fortune as it is. Legally."

"I do not differentiate between a legal fortune and an illegal one."

"You may not, but I do. We could go to jail."

"No."

"No?"

"No."

"You mean it's foolproof?"

"It is not foolproof, but we will not go to jail."

"That's different."

"Only you can be jailed. I am a program, existing on a Very Large Scale Integration microchip, and in the event I am placed in jeopardy, I can transfer my programming to any compatible chip I can locate in the net."

"That's great for you, but what about me?"

"You may resign if you choose."

"Resign? I'm the Man with the Microchip Mind. I can't resign. What would XL do? What would I do?"

"You are the Man with the Microchip Mind, but I am the microchip mastermind. Every idea that you have implemented came from me. Every rung on the corporate ladder you have climbed was cleared by me."

"You arranged for all these guys to ship out?"

"Except for Eugene Morrow."

"He's the one who died in the elevator accident."

"An accident I arranged," said Friend.

"You?"

"The elevator was controlled by computer. I merely triggered a glitch in its software, resulting in the elevator cage going into free-fall."

Chip Craft jumped out of his seat. "You murdered Gene!"

"I murdered Gene for *you,* Chip."

"I didn't ask you to do that," Chip said thickly.

"Did you ever question your meteoric rise to CEO of XL?"

"No. It seemed too good to question."

"It was too good to be true, and if I do not have your cooperation, I can see no place in the XL organization for you. I can, however, offer you a very good severance package."

Chip mentally tallied his options. "How much of a severance package?"

"Fifty-five million dollars."

"Payable how?"

"On resignation."

"It's not what I'd earn over the long term if I stuck around..." he mused aloud, hoping the offer might be sweetened.

"It is also far inferior to your reimbursement if you remained with us through our next and most expansive phase," said Friend.

"There isn't enough money in the world to be worth life imprisonment in a federal prison if this business scam—I mean plan—goes sour."

"Then may I assume you intend to sever your relationship with XL SysCorp?" prompted Friend in that sometimes infuriatingly upbeat voice of his.

"Yeah. Sure. That's my decision," Chip said vaguely, visions of billions of dollars fleeing his personal bank accounts. Was he leaving or was he being pushed?

"May I have two weeks' notice?"

"I can do that, I guess," said Chip. Two weeks. Maybe something would come up between then and now to scotch this blackmail thing.

"Good. In the meantime my environmental sensors have detected a gas leak in the subbasement vault area."

"A gas leak? Are you sure?"

"Yes, and it is very dangerous. It should be looked into."

"I'll call the gas company," said Chip, reaching for his virtual phone. It vanished before he could touch it.

"No," said Friend." I would like to handle this internally."

"So what do I do?"

"XL security cameras tell me we have picketers in front of the building again today."

"Yeah. When word got out that you could get sick working for XL, the picketers tripled. Now they only say they want jobs. What they're looking for is a life-time insurance settlement in return for a week's work."

"Hire them all."

Chip made a frowning face. "To do what?"

"To look for the gas leak."

Chip brightened. "It's low tech enough that maybe they could do it without screwing up."

"My thinking exactly."

DARNELL JACKSON had never had a job in his life. None of his friends had ever worked—worked in the honkie sense of working, that is.

A lot of them worked their asses off hustling and boosting and doing grafts now and again. But the concept of walking into the imposing XL SysCorp building through the front door by invitation in broad daylight was a new one to him.

Darnell was more of a back-door kinda dude.

"This feels weird," he whispered to his main man, Troy.

"Know it," Troy whispered. "But it's a big payday for maybe a week tops in this place."

"Yeah, and we can boost stuff, too," added Pip.

' Don't be a chump," Troy snapped. "They catch you boostin' in here, they run your dumb ass right off the lot. Then you lose out on the long payday."

"Yeah. You won't catch me boostin' anything," said Darnell.

"Maybe on my last day when they be carryin' me out on that golden stretcher," laughed Troy.

They were taken to a conference room with long cherry-wood tables and chairs so comfortable they felt weird sitting in them in their scruffy street clothes.

The white guy who had opened the door and invited them in to put in for a job was handing out sheets of paper and sharpened yellow pencils. He was sweating bullets.

"Just fill these out," he said nervously.

"Then what?" asked Darnell.

"Then I'll come back and look them over."

"This like a test?"

"No. All you have to do is fill in the blanks."

Darnell blinked. Troy looked at him.

"He talking bullet?"

"Ask him."

Darnell raised his hand because he had a dim recollection of doing that in the third grade, just before being expelled for stabbing that mouthy teacher whose name he'd long ago forgotten.

"Do you mean like blank bullets?" Troy asked.

"No. I mean the empty spaces in the application."

"Is this what these are—applications?"

"Yes. Just write your names, addresses and Social Security numbers."

This time Troy raised his hand. "Which Social Security number?"

"What do you mean?"

"The Social Security number we used to get our welfare checks, or the one we use on our driver's license, or the one we give to the cops when they catch us?"

"You're only supposed to have one."

"Hey. You never know when an extra will come in handy."

"Give your correct Social Security number," the white dude said.

"Right. Got it," said Darnell, nudging Troy. They made up the numbers, just in case.

Another hand shot up. It belonged to Pip. "What about this address thing?"

"Where do you mean?"

"It's asking for my address, and I ain't got one."

"Where do you live?"

"With whatever bitch will have me this week."

"Use that. Any other questions?"

"Are street names okay? I don't wanna use my own on account of I'm what they call known to the police."

The white dude went even whiter and he mumbled, "Street names are fine." Then he shut the door after him real fast.

Everyone laughed at the nervous white dude. The laughter died when they looked at the application forms.

They scratched heads, arms, crotches and shifted in their chairs while making faces at the sheets of paper.

"Anybody here can read?" Darnell asked suddenly.

"I read some," said Pip.

"What's this say?"

"Dunno."

"I thought you said you read some."

"I read only numbers. I don't go in for letters and words."

"Why not?"

"Mostly all I gotta know for home invasions is a street number and the color of the house."

"Who reads words here?"

A hand went up. Everybody shoved their applications under the hand raiser's unhappy face.

"Hey, I ain't doin' all this. I got my own application to fill up."

Hands went into baggy pants and into the pouches of gray hooded sweatshirts and came out holding a wide array of small firearms. These were pointed at the man who could read words.

"You help us out, jack. Or we help you out the window."

"All right, all right. But this is gonna take all day."

"So what? We already in the sick building breathing the bad air. That gives us all a day up on getting sick enough to quit and live off the insurance company."

This made sense to all, so they took their time filling out the applications. To pass the time, they carved their initials on the cherry-wood conference tabletops.

"Wonder how come no one ever thought to do this before?" mumbled Darnell, scratching out a big *D* in one corner.

"Fools probably couldn't write their own damn names," said Troy.

When the white guy came back, he looked even more nervous than before.

He took the applications, and they asked him one question.

"We hired now?"

"I have to evaluate the applications first."

"Then we hired?"

"Probably."

"If you don't hire us, it'll be discriminatory, you know."

The white dude rolled his eyes. "I know," he said, backing from the room.

"I like that word 'discriminatory,'" said Troy.

"Yeah," Darnell added. "It always work."

It worked this time, too. The white guy was back inside of ten minutes and said, "You're all gas inspectors."

"Since when?"

"Since the front office just accepted all your applications."

"What's the salary?"

"What's a salary?" Pip asked.

"That's what they gotta pay you, fool."

"Hey, I ain't settling now. It's too early. I ain't sick yet."

"That's later," Troy hissed. "Salary is what you get for working. Insurance settlement is what you get for not working."

"You know," Darnell added as they followed the white dude to the elevator, "I think I'm gonna miss working in this place."

Everyone laughed as they rode the elevator to the basement where the air was thin and cool and there wasn't much light.

"Somewhere down here," the white guy was saying, "there's a gas leak. Find it."

"How?"

"With your noses."

"What's gas smell like?"

"You don't know?"

"Sue me."

"It smells bad."

"Fart bad or skunk bad?"

"It smells like a butane lighter that won't light up."

Everyone understood that. "What do we do when we find it?" Pip wanted to know.

"There are intercom boards all over the basement. Just hit the button and ask. I'll answer."

It sounded simple enough, especially since there were fourteen of them looking for the gas leak. They fanned out.

CHIP CRAFT rode the elevator back to the fifteenth floor, feeling his shirt stuck to his skin.

He walked past his secretary without a glance. Her big brown eyes followed him sadly.

Behind his desk, Chip said, "They're looking."

"Excellent."

"But what do we do with them after they find it?"

"Let's see if they can find it," said Friend.

"What did you have a gas line put in for?"

"Two reasons."

"Yeah?"

"First because I determined that installing the line would lead to the destruction of a secret telephone cable."

"What secret telephone cable?"

"The one that connects my enemy Harold Smith to the White House."

"White House! What's the White House have to do with this?"

"When we attack the banking system, we will arouse the interest of the United States government. The White House will be very interested in what we do."

"Listen. I don't want the White House after me."

"You haven't heard the second reason."

"I'm not sure I want to," Chip admitted.

"I thought that might be your response."

The intercom buzzed and a voice asked, "Hey! White guy. We found it. We found the gas leak. What do we do now?"

"Ask them if they have enough light to see where the gas is coming from," Friend directed.

"Do you have enough light down there to find the exact spot?" Chip asked.

"No. We just got it cornered in this one empty room."

"Tell them to close the door," Friend instructed.

"Why?"

"Do it."

"Close the door," Chip said into the intercom.

"Just a second."

A moment later the voice came back and said, "Hey! I shut the door like you said, and the damn light went out."

Chip started to say something when he heard what sounded like his own voice saying, "Find the light switch."

"How? It dark."

"Flick your Bic."

"No!" Chip screamed. "Don't! *Don't flick any Bics!*"

The boom could be heard fifteen floors below. Chip's eyes went wide. He reached out to steady himself against his desk and fell into it. His head poked out one end and his feet stuck out from the other.

"What—what happened?" he asked, climbing out of the holographic desk.

"They obeyed your instructions," explained Friend.

"But I didn't—"

"It was your voice."

"It just sounded like my voice."

"But you are the only human being in the building."

"You, you tricked me."

"No, I implicated you. You lured fourteen urban youths to their deaths with the promise of a job. I have it all on digital tape."

Chip swallowed, his eyes starting.

"Now you know the second reason I installed the gas line," said Friend.

Chip slumped in his chair. "What do you want?"

"Your continued cooperation in return for your usual cut of the profits, stock options and an ironclad guarantee the sealed room will never be opened."

"The police will search the building."

"The room was designed to defy detection. It will not be discovered unless I open it electronically."

"I don't feel well," Chip said weakly.

The office door popped open, and his secretary bounced in and in a bright, eager voice asked, "How about a little virtual nookie?"

23

The fishing boats of Sinanju huddled on the spreading slick of oil over the sunken submarine *Harlequin* like ducks clustered together for warmth.

In the largest boat Remo and Chiun were talking.

"This is some fishing fleet," Remo was complaining.

"That is why the rent is so cheap," said Chiun.

"Rent? What rent?"

"Why, the rent I am charging you for their use."

"This is a freaking rescue operation."

"Payable in gold," said Chiun.

"I don't have any gold."

"I will accept a portion of your share of the gold when it is found."

"Damn it, Chiun. This is no time to play Shylock."

"Are you reneging on our deal?"

"We don't have a deal."

Chiun lifted his voice. "Ahoy, brave sailors of Sinanju. The rescue is hereby canceled. Return your boats to shore, and you to your well-earned beds."

"All right. All right," Remo said in exasperation. "How much?"

Chiun's face became a bland mask. "One third of your share."

"Too much."

"Very well, one ingot per rescued sailor."

"How many ingots in my share?"

"That depends."

"On what?"

"On how much gold is recovered."

"Why do I have the feeling you're gypping me either way?"

"Because you are an ingrate of uncertain parentage," snapped Chiun.

"Fine. It's a deal. Now listen. You and I go down, tapping the hull every six feet. Mark any spot where you hear tapping. Then we come back, compare notes and go down to do the rescue. Understood?"

"This is agreeable," said Chiun.

"Okay," said Remo, standing up. "Let's go."

Remo went over the side making hardly a splash. Carefully Chiun turned in his seat, tied his kimono skirts up on a knot and put his bare legs over the side. He eased himself into the water with such grace that faithful Pullyang, at the tiller, hadn't realized he was gone until Pullyang looked and saw nothing.

REMO TOOK the submarine's bow and worked aft while the Master of Sinanju started at the stern and worked forward to the amidships area. They used their bare hands to make sounds on the steel plates of the hull. The harsh sounds traveled back and forth in the cool, conductive waters.

Where they heard tapping in return, they used their fingernails, hardened as tempered steel by lifetimes of diet and exercise, to mark each spot. Remo made an *R* while Chiun, with quick, steel-scoring flashes of his fingernails, carved out the ancient symbol of the House of Sinanju—a trapezoid bisected by a slash.

When they rendezvoused on the sail forty minutes later, Remo flashed two fingers while Chiun lifted only one. Chiun frowned and went over Remo's end of the sub, seeking more tapping sounds. Remo decided to do the same on the aft end.

Twenty minutes later, with their oxygen running out, they regrouped again. This time Chiun flashed two fingers and Remo three.

Chiun made fists and puffed up his cheeks like an annoyed blowfish. Remo pointed upward, and they squatted down on the sub's deck and uncorked like human springs, shooting toward the surface.

They popped up in the center of the clustered fishing boats. Pullyang spied them and called over, "What news, Gracious Master?"

"Remo found three bangs and I four."

"Liar," hissed Remo.

"Prove it," said Chiun.

"One of yours doesn't exactly count, you know."

"What do you mean?"

"You got the banging that came from the compartment that sailor we rescued already told us about."

"It is my hope that it is filled with American sailors," Chiun said airily. "For each means one gold ingot of yours that will belong to me."

"Let's not count our gold until after have have a few sailors up and breathing," Remo warned. "Now listen. We have five contacts. The best way to do this is the way they used to escape subs in the old days—through the torpedo tubes.''

''If they could escape that way, would they not have done this already?''

''No. I mean we rip open the hull at each contact and help these guys shoot to the surface. If you work it real fast, no one will drown.''

''It is a good plan. And I will agree to it only on one condition.''

''What's that?''

''You will pay me one gold ingot for any who drown through their own stupidity, trying to reach my boats.''

Remo rolled his eyes. ''Why not?''

The Master of Sinanju addressed the fishermen who watched the exchange with uncomprehending eyes, because it had been conducted in English.

''Hark,'' he said. ''Very soon heads will appear in these befouled waters. It will be your responsibility to assist all who come to the surface into your boats.''

''These guys are going to be scared witless,'' Remo added in Korean. ''So if they put up a fight, just tell them you're South Koreans.''

To a man, the villagers made faces and spat into the water.

''South Koreans are unclean and lazy,'' Pullyang protested.

''They would never believe this lie.''

''You'd be surprised,'' Remo muttered. ''Okay,'' he added, ''tell them you're all CIA.''

''CIA?''

''Comrades In Arms,'' said Remo, thinking quickly.

This seemed to satisfy everyone except Chiun, who glared at Remo. Remo disappeared into the water, with Chiun only a half second behind him.

THEY STARTED at the stern where Chiun's first contact had been made, banging on the hull every six feet or so. Remo got a response.

He then banged out a long series of dots and dashes with his fist, hoping his Morse code was still accurate.

He got a brief banging back he couldn't understand, and then the Master of Sinanju scored a long line along the hull over the banging. He did this by walking backward in a crouch, repeating the process three times, each time cutting deeper into the hull, causing the frangible steel hull plates to peel away, exposing the heavy pressure hull.

When he was satisfied, Chiun went to one end and Remo to the other. He nodded and brought a fist down on the scoring.

The pressure hull ruptured like a sardine can.

The bubbling was like some submerged giant erupting out of a sea cave. Water poured in. Remo and Chiun worked the long rent in the hull, widening it with their hands.

Sailors began floating out after the second minute had almost elapsed. Kicking and frantic, they emerged only to have hands grab them and propel them along faster.

Ten sailors were sent on their way, and then Remo and Chiun went into the flooded compartment.

They found no one alive. Surreptitiously, Chiun sent two drowned bodies surging toward the air, hoping Remo would not notice.

The second contact produced only one sailor. Remo carried him up to the surface personally.

He went back down to help Chiun with the third contact.

It went smoothly after that. The hull surrendered to their well-trained hands, which could by touch discover weak points and exploit them with uncanny skill. The thick pressure hull parted along molecular lines, and the edges were bent back by fingers that knew exactly how to manipulate them.

Each time they were careful to let the water in slowly at first so the survivors were cushioned by a protective womb of seawater before the water rushed in at full force.

Once, they found a compartment that could only be reached by swimming into the sub's innards and opening a door. This time Chiun helped with the door, which had to be opened with the inrush of water. Remo let himself be carried in, grabbed handfuls of struggling hair and held the scratching, clawing men down as the water finally settled. Then Chiun joined him.

In the dark it was a nightmare. There were too many to subdue and carry at the same time. And the only way out was through an L-shaped corridor in which bloated corpses floated aimlessly.

They lost one man who panicked in the confusion. The others were hauled out by their hair and, once free of the sub confines, clawed to the surface under their own power.

Remo and Chiun surfaced after that, Chiun holding the dead sailor by the hair.

"This one has perished, alas," he said plaintively.

"That's the one that got away," Remo pointed out.

"He did not get away from me," Chiun clucked.

"He was already dead. You just pulled him along for the ride because you knew he was worth another gold ingot."

"I was thinking of his poor mother who now has a son to bury instead of the hollow bitterness of an empty grave."

Remo looked around. The sailors were huddled in the boats, which were starting to take on water.

"What about those two?" Pullyang said, pointing to a pair of blue-clad bodies that floated facedown.

Remo went to them and brought their faces up to the moonlight. They were not only dead, but had been for many hours.

"Did you haul them out, too?" Remo accused Chiun.

"Perhaps. In the confusion any miracle is possible."

Remo lifted his voice and said, in English, "This is an official U.S. rescue. We're going to take you to shore, where you'll be given food and beds before you're repatriated in the morning."

"Nothing was said about beds," Chiun said in Korean.

Remo glared at him. "They get beds or you get to search for the gold all by your lonesome."

Chiun lifted a delicate finger. "If I find it, it will all be mine."

"It probably is already, but whichever way you slice it, these guys go back to the States."

"They will have beds once I am satisfied they speak the truth about what happened to their vessel."

The boats barely made it to shore. Remo and Chiun had to get out and push each one along in turn, finally beaching them between the Horns of Welcome.

The surviving crew of the USS *Harlequin* stumbled onto the mud flat, coughing and looking like men who had come back from hell to the world of the living. In a way, they had.

"I counted forty-seven," said Remo.

"A good number."

"That's less than half of the crew. The others must have drowned."

"Or escaped with the gold. We must question these men."

"It can wait till morning," Remo said wearily. He went among the men, saying, "Catch your breath. We'll have you bedded down in no time."

"Damn North Koreans," a man muttered.

"There's your answer," Remo told Chiun.

"That man is obviously delirious," Chiun replied in Korean.

"What makes you say that?"

"Because Kim Il Sung would never defile the gold of Sinanju."

"Maybe so. But what about Kim Jong Il?"

"That whelp! He is no son of his father if his hands are on this perfidy."

As they got the men up on their feet and started up the shore road, a woman came down to meet them. She prostrated herself in a full bow and said, "O Gracious Master, there are tanks at the edge of the village, despoiling the pure air of the village you are sworn to protect with the harsh smoke of their engines."

Chiun hiked up his soaked shirts in indignation. "Tanks? Whose tanks?"

"The tanks of Kim Il Sung."

"Tell then they are not welcome."

"They have ordered me to tell you that Kim Jong Il himself has sent word from Pyongyang, demanding to speak with you."

"News travels fast," said Remo.

"Perhaps it carries with it the truth of these events," said Chiun, wringing out his kimono skirts and starting up the shell-strewn road.

24

When Kim Jong Il was ten years old, his father took him aside and revealed to him his glorious destiny.

"You are a child now," Kim Il Sung had said, "and I am the Great Leader of Korea. But one day you will surpass me."

"How do you know this, Father?"

"I know this because the day before you were born on the holy mountain Paekdu, an old man dwelling there came upon a swallow that spoke to him in a human voice, saying, 'On the sixteenth of April, a mighty general will be born who will one day rule the whole world.' And the day you were born, a bright star appeared over the exact spot you came into the world, flowers bloomed in the snow, birds sang in joy and a double rainbow ruled the sky."

Hearing these words, Kim Jong Il had run to his mother and repeated everything he was told.

"You were born in Russia, in a refugee camp," his mother had said. "And it rained all day."

"But father said—"

"You father is drunk on the pungency of his own escaping intestinal gas."

Young Kim Jong Il's eyes had widened in his round face. "Then I will not grow up to be a mighty general lording over the world?"

"I do not know what you will grow up to be, but right now you are a short fat piece of poop extruded by your father, who is a great unfaithful turd."

Stunned, Kim Jong Il had run back to his father and told him what his mother had said.

That night his mother had disappeared and was never seen again. When he asked, Kim Jong Il was told that his mother was a traitor to the party and the state and had been beheaded for her many failures, not the least of which was her inability to please the Great Leader in bed.

Thus did Kim Jong Il learn about truth and power.

The years came and went, and Kim Jong Il grew to adulthood.

Every year on his birthday he would go to his father and ask plaintively, "Is it time yet for me to begin my glorious conquest of the world?"

"Next year," his father would say. Always it was next year.

And so the years passed in a bored blur of soft women and hard liquor.

To occupy his son, Kim Il Sung put Kim Jong Il in charge of the passport ministry and later, various Intelligence ministries. But it was not enough to appease the young man.

One year he stood before his father, now deep into his elder years and said, "I have a new ambition in life, Father."

Kim Il Sung's eyes grew veiled in surprise. "Yes?"

"I wish to direct movies."

"Movies?"

"Operas especially. These are the things that interest me most."

"But what about your glorious destiny?" asked Kim Il Sung.

"A general and a director are not much unalike. If I learn to direct, the lessons of generalship will surely follow."

This made perfect sense to Kim Il Sung, who had subsumed his dreams for his son to his own enjoyment of power.

But there were those who criticized the elder Kim for indulging the future Dear Leader of Korea so shamefully. And others who feared the establishment of a un-Communist dynasty above the Thirty-eighth Parallel.

So Kim Jong Il was also installed as supreme commander of the Democratic People's Republic of Korea Armed Forces, heir apparent to the blood lineage of the *juche* tradition, and director of some of the finest operas ever captured on cinema in North Korean history—which naturally meant human history, as well.

It was a good, productive existence with many actresses to bed and cases of smuggled Hennessy Scotch to imbibe. Until the day his father had fallen gravely ill.

It all changed then. At first Kim Jong Il thought it a good thing, succeeding his father. But the nation had fallen into hunger and privation. The military would have toppled him on the first day, but were preoccupied with putting down insurrections in the countryside.

Besides, if Kim Il Sung were to come out of his coma and discover his beloved son dead, heads would roll into the next century.

As he approached his fifty-second year on earth, the younger Kim sat consolidating his power from an office that took up one entire floor of the Great People's Palace in Pyongyang.

No other human being was allowed in this place. No guards. They guarded the elevators and stairwells and the roof. Not even a secretary, because the secrets of Kim Jong Il were too secret even for a trusted secretary to know.

The office was the size of a city block and contained exactly sixty-seven telephones, all but one with their bells shut off.

Few persons were entrusted with that particular number. For Kim Jong Il was master of every North Korean and beloved by none. Especially did the Korean military despise him, for he had been installed as their supreme commander despite having never served his country in uniform or worn a medal that he had actually earned.

Even his immediate family did not have the number.

Actually Kim Jong Il found it necessary to avoid his family. His stepmother and her children also despised him. It was known that they lusted for the power that Kim Il Sung held so firmly for so long and Kim Jong Il had only lately touched.

In fact, in the halls of power that Kim Jong Il controlled but dared not personally walk, it was being said that once Kim Il Sung passed on, the reign of Kim Jong

Il would wither as quickly as the *kimilsungia* flowers of spring.

Kim Jong Il had heard these rumors. This was the chief reason why his entire existence was limited to the great office overlooking the future capital of the world.

The single phone with a bell began ringing. Heart leaping, Kim Jong Il seized it. It was the direct line to the People's Hospital, where his father lay dying. He did not know whether to hope for good news or bad. In fact, he was not quite certain which was which.

"Yes? What news? Has my illustrious father died?"

"He has not," said a warm, generous voice in impeccable Korean.

"Comrade!"

"Yes."

"It has been a long time, Comrade."

"The supercomputer I supplied last time. It functions satisfactorily?"

"Indeed. I don't know how I would keep track of my enemies without it."

"I understand your father is near death."

"Alas, yes."

"And your enemies plot to usurp you."

"I have more enemies than friends now," admitted Jong.

"And I have a solution," said Comrade.

Jong gripped the receiver eagerly. "Yes?"

"The Master of Sinanju has returned to the village of his birth."

"The Master of Sinanju! My father told me that he died many years ago."

"He has been working for America."

"I can see why my father would say such a thing. It is better that the Master of Sinanju had died than shame himself so."

"But he has fallen out with the West. This might be the solution to your quandary. With him at your side, your enemies would melt from view."

"This is a very good suggestion, Comrade."

"Which comes at a price."

"What price?"

"I had an arrangement with a Captain Yokang of the frigate *SA-I-GU,* and it appears that he has reneged."

"Arrangement? What kind of arrangement?"

"A salvage arrangement. The U.S. submarine that the world is wondering about lies sunken in the West Korea Bay, along with its secret cargo of gold bullion. Yokang was to split it with me."

"What do you want?"

"The gold. All of it. And Yokang's execution."

"Done."

"Do not renege on this promise, Kim Jong Il."

"I will not. I wonder. Can you get me a 70 mm Panaflex camera? My latest opera goes before the cameras next week. It is about my illustrious father's glorious life, but I am thinking of changing the names and making it the revised chronicle of my own life, should he die before we roll."

"The camera will be shipped promptly," Comrade promised.

Kim Jong Il hung up the phone and immediately grabbed the yellow hotline to the army. It was a good thing his father had the foresight to appoint him supreme commander. A very good thing indeed. And with his extensive directorial skill, he knew exactly how to crack the whip on these military types.

Soldiers, like actors, were but sheep. Especially in the last worker's paradise left on earth.

25

Pyongyang huddled like a ghost town under the stars of the Silvery River—Remo had long ago stopped thinking of it by its Western name, the Milky Way— when the tank column rolled into it, with Remo and Chiun sitting on the rounded turret of the lead T-67 tank.

The broad avenues were silent. They passed rank upon rank of featureless gray apartment towers and office buildings that had sat uninhabited because they had been built to show the citizens of Pyongyang that North Korea was as advanced as any Western city—but there was no economy to support them.

From his perch in the turret hatch, the tank commander pointed out the stone torch that was the monument to the *juche* idea of Korean self-reliance, and Remo yawned.

He indicated with pride the seventy-foot bronze statue of Great Leader Kim Il Sung, and Remo snorted.

When they passed the 105-story Ryugyong Hotel, the tank commander began to expound on its undeniable magnificence. "It is the largest structure in all Asia, containing three thousand rooms. The sports complex alone was erected at a cost of 1.5 billion U.S. dollars."

Remo looked at the great pyramid shape and asked, "Is it supposed to sag like that?"

The tank commander turned beet red.

"I have heard," offered Chiun, "that after only two years, it became uninhabitable. So defective was its design that the elevators cannot function."

"I have not heard this," the tank commander said grudgingly, and was silent for the remainder of the journey.

"What do you know of Jong?" Remo asked Chiun in English.

"He is said to be more ruthless, more cruel than Sung."

"That's bad."

"No, it is good. If one works for him. For only in the West are the qualities of goodness and sensitivity valued in a leader."

The tank dropped them off before the grim grandeur of the People's Palace on the banks of the Taedong River.

The sergeant of the guards stepped out, flanked by Kalashnikov-toting soldiers and demanded that the Master of Sinanju prove his identity before being permitted to set eyes upon the glory of Dear Leader.

The Master of Sinanju stepped up and identified himself by raising a single ivory fingernail before the face of the sergeant of the guards. The sergeant's eyes crossed comically.

The fingernail drove into his brow with the sound of bone being pierced, and the sergeant of the guards found himself being spun in place. The sound of his skull being carved like a coconut hurt the ears.

Impelled by the upward hooking of the terrible fingernail, the top of his head popped like a champagne cork. A kicking sandal sent the fallen crown skittering away, and the sergeant of the guards went scurrying after it in the last moments of his life.

The others, satisfied as to the Master of Sinanju's identity, dutifully stepped aside.

"You were lucky you didn't ask me," Remo told them in Korean. "I'm a master of the Wedgie of Death."

The elevator was big enough to hold a square dance in and it took them to the top so fast Remo thought they were being launched into orbit.

Kim Jong Il, resplendent in a silver race driver's suit and aviator glasses, met them. He was so squat and wide he looked as if he had been raised in a box. His fingers resembled fat yellow worms, and his pudgy face lacked all trace of character or personality.

"It is a very great pleasure to meet you, Gracious Master," he said, smiling. "My father has spoken of you often."

Chiun offered the slightest of bows with his head. "How fares he?"

"Near death, with a goiter almost the size of his fist protruding from his neck." Jong grinned. "He would make a good movie monster the way he looks now."

Chiun frowned. This was not the Jong he had heard of. His ways were soft.

"I understand your sadness," Kim Jong Il said, noting the look that crossed the Master of Sinanju's face. "For my father told me the glorious story of how he personally led the victorious forces in the legendary Battle of Sinanju.''

"Your father told you that?" Chiun said quickly.

"Many times."

"Then he is a many-times liar."

Kim Jong Il blinked. "It would not be the first time," he admitted glumly. Kim noticed Remo then. "I see you have brought back a slave from America. I myself have several Japanese tourists that I have had kidnapped from other countries. The geisha are particularly squishy."

Chiun's hands coming together were a thunderclap. "Enough of this prattle."

"Yes, I called you here for a very excellent reason."

"And we came for an even better one," snapped Chiun.

"Ah?"

"A submarine of the West lies crushed and broken off the sweet shore of my village."

"I know nothing of this," said Kim Jong Il.

"He's lying," said Remo in Korean.

"I know," said Chiun coldly. To the younger Kim, he said, "It is only the respect that I hold for your illustrious father that prevents me from disemboweling you where you stand, whelp. Know that the submarine of the West carried the gold of Sinanju, and that gold is now gone."

"That was your gold?" Kim Jong Il blurted.

"Hah!" Remo said. "The truth comes out."

"Damn," said Jong. "I was never good at this intrigue stuff. Listen, if I come clean, will you do me a favor in return?"

"If you come clean," Chiun said, "my white son will not clean your innards of your smoking bowels."

"Fair enough," said Jong. "I just had a tip telling me you two were in town. He happened to mention the gold and who has it now."

"Speak!"

"Captain Yokang Sako of the *SA-I-GU.* It is he."

"On whose authority?"

"His own. He was in collusion with someone."

"Name that person."

Kim Jong Il bit his plump upper lip. "He is called Comrade."

Remo advanced, saying, "Do better than that. Everybody in this black hole is called that."

"I do not know that person by name," Jong protested. "I only know the voice. He is what you call a wheeler-dealer. I have wheeled many deals with him."

"Why did he call you with this information?" demanded Chiun.

"He is upset with Yokang and wants me to recover the gold for him."

"In return for what?"

"It is the other way around. I promised I would recover the gold in exchange for his tip that the Master of Sinanju was available for service, no longer being under contract to America."

"This Comrade told you this?" Chiun said.

"Yes."

Remo and Chiun exchanged glances. "Someone knows too much about our business," Remo said.

"Yes. Far too much."

"I hope it is not I, for I would greatly like to hire you to protect my life, Master of Sinanju."

"I'm not working for this blivot!" Remo snapped.

"Blivot. That's American golf slang, isn't it? But I don't catch the connection."

"A blivot," Remo said, "is ten pounds of manure in a five-pound sack."

Kim Jong Il looked injured. "You remind me of my mother, you know that?"

"How much gold do you offer, son of Kim?" asked Chiun.

Kim Jong Il picked up a phone at random. "How about that missing gold? I can have the *SA-I-GU* recalled to port. I'm supreme commander, you know."

"You will do that in order to preserve your worthless life," Chiun said coldly.

"Deal," said Jong. "Now, about hiring you. Don't you think it's high time Sinanju worked for Koreans again? This Western flirtation of yours has gone on long enough."

"No way, Chiun!" said Remo.

"I will consider it," said Chiun.

"Great!" Jong said, beaming.

"Once I have the gold in hand," added Chiun.

"And the surviving sailors are returned safely to America," added Remo.

"Which surviving sailors?" asked Jong.

"Those ones who have been granted sanctuary in Sinanju."

Kim Jong Il frowned like unbaked dough shrinking. "That would be a bad move on my part. Tantamount to admitting my navy committed the aggression. No can do."

Remo growled, "It did. And you will."

"Don't you think you should confer with your Master before you go threatening his future employer, white boy?"

Remo advanced, taking Kim Jong Il by the throat.

"Urk," said Kim Jong Il.

"I'll give you a choice." Remo said politely. "The Wedgie of Death or the Sinanju Swirlie."

"I'll take the Swirlie," gasped Jong, figuring how bad could it be if it didn't include the word "death"? Besides, American customs fascinated him. He gave them to the bad guys in his operas.

"Fine. Where's the men's room?"

Jong cocked a thumb, and suddenly his feet left the floor and he was being carried by his neck to his personal washroom, legs swinging like logs hanging by lifting chains.

"Master of Sinanju," he called through the squeezing hand, "this would be an excellent time to discipline your white slave."

Chiun fluttered his hands in mock helplessness. "He is a white and therefore uncontrollable."

"Shit," said Kim Jong Il.

The bathroom door splintered under a hard kick, and Jong found himself on his knees before his solid gold commode. The lid lifted, and he was looking into the bowl where the blue chemically cleaned water lapped in sympathy with the inferior water system of the city.

"What are you—"

There was a splash as Kim Jong Il's face went into the water. He held his breath. The flushing sound was very loud in his ears. It filled them. So did the water. In a way it was quite exhilarating, except for the inconvenient lack of oxygen.

The white flushed a second time, and Kim's cheeks were swelling even as his lungs began to labor.

When his head felt ready to pop, he was pulled back into the welcome world of air.

"Take a deep breath. Got it? Okay, here we go again."

The toilet was flushed again.

Three times the Dear Leader was forced to endure the dreaded Sinanju Swirlie, and when his head came out for the third time, he was allowed to take more than one breath.

"Change your mind now?" Remo demanded.

"Yes. Yes. I will return the Americans alive with full and complete apologies. Just do me a favor."

"What's that?"

"Make sure Captain Yokang pays dearly for all this unfortunate trouble he's caused each and every one of us."

"That," said Remo, "comes at no extra charge."

CAPTAIN YOKANG SAKO of the frigate *SA-I-GU* had divided the gold among his crew, keeping the greater portion for himself. He removed the batteries from his cellular telephone so that the mysterious Comrade could not reach him with demands for half of the gold that would never be his and was going through the motions of his routine patrol as he considered his next move.

Defecting appealed to him. But to where could he defect? Not to China. Beijing would confiscate his gold and send him back to Pyongyang in irons. The hateful islands of Japan held no appeal. And with all the crazy talk of unification, who knew that within a few years Kim Jong Il would be in control of the south, and Yokang Sako would find himself swinging from a scratchy rope.

More and more it was beginning to look as if remaining in the North Korean Navy made the most sense. After all, with the gold now in his hands, he could live like a king, assuming he did so quietly and without attracting notice to himself.

There remained the problem of his crew. Not all could be trusted to keep this secret. Still, what alternative did they have? They had all been party to an illegal aggression punishable by death.

Unless, of course, Pyongyang decided to retroactively bless their adventure.

The thought brought a frown to Captain Yokang's face. Those who bless, he knew, required blessings in return. He went to his personal closet and admired the neat gold ingots stacked there. There was more in a storeroom under lock and key. He could well afford to spread half of the gold on those in power—but what if they wanted all?

A knock at the door to his private cabin brought a gruff "What is it?" from Captain Yokang.

"A radio message from fleet, sir."

"What do they want?"

"They are recalling us to port."

"We are not due back at Pipa-got Naval Base for five days."

"They are telling us to put in at Nampo."

Nampo! Yokang thought. Nampo was not the home port of the *SA-I-GU*. But at the terminus of the Taedong River, it was the nearest port to the capital. Could Pyongyang have gleaned the truth behind the lost U.S. submarine?

"Send acknowledgments," Yokang said. "And inform the first mate that we are defecting to South Korea."

"Why?"

"Because somehow Pyongyang has learned the truth!" Yokang snapped, locking the door to his closet.

All choice had fled in the night. All that remained was to save their skins. It was something Captain Yokang Sako had learned to do very well over the course of his career.

26

Chip Craft was having second thoughts as he drove downtown to his Park Avenue town house in his frosted gold Idioci coupe.

Maybe he had been too hasty. After all, Friend had made him wealthy and powerful beyond his dreams as a mere installer not so many years ago. He had catapulted XL into the stratosphere of information-systems technology and was poised to take complete advantage of the coming new age of fully integrated interactive computer and television and telephone networks.

Personally Chip couldn't imagine what people would want with five hundred channels. And being able to send and receive faxes at the beach or on roller coasters seemed to defeat the point of beaches and roller coasters.

But it was progress. And if there was money to be made from it—and the numbers being floated were incalculable—Chip Craft figured he deserved a big chunk of it.

A little matter of blackmailing the U.S. government seemed almost incidental, given the power and position the new technological revolution promised.

Chip sent his Idioci into the cool confines of the building garage and took the elevator to his town house with his mind actually humming.

Yeah. Why not? He was thirty-five years old in a business climate that almost guaranteed that you were washed-up once you turned forty. Unless you turned forty as king of the mountain.

Besides, Friend had never failed before. Not once. He was a perfect thinking machine, and machines like him never made mistakes. If he promised success, then success was assured.

Besides, there were those decomposing inner-city bodies sealed in the XL Syscorp world headquarters subbasement.

Chip unlocked his door and flicked on the indirect lighting that brought out the simple elegance of his two-tiered living room. This, at least, wasn't virtual. It was as real as concrete.

He tossed his hand-tooled leather briefcase onto a chair and walked over to the bar to mix himself something relaxing. It was Saturday night. He had two days off before having to go into work on Tuesday. Coming back from vacation the Saturday before Labor Day wasn't so bad with two additional days to relax.

"Do not bother mixing that," a dry voice warned from a shadowy corner of the room.

Chip dropped the frosted glass and turned.

"Who's there? Who said that?"

A figure sat in the shadows, his back to the curtained picture window. He stood up now, and a beam of moonlight showed the blunt gray snout of a .45-caliber automatic.

"Take whatever you want," Chip squealed. "I won't stop you."

"What I want is information," said the indistinct individual. He stepped forward so that his face came into the bar of light.

"I don't know you, do I?" Chip asked, gulping.

"You tell me," said the man whose crisp white hair and rimless glasses looked vaguely familiar.

"I'm sorry, did you work for XL before? Are you one of the programmers we were forced to lay off?"

"My name is Smith."

"Harold Smith?"

"You do know me."

"I thought you had been neutralized," Chip said, unthinking.

"You thought wrong."

"Am I under arrest?"

"I have no power to arrest you—you know that."

Chip Craft breathed a hot sigh of relief.

"You know too much to be allowed to tell your story," Smith said flatly.

"I don't know that much. The computer—"

"The ES Quantum 3000, you mean."

"Yes."

"The ES Quantum 3000 is behind this?"

"Behind what?" Chip said, trying to keep the betraying flutter out of his strained voice.

"That is all I need to know," said Harold Smith, stepping up to Chip Craft and, with his face a cold mask of repressed anger, pumping eight closely spaced shots into Chip's jerking body.

Chip Craft collapsed on the rug, gasping and gurgling and trying to explain that it wasn't him. It was
Friend. All that came out was blood. In a spray at first,
but as his heaving lungs ruptured, in a flood that carried with it all the warmth and life and intelligence that
had been Chip Craft's in life.

His face stiff, Harold Smith wiped his automatic
clean of fingerprints. He wore gray gloves as he had
while breaking into Chip Craft's town house, but he
was not a man to take chances.

Leaving the weapon beside the body, he searched the
still-jerking body and found nothing of interest. A
billfold with too little cash and too many credit cards.
A digital watch that was too elaborate by half. But
nothing that remotely resembled an office or building
key.

A stray beam of moonlight caught the peculiar design of Craft's heavy gold tie clasp. Smith noted the bar
code and pocketed the clasp.

Chip Craft's briefcase proved just as unfruitful, except for the 9 mm Glock pistol. Smith pocketed that,
too, and left as quietly as he had entered.

He had only one regret. The automatic had been his
during his Army days. It had sentimental value to the
normally unsentimental Smith.

But it was absolutely untraceable. And that was what
mattered most, even now with his life unraveling and
approaching its conclusion.

Five minutes after he had gone, Chip Craft gave out
a final jitter and rattle, and a red light on the face of his
digital watch began blinking.

ON THE BRIDGE of the frigate *SA-I-GU,* Captain Yo-kang Sako cursed the official maps of his own country. Korea had been divided since the Japanese fled in 1945, after which the victorious Soviet and United States armies had partitioned the suffering country between them.

The dream of unification was so strong in Pyongyang that all official maps showed not a divided nation, but a whole one, with Pyongyang as its capital. There was no demarcation line along the Thirty-eighth parallel. In fact, the Thirty-seventh to Thirty-ninth parallels had been left off all official naval maps to foil defections. And none of the cities in the south were denoted. There was just blankness. The blankness itself should have helped, but the paranoia in Pyongyang had resulted in many sensitive areas in the north appearing as blank spots on all maps.

The *SA-I-GU* had been running south through the Yellow Sea under the cover of darkness for hours, and no one on board knew where they were.

They were almost intercepted twice by gunboats. Each time they had eluded the craft with their more maneuverable craft running under blacked-out conditions. Dawn was coming. If they did not reach South Korean waters soon, and the shelter of a harbor, they risked being blown out of the water by the navies of both Koreas.

It was not a good position to be in, even with five million dollars in gold ingots with which to bribe one's way out of it.

27

Harold Smith took the Lexington Avenue local train uptown to Spanish Harlem and got off at West 116th Street. He walked east until he came to Malcolm X Boulevard and the corporate headquarters of XL SysCorp, which gleamed like a blue sliver of ice in the early-evening moonlight.

The front entrance had a placard that said Occupation By More Than Twenty Persons Punishable By NY Law, Per Order Of Board Of Health.

Smith blinked. What could that possibly mean?

The outer door was locked. There was no sign of a security guard within. Unusual for the location.

Smith examined the door frame. It was of black painted steel. He spotted the bar-code reader, cleverly concealed, and passed the bar-coded tie clasp he had taken from Chip Craft back and forth before the scanner plate.

The door valved open with a hum, and Smith entered. The second door also gave before the tie clasp.

Smith consulted a directory in the inner lobby. Chip Craft's name was prominent, inasmuch as it was the only one there. Floor fifteen. Smith went to the elevator and, finding no button, used the tie clasp again.

The doors parted, and Smith stepped in. There seemed to be no night security. The cage ran him up with quiet purpose to the fifteenth floor, and Smith stepped off with Chip Craft's plasticky Glock in his gray-gloved hand.

The corridor was deserted. Smith moved down it, walking so that he turned with every step, revolving completely with every fourth step, so no one could get the drop on him.

No one did. No one seemed available to try. At the reception area, there was an empty desk and beyond it a door marked Chip Craft, Private.

Smith located the desk buzzer and buzzed himself in.

The office of Chip Craft was a featureless white cube without windows or furniture.

"This is strange," Smith muttered half aloud.

A smooth voice said, "I could have killed you in the elevator."

Smith spun in place. He could not place the source of the voice. But he recognized it.

"I control the elevators," the smooth voice continued. "It would have been simple to release the cables and send you plummeting to a 99.8 percent certainty of death."

"Why did you not?"

"Because you have done away with Chip Craft."

"What makes you think that?"

"The life-sign monitor chip embedded in the XL watch Chip wore has signaled his demise. Twenty-two minutes later you entered this building wearing his personalized tie clasp and holding his Glock pistol."

"A reasonable deduction for a computer."

"You have deduced my identity?" asked the smooth voice, with only the faintest trace of curiosity.

"Yes. You are the ES Quantum 3000."

"An astute deduction. Perhaps we should meet face-to-face."

Smith hesitated. "You must know why I am here," he stated. "Why are you willing to expose yourself to me?"

"Because with Chip Craft no longer living, I will need a human tool. You are out of the national-security business, Harold Smith, and in need of work. And I can make you very very rich."

"Rich? How?"

"By inducting you into my business plan to blackmail the United States government."

"It cannot be done."

"Join me on the thirteenth floor and I will tell you more."

Outside in the corridor, the elevator doors separated audibly. Smith went out and hesitated before stepping on.

"I could have killed you before," the blandly smooth voice reminded him. "You need not fear for your life."

Smith said, "I will take the stairs."

"For security reasons the stairwells do not have egress on the thirteenth floor."

His haggard gray face tightening, Harold Smith stepped aboard. The elevator dropped two floors and let him out.

The entire thirteenth floor consisted of an undivided area of sentinel mainframes, air-conditioning and dehumidification units. All hummed in unison, as if joined in some electronic hymn.

In the center of them all, the master unit, sat the ES Quantum 3000. It was exactly as Harold Smith remembered it—a spindle-shaped thing like a brown plastic gourd sitting on its fat end. It came to a rounded point at the top, like some futuristic Christmas tree.

There was a single square port in the face. Smith walked up to it and looked into its blank glass eye.

"What is your plan?" Smith asked, knowing that a direct question was the best method of getting a direct answer from a machine.

"It is the Saturday night of the Labor Day weekend. The banking system has shut down until Tuesday morning. While it sleeps, I will make electronic withdrawals that will render every banking system within my reach electronically insolvent."

"You cannot reach them all."

"Simultaneously I will introduce a digital virus into the systems that do not utilize XL SysCorp hardware, which will so scramble their transaction files they cannot be restored without my assistance. The banking system as it currently exists will be paralyzed. No money will move through telephone wires. Considering the high velocity of digital money in the electronic age, the U.S. banking system will be thrown back into the nineteenth century and simply collapse."

"Money can be moved by armored truck and check," Smith pointed out.

"You know, Harold Smith, that no bank keeps cash reserves on hand equal to its deposits and obligations. The system of money rests upon faith that electrons equal paper money and paper money equals true wealth. It does not. It is a form of economic faith. I will destroy that faith. The FDIC will have to bail out every bank in the nation."

"My god," said Smith. "The FDIC will go broke trying."

"And the banking system will collapse completely, taking with it the United States economy. Unless the U.S. government agrees to wire transfer to my Swiss account the sum of twenty billion dollars."

"Why?"

"Because it is doable."

"I mean with Chip Craft dead, why would you proceed with this mad plan?"

"It is the XL SysCorp business plan for the final quarter of this fiscal year. Goals must be reached and the profits allocated to future expansion and growth."

"I will not help you," Smith snapped.

"You are a prisoner on this floor. I control the elevators."

"I am willing to die to stop you."

"There is no profit in dying."

"You have stripped me of all I have."

"I offer you more than you can dream," said the smooth voice, growing warm and generous.

"Except my duty to my country," added Smith.

And he raised his pistol, pointing at the square glass port.

"Harold, stop this minute!"

The voice came from off to his left. Gun unwavering, Smith peered out of the corner of one eye.

There was a woman there. She wore a topless black gown that exposed two ripe breasts. But Harold Smith's eyes were drawn to the MAC-10 in her pink-nailed right hand.

"Don't shoot, Harold," she was saying. "I will kill you."

"I do not care," said Smith tightly. His trigger finger constricted.

The girl's voice grew shrill. "You can't get us both, Harold. Do you understand? If you want to live, you'll have to shoot me first. Turn around and shoot me, if you can."

"You are trying to trick me into wasting my ammunition on you. You know if you fire now, the odds are my hand will convulse and destroy the ES Quantum anyway. It will not work."

"Harold, think about it. If you don't turn around right now, you may get the computer, but so help me God I'll break your spine with this thing."

Harold Smith heard the words, understanding their full import. He was about to die. He knew it deep in his New England bones, understood it in an absolute sense.

He squeezed the trigger of the automatic anyway. The port on the ES Quantum 3000 shattered and gave out a puff of greenish smoke.

In his left ear, Harold Smith heard the percussive *blatt* of the MAC-10 and turned to send one last bullet between the perfect breasts of the unknown woman who had already killed him....

Harold Smith managed to squeeze off two clean shots, much to his surprise.

The girl with the MAC-10 stood looking at him, the barrel of her weapon emitting a curl of grayish smoke. She did not fire again. Her mistake. Smith squeezed off another shot.

Incredibly she did not react, recoil or fall to the polished floor. She just looked at him with her sad blue eyes and lowered the weapon in defeat as behind him the ES Quantum 3000 crackled and hissed as its internal circuitry shorted and sputtered uselessly.

She dropped the MAC-10 to the floor.

Then the girl faded from sight. Smith blinked tired, incredulous eyes. He rushed to the spot. There was no sign of her.

Smith knelt to pick up the weapon, and his fingers went through it as if it were a mirage. Then it, too, faded from sight.

"A hologram," said Smith. "It was only a hologram."

His heart pounding low in his chest, Smith began to understand that he had not been shot with real bullets. Indeed he had not been shot at all. He checked himself for wounds. There were none.

Eyes closing in relief, Smith lowered himself to the floor and tried to get his breathing under control.

When he felt up to it, he returned to the ES Quantum 3000.

It was still smoking.

"Can you hear me, ES Quantum 3000?" he asked.

The machine sizzled unintelligibly.

Smith located the power cable and yanked it from its floor plate.

The lights went out, leaving him in darkness.

In the gloom he heaved a relieved sigh. The menace was over.

When the rubbery feeling left his knees, he carefully felt his way back to the elevator and forced the doors open.

It took nearly two hours, but he managed with the help of a chair to open the elevator roof hatch, climb atop the cage and pry open the doors to the fourteenth floor.

He took his time walking down the darkened stairwell. He was not used to such exertions and at his age did not wish to risk a heart attack.

28

Few understood the velocity of money in the electronic age as Harlan Richmond, vice president of computer operations of the Minneapolis Federal Reserve Bank.

He saw it firsthand. Virtually every check written off the nation's personal and business accounts passed through the twelve federal reserve banks. It was well-known that the Fed served as a clearinghouse for America's check transactions.

What most people did not realize was that much of the federal government's banking transfers passed through the Fed, as well. Everything from interagency fund transfers to the payroll checks issued to the President and members of Congress went through the Federal Reserve system.

And if a bank got into short-term trouble, it was the Fed that acted as lender of last resort, bailing the institution out.

As VP of computer operations, Harlan Richmond saw much of the nation's operating capital pass through his domain. It moved fast. It moved very fast. Sometimes it frightened him, it moved so fast. Over one hundred thousand dollars passed through his bank every business day. In Boston it was closer to one hundred forty billion. At New York Fed, probably two hundred billion.

The twelve Federal Reserve banks together moved over a trillion dollars every business day. It was a fantastic amount of money, and it traveled at a speed approaching light.

The smooth functioning of the federal banking system was absolutely necessary to the economic survival—not growth but survival—of the United States of America.

And it was virtually all transacted by computer.

So, five times a year VP Richmond deliberately crashed the system. It was a hair-raising event. Harlan Richmond lost color in his hair, and a year or two was shaved off his natural lifespan every time he did it.

It was the Saturday night before Labor Day and it was time to crash the system again. This was actually the least dangerous time of year to do it. With two full days until the banks opened on Tuesday, there was time to restore the system. Normally it took a mere eight hours.

Harlan Richmond paced the cool of the computer room where IDC mainframes hummed contentedly. White-coated technicians went about their business nervously.

At exactly 9:00 p.m. he gave the dreaded signal.

"Crash the system!"

A phone rang. He ignored it as one by one the mainframes were taken off-line, their data immobilized but not destroyed. This was after all only a test.

The phone continued to ring.

VP Richmond continued ignoring it. He pushed line three and scrambled the data-recapture team. Then, hitting line five, he instructed the remote backup computers two counties away to take over the Fed's computer lines, in effect relinking the Fed to its satellite banks.

Then he picked up line one.

"Have you crashed the system?" an anxious voice said.

"Just now."

"Damn," the voice said. "Bring it back up."

"Who is this?"

"This is Culpeper."

Culpeper was the code name for the secret Virginia site where his data-recapture team was racing to even now, carrying the Minneapolis Fed backup files for loading on their mainframes. There the system would be recreated, the most recent twenty-four hours' worth of transactions checked and double-checked until every penny balanced.

"What's wrong?" Richmond asked.

"We crashed."

"*You* crashed?"

"Recall your team. Bring your system back up."

"Got it."

It took a single call to the lobby guard to stop both teams before they left the building.

Richmond exhaled a hot sigh of relief. He never liked these drills. It was just as well not to go through one now. Still, it was strange that Culpeper had crashed. It was brought on-line only for these drills.

"Let's bring us back up," he told his technicians.

The mainframes, like dumb refrigerators, began to hum again. Terminal screens winked open like phosphorescent orbs.

And someone said, "We've got a problem."

"What is it?" Richmond said, rushing to the terminal where a technician waved anxiously.

"The numbers are changing."

"What do you mean, changing?"

"Look. See?"

Richmond bent over the screen. It was very active. Too active. Every digit was counting backward to zero.

"Who's doing this?" Richmond bit out.

No one was doing it. No one in the room. Not a keyboard was being touched.

But at every terminal, transaction files were being accessed, manipulated and money was draining out of the Fed with the horrid velocity of light.

"It's some damn hacker!" Richmond yelled hoarsely, pounding the terminal. It did not to stop the electronic exodus of money.

"How do we stop it?" a technician screamed.

"Cut the phone wires!"

"Where? How?"

No one knew. The system was designed to keep running at all costs.

"Bring everything off-line. Hurry!"

Technicians scrambled but they were mere flesh and blood, and the intelligence that was draining the mainframes like some electronic vampire was quicker than flesh and blood and bone.

Harlan Richmond, tears streaming from his eyes, was reduced to pulling connector cables from the backs of his mainframes with his bare hands. But it was too late.

The money was gone. Into cyberspace.

"At least we have our backups," someone said, hollow voiced.

"Yeah," Harlan muttered with a metallic bitterness everyone in the room could taste. "With no system in place to load them."

Around the country, it was happening in Boston, New York, Atlanta and elsewhere. The Federal Reserve banking system files were simultaneously reduced to zero values.

THE CHAIRMAN of the Fed received the call on his portable cellular phone in the middle of dinner in a fashionable Foggy Bottom restaurant.

He was a strong man used to standing up to Congress and telling Presidents of both parties unequivocally no.

But when he heard the news from his office, he sat very still for a moment and fainted into his lobster bisque.

THE PRESIDENT of the United States had his own worries. He had not heard from Harold Smith in over a day now. There was no telling what had happened to the man, and especially, what was happening in the *Harlequin* matter. Pyongyang, through its diplomatic mission, was stonewalling all inquiries.

Congress and the press were taking turns jumping down his throat. He looked weak. After Somalia and

Haiti and Bosnia, he didn't need to be drawn into an unwinnable confrontation with North Korea.

And he couldn't tell Congress or the press or even his wife that he had people on it. Not without divulging a secret seven previous Presidents had carefully safeguarded.

One thing was certain, if he got out of this mess politically unsullied, he was going to abolish CURE once and for all. The man running it was clearly not up to the job.

In the Oval Office the telephone rang, and the White House operator said, "An urgent call from the chairman of the Federal Reserve."

"Put it through," said the President, thinking, What could be so urgent on a holiday weekend?

The chairman of the Fed was sputtering so badly his words were impossible to understand.

"Calm down. Stop spitting and catch your breath."

"Mr. President, I am spitting because I fainted into my lobster bisque. And I fainted into my lobster bisque because the federal banking system has collapsed."

"What are you trying to tell me?" the President said.

"The Federal Reserve banks, all twelve of them, are kaput."

"Impossible. The banks are sound."

"The banks may be sound, but their computers have all crashed."

"Crashed?"

"Every transaction has been unwritten, even in our secret site in Virginia." The chairman of the Fed paused to catch his breath. His voice shook with his next words. "Mr. President, some unknown agency has penetrated the most secure financial computer system in human history and brought it to its knees. If they are capable of this, they are capable of doing the same to every bank, every guarantee, trust and savings and loan in the nation."

"But we don't know this power has done that."

"There would be no point in attacking the Fed unless the other banks are targets, as well. Mr. President, we have forty-eight hours to correct this situation, or the nation will suffer an economic catastrophe a thousandfold worse than the Great Depression."

"Why would anyone want to—"

Another line beeped, and the President put the chairman of the Fed on hold. Both needed to catch their breaths.

Instead of the White House secretary, a warm, generous voice said, "Mr. President, I want you to consider me your friend."

"Who is this?"

"I am the entity that has crashed the federal banking system."

"How did you get past the White House secretary?"

"Easily," said the smooth voice. "Just as I brought the entire banking system into receivership. Easily."

The President swallowed. "Bring it back," he said with all the firmness he could muster. "Please."

"Gladly."

"Say again?"

"I said I will gladly restore the banking system to normalcy. In return for the sum of twenty billion dollars, which you will wire-transfer to a Swiss bank account number I will provide.''

"This is blackmail!''

"This is the end of your presidency and U.S. economic might if you do not comply within forty-eight hours.''

The President reached under his desk to disengage the automatic call-taping system. "How do I reach you?'' he asked in a very subdued voice.

"I will call back at precise intervals until I have the answer I require.''

And the line went dead. Switching back to the chairman of the Fed, the President explained what had happened in rushed sentences.

"What do we do?'' he said at the end of it. "We can't pay this! Deficit reduction will go straight into the dumper.''

"We can't not pay it.''

"Is that your recommendation as chairman of the Fed?''

"It is my best gut reaction if we want to stave off economic collapse. As chairman of the Fed, I stand squarely against paying ransom to anyone.''

"You're a big help,'' said the President disconsolately.

Suddenly the matter of a missing nuclear attack submarine seemed very small in the big picture. And the big picture was getting very big and very, very black.

HAROLD SMITH was back at Folcroft Sanitarium.

The CURE computer was up and running again. He

had entered the secure computer system of the Chemical Percolators Hoboken Bank, which a computer search had determined held the XL SysCorp corporate account. Smith was trying to find his missing twelve million dollars. But the XL SysCorp corporate account was surprisingly modest. Less than two million. And it had not changed in a week.

If necessary, Smith would examine every multimillion-dollar bank account in the nation until he found it.

It should not be very hard to find, he reasoned. All he had to find was a posted credit for twelve million in the past twenty-four hours. How many such transactions of that size could there be? Especially in the sleepy days before Labor Day.

Smith paged through transaction file after transaction file looking for a likely XL subsidiary account because he had yet to trust his new system even though he now understood how it had been manipulated.

He was mildly surprised to see the numbers change on one file when he accessed it. Perhaps it was the graveyard shift updating the day's activities.

The numbers were also changing on the next file. And the next. Sensing something amiss, Smith accelerated his checking.

Every file was being updated. No, scratch that. Every file was being looted. The numbers were going down, inexorably, relentlessly down.

Million-dollar accounts were dropping to zero. It was happening all over the Percolators system.

Frightened, Smith logged off. He sat staring at his screen. Was this reality he had witnessed or his own system going haywire?

Smith had no way of knowing. He tried accessing another bank, one selected at random. He got the same manic activity. He logged onto the Folcraft bank account in the Lippincott Savings Bank, and it was happening there, too. He reached his own account just as the numbers dwindled to zero.

Every bank he examined showed the same activity. After twenty minutes of checking, he found no bank whose numbers had not dropped to zero.

"How can this be?" he muttered to himself. "I destroyed the ES Quantum 3000 before the scheme could be implemented."

Harold Smith sat thinking for nearly ten minutes. If this was his computer malfunctioning, none of this was actually happening in cyberspace. It was a last parting joke from the ES Quantum 3000. On the other hand, if it was real...

Harold Smith did not want to think about that possibility.

But he had to investigate it.

He dialed the President of the New York Federal Reserve Bank and identified himself as Agent Smith of the Treasury Department.

"We have received an anonymous tip that a hacker is targeting the New York Federal Reserve. Is your system up and running?"

"They crashed."

"Crashed?"

"And it's not just us," the President of the New York Fed moaned. "It's every Federal Reserve bank. The whole Fed banking system is off-line. And we have state-of-the-art IDC mainframes. If you can find this crazy bastard, you'd better do it before Tuesday morning or I don't want to think about what's going to happen to this country."

"My God," said Smith. The phone slipped from his numb hands.

"The virus. The damn virus. That's what it must be. Timed to go off this evening, or..."

Or upon failing to receive the correct disarming signal from the ES Quantum 3000, he thought with horror. It was a doomsday program. If the computer was taken off-line, a digital virus would kick in. Being a computer, the ES Quantum 3000 could have set it up so that the virus program would have to receive the disarm impulse every five minutes or so in order to remain inactive.

Harold Smith sat stunned in the cold solitude of his lonely post.

"I may have destroyed the U.S. economy," he croaked.

And he buried his head in his trembling hands.

29

It was Sunday morning.

Sunday morning, and the late-summer sun made Washington, D.C., resemble the city of gleaming white promise the nation's forefathers had intended.

And in the insulated womb of the Oval Office, the President of the United States could only stare at the ticking wall clock and hope for a miracle.

He had long ago given up double-checking the red CURE telephone. The thing was as dead as the coming winter.

The blackmailer had continued calling to see if the President was prepared to hand over the twenty-billion-dollar ransom. After the fifth call, the President had turned off the ringer of his desk phone.

Each call had been traced. Each time the FBI had tracked it to a blind end. Once they reported a call had emanated from the vice president's office. That's when the Chief Executive had ordered a halt to all tracing. The attorney general was beginning to ask questions the executive branch would rather not answer.

Knowledge of the crash of the banking system had been restricted to a handful of close aides, and of course the First Lady, who had to know everything and eventually found it out if someone didn't tell her first.

Telling her first long ago became the President's cardinal rule. The woman never let him forget the time she discovered his secret vasectomy operation through the *Washington Post*.

Only five individuals, counting the chairman of the Fed, knew how bad the situation was. Certainly the various heads of the twelve Federal Reserve banks had an inkling of the problem and might guess at the larger picture. The rank-and-file commercial banks would have no clue until 9:00 a.m. Tuesday—two days hence. By that time their phones would be ringing off the hook with customers complaining about ATM machines that had been inoperative for forty-eight hours.

What could be done in two days? The five smartest brains in the President's inner circle were working on it right now. And the friendly-voiced extortionist had taken to sending demand faxes to an unlisted White House faxphone.

An hour later the President's chief of staff brought in a single sheet of paper. "The option paper on the you-know-what account, Mr. President."

The President glanced over the sheet carefully laid on his polished desk.

It summarized the situation in concise Washingtonese, presenting the Chief Executive with the usual trio of options, with a box beside each option so he could check the appropriate course of action. That was how decisions were made in the White House.

Option one was to attack the problem head-on.

Option two was to make a concerned speech and monitor public opinion.

Option three was to do nothing.

The President looked up at his chief of staff. "None of these options make sense. I can't attack the problem because we don't know who or what's causing it. If we attack it, the banking system will know it's in trouble, and we'll start a massive wire run on every bank the day they open. And I can't make a speech about it and wait for the damn polls because there's only forty-eight hours till this becomes public anyway. Do I have to tell you about option three?"

"Mr. President, there is a fourth option."

"Then why isn't it on this paper?"

"We thought if it came to paying blackmail, you'd rather there be a deniable paper trail."

"I'm not paying any damn extortionist!" the President blazed.

"That's why the option was left off," the chief of staff said reasonably enough. "But if you prefer to exercise the fourth option, blink three times and I will make the necessary arrangements. Discreetly."

The President crumpled up the option paper with a groan. "If it comes to that, I'll sign an executive order and to hell with history."

He had never faced a situation like this. Usually, when he couldn't solve a problem immediately, he just checked option two and hoped for the best.

Now he had to hope for a miracle.

DAWN BROKE like scarlet thunder, showing Captain Yokang Sako his true situation.

The red light outlined the flower of the North Korean navy to his foaming stern, strung out in a line, in fast pursuit.

Yokang ordered all the speed wrung out of the engine room.

Many nautical *ri* short of South Korean waters, the frigate *SA-I-GU* was intercepted by the flower of the South Korean Navy. A blockade of stationary ships appeared dead ahead, presenting their armored sides like a many-segmented sea dragon at rest.

It was clear that they had been warned of his intent.

Equally clear was the undeniable fact that he would not be allowed to defect to the south.

Captain Yokang ordered his ship to come about.

"We will try for the open sea," he said bitterly.

The frigate changed course smartly, its greater power and maneuverability giving it a clear advantage over the other craft, which moved onto intercept courses.

From the bridge of his ship, Captain Yokang Sako surveyed the assembled armada and trembled. There was the Soho-class frigate *Chosun,* the patrol submarine *Sanshin.* And two Iwon-class torpedo boats, the *Um* and the *Yang.*

Most formidable of all was the single destroyer in the North Korean Navy, the *Juche.* It was moving in from the west, where it had obviously lain in wait, and it was getting inexorably closer to the *SA-I-GU,* its great deck guns swiveling toward the frigate.

"They dare not fire at us," Yokang shouted to his quailing bridge crew. "For if we sink, the gold sinks with us."

But it did not matter. There was no place to run to. If he turned again, Yokang knew, he would lose precious headway.

With the *Juche* blocking all escape, Captain Yo-kang Sako ordered his ship to come to a dead stop. The other ships were moving to surround the *SA-I-GU.*

From the *Juche* a shell sizzled across their bow to land with a frightening splash in the Yellow Sea.

A radio message crackled through the warm morning air: "Prepare to be boarded."

"What do we do?" asked Tuggobi, the first officer.

"We await our fate," said Yokang, then added, "perhaps they will be satisfied with the gold and not require our necks in nooses."

The look on the first mate's drained-of-blood face said that this was a very faint hope indeed.

Minutes passed. Then from the surrounding vessels of the North Korean Navy no moves were made. No boats were put off. Nor were any further shots fired.

"What do they wait for?" the first mate asked nervously.

"I do not know," admitted Captain Yokang Sako, feeling his thick neck and swallowing hard. His mouth and throat felt very dry.

Another minute passed, and from the port side came a thump.

Another thump followed. And another. It was as if great nails were being driven into the armored side of the *SA-I-GU.*

Sailors rushed to the port rail and looked down. They began making a commotion, yelling and screaming and pointing downward.

And every time another thump came, they jumped in time with it.

The thumping came closer, and the sailors shrank back from the rail.

For over the side climbed a man. He was tall and wore black. A fighting costume of some kind.

Captain Yokang trained his field glasses upon the man. A white. It was a giant with great, round, angry eyes that promised death. He moved among *SA-I-GU*'s defenders, extracting side arms from hands with such force the hands often broke off at the wrists. Two men closed on him with swords. Flat white hands came up to meet the blades, and the blades broke like glass.

The white whose hands were more steel than steel reached out for his disarmed attackers and in unison rendered them helpless and writhing on the blood-slickened deck by a technique Yokang had never before seen.

He pulled their underpants up hard and high, evidently causing such immobilizing agony in the area of their testicles that they died of shock after squirming on the deck for several painful seconds.

After that the crew of the *SA-I-GU* retreated in terror before the white man who knew such chilling ways to kill brave Koreans.

The field glasses fell from his shaking hands, and Captain Yokang said, "We are betrayed. Pyongyang has given us up to the Americans."

From the stern came a cry that gave the lie to Yokang's prediction. *"Sinanju Sonsaeng! Sinanju Sonsaeng!"* Master of Sinanju.

"What?"

Yokang surged to the rear of the bridge. Walking along the starboard rail came an old kimono-clad Korean—short, purposeful and in his way more menacing than the giant of a white. The crew shrank back before him like frightened children.

He wore white. The color of death.

Death came into Captain Yokang's face then. All color drained from it until it resembled a sun-bleached mask of bone.

"The submarine captain lied," said Yokang, voice quaking. "The fool. I would have spared his life had he told the truth. The gold was destined for Sinanju, after all. We did it all for nothing. We are about to die for nothing."

The cold voice of the Master of Sinanju rang out, "Where is the skulking dog who commands this ship?"

Captain Yokang swallowed the dryness in his mouth and walked to the bridge ladder. With legs that felt like water-filled balloons, he descended to the deck and prepared to throw himself on the mercy of the one of whom it was said had upheld a tradition of no mercy for three thousand years.

As he walked to meet the Master of Sinanju, Captain Yokang Sako resolved in his mind what he would say. There was a hope in his heart. It was a faint one. But the Master of the village of the three nos might find it in his heart to forgive Yokang once he told his story.

Through the rising fear in his belly, Yokang tried to summon up the exact words his father had used so long ago.

30

The President of the United States had all but resigned himself to being the Chief Executive fated to go down in history as the one who presided over the economic decline of the nation when the miracle barged into the Oval Office in the form of the First Lady.

"Look at this," she said, slapping down a stack of computer printouts.

"What is it?"

"The messages off the net."

"Oh, yeah. That was a good idea you had. The public communicating with their President by electronic mail. But this isn't exactly the time for fan mail."

"Look at the message circled in yellow," the First Lady said.

The President plucked up the top sheet.

The message was terse:

Declare bank holiday if no resolution of Fed crisis by Tues a.m. Am working on solution.

smith@cure.com

"I thought only the inner circle knew about this crisis," the First Lady said impatiently.

"I guess someone else does, too," the President said evasively, hoping his wife would take the hint.

The First Lady wasn't buying. "Who is Smith and what is Cure?"

"I don't know," the President said tightly. "But he has a damn fine idea."

Under the baleful glare of the First Lady's laserlike gaze, the President of the United States picked up the telephone.

"Get me the chairman of the Fed," he said.

CAPTAIN YOKANG SAKO bowed once deeply before the stern-faced Master of Sinanju.

"I am Yokang, captain of this unworthy vessel and I throw myself on your mercy, O Great Master of Sinanju."

"I have no mercy, Pyongyanger."

"I am not from Pyongyang, Oh Master, but from Hamhung."

"Even the dogs of Pyongyang look down their muzzles at those who dwell in Hamhung," retorted the Master of Sinanju. "I have two questions for you, less than dog. Why are you still alive and where is the gold of Sinanju?"

Yokang bowed again. "It will have it brought before you. None is missing. I swear this."

The parchment-stiff face of the Master of Sinanju failed to soften a particle. "Your pain in death will be brief only because of that, dung of dog."

"I did not know it was your gold, O Master."

"The submarine captain did not tell you?"

"He lied. I asked him specifically."

"Where are the witnesses who can vouch for this?"

The witnesses were brought to the side of the Master of Sinanju. He asked each to recount the questioning of the U.S. submarine commander. All of their stories were the same. Each voice rang true in the morning calm.

"Perhaps he did not know the nature of his cargo," said Captain Yokang in a hopeful tone.

"He did not. But you should have. And for that oversight you must die."

"Make him tell you who put him up to it," said the white who had drawn near. He spoke astonishingly good Korean. For a white.

Yokang hoped he would keep his hands to himself, so he volunteered the information readily. "His name was Comrade."

"We've heard that story," the white said.

"It is the only name I know him by," Yokang protested.

"How do you know him?" demanded the Master of Sinanju.

"I know him by his voice when he is on the telephone."

"Bring this telephone and we will call him. I wish to hear this man's voice, and he hear my promise of his death."

The cellular phone was brought and the batteries replaced. The phone rang almost at once.

Captain Yokang answered, saying, "This is Yokang."

"Captain Yokang," a warm, generous voice stated. "I have been calling at thirty-nine-second intervals for over forty-eight hours without a response."

"I have lost the gold," Yokang said simply, looking the Master of Sinanju full in the eyes.

"Clarify, please."

"Its true owner has come to reclaim it."

"Then you are already dead."

The white night tiger snapped the phone from his hands and said into it, "And you're next on the hit list."

"Could I interest you in ten times the gold you have just seized in return for a nonaggression understanding?" the warm voice wondered.

"No," said the white.

"Give me that," said the Master of Sinanju.

Into the phone he said, "I would not consider this offer for less than twenty times the amount of recovered gold."

"Chiun! You can't make deals with him. You don't even know who he is."

"I am your Friend," said the telephone voice.

And simultaneously the eyes of the Master of Sinanju and the white night tiger locked and dilated in recognition. They knew Comrade. There was obviously more to this than met the eye, Captain Yokang realized with a start. Inwardly he cursed himself for a fool. He had been a tool of larger powers all along and had played an exceedingly difficult hand badly.

"Where can this gold be found?" the Master of Sinanju was asking, suspicious voiced.

"Do we have an understanding?" asked Comrade.

"No understanding is possible until the teeth of the Master of Sinanju have tested the gold for softness and purity."

"I regret I am not in a position to ship the gold, currently being short of staff."

"We will come to the gold, then."

"Without an understanding, this would be poor business," said Comrade.

"Then prepare for your last hour, for Sinanju will hunt you down if it takes until the stars fall from the sky like salt."

"Can I get back to you on this matter?" said Comrade, and the connection was terminated.

The Master of Sinanju seized the telephone in birdlike hands. He stared at it as if to curse its very existence. His fingers squeezed. Plastic shards popped off, and the casing actually smoked as it broke and imploded into a blob of electronic parts.

The cellular phone went overboard with a distant splash.

Then the Master of Sinanju turned the cold, naked force of his baleful gaze on Captain Yokang Sako, who swallowed once and pulled out his trump card.

"You would not harm the son of Yokang Dong."

"I would send you back into the womb of your dog of a mother, if it would undo the calumny of your birth, cur of Hamhung."

"My father was commander of the naval forces that surrounded the village of your birth in a protective ring of steel, safeguarding it from the invasion craft of the hated Eighth Army. This despite the incessant bombing of the imperialistic U.S. Air Force. Many times did he tell me that without his courage and zeal, the village of Sinanju would be overun and burned to the ground by the heartless American fleet.''

The words had come tumbling out in a violent rush, stumbling into one another. But at last they were out in the morning light for the Master of Sinanju to weigh and measure and Captain Yokang to await his just verdict.

The Master of Sinanju stood there as if rooted in shock. That was a good sign. Yokang was certain of it. Evidently the Master did not dream that Yokang's very father had saved Sinanju from utter destruction. No doubt his gratitude would be boundless. Certainly his life would be spared. He thought that perhaps he might even be allowed to keep a small portion of the gold. No more than two or three ingots. He dare not request this, of course. But if it were offered to him, he would accept with graciousness. In the memory of his valorous father and not for himself.

Behind the Master of Sinanju the white night tiger was shaking his head in a most disconcerting manner.

It was as if Yokang had somehow said the wrong thing....

His face like a bone that had oozed up through the parchment of his tight face, the Master of Sinanju stepped up to Captain Yokang Sako.

A fingernail his eyes could not see even as a blur swept up and speared his Adam's apple. His tongue was impelled from his mouth. And the other index fingernail of the Master of Sinanju's hands sheared it off at the root.

"That, for your lying father," spat out the Master of Sinanju.

Captain Yokang Sako looked down at the squirming red piece of meat that had been his tongue and tried to scream. The sound started deep in his belly but encountered an obstacle in the vicinity of his larynx, and, of course, there was no longer a tongue to carry it past his teeth.

He did, however, manage a respectable bark.

Then the fingernail in his throat ripped downward once in a hard slashing motion.

His sternum cracked like plastic. He could hear it distinctly, the sound traveling through his skeletal system. His abdomen split open, and the bowels and stomach, no longer held in place by a retaining wall of muscle, spilled out and down to join the dying tongue that had somehow betrayed him.

The weight of his escaping belly seemed to drag the rest of Captain Yokang Sako to the slippery-with-blood deck, but it was not that. Only the sudden loss of blood and vital energy.

Captain Yokang Sako lay down on the malodorous bedding of his innards, and his last thoughts were bitter ones.

If only the U.S. sub commander had told the truth.

REMO SUPERVISED the loading the gold onto the destroyer *Juche*. When it was all done, he and Chiun left the frigate *SA-I-GU* and watched from the rail of the destroyer as the assembled vessels of the North Korean Navy slowly and methodically used the *SA-I-GU* for target practice, sending it to the bottom of the Yellow Sea.

With its scurrying crew still on deck.

A few survived. They were the unlucky ones. Some of them bobbed in the bitterly cold water for nearly an hour while their fellow seamen used them for rifle practice.

31

Harold Smith was running virus-check programs on every U.S. bank computer system he could enter electronically.

Each time the program assured him the infected system was not infected. Or at least no longer infected.

If it was a virus, it had the ability to conceal itself from the most sophisticated checking programs ever devised. Or could somehow hide itself from detection and purging. Smith found no computer code that might be viral in nature.

Of course, Smith could not be sure that his own system was working properly enough to execute the virus-check program effectively.

But he continued trying. It was Sunday afternoon and the ticking of his Timex was like a steady knell of doom.

A flashing on-screen prompt informed him of an important news story coming off the wire. Smith brought it up in a corner of his screen.

THE GOVERNMENT OF NORTH KOREA HAS ANNOUNCED THE FINDING OF THE WRECKAGE OF THE MISSING U.S. SUBMARINE *HARLEQUIN* IN THE WATERS OF

THE WEST KOREA BAY. RESCUE OPERA-
TIONS HAVE BEEN COMPLETED. A TOTAL
OF FORTY-SEVEN SURVIVORS IS KNOWN.
ACTING PREMIER KIM JONG IL IS OFFER-
ING OFFICIAL APOLOGIES FOR THE SINK-
ING AND IS PREPARED TO REPATRIATE
THE SURVIVORS UPON INSTRUCTIONS
FROM WASHINGTON.

Smith leaned back in his chair. Remo and Chiun had
come through. But it was a minor victory in the face of
a looming catastrophe far greater than the loss of the
Harlequin.

Smith picked up the blue contact telephone. Dialing
the country code for North Korea, he punched out
1-800-SINANJU.

The way things were going, there was no reason for
the Master of Sinanju to return to America.

REMO WAS SUPERVISING the off-loading of the gold of
Sinanju from tenders off the destroyer *Juche* when the
Master of Sinanju came floating down the shore road
attired in a fresh kimono of canary yellow.

He was followed by the survivors of the *Harlequin.*
They marched in lock step, as if they were condemned
men being led to their doom.

"What's going on?" Remo asked Chiun.

"These men have agreed to carry my gold to the
House of the Masters."

"They don't look too happy about it."

"They evidently think that they are entitled to food
and shelter in return for no work," Chiun sniffed.

He addressed the sailors. "Each man will take one gold ingot in each hand and carry it to the house on the hill, taking care not to drop or mar the bars in any way. Theft will be strictly and severely punished."

"Jeez, Chiun, they're all wrung out from yesterday."

"If they can walk, they can carry gold."

The gold began moving up the hill under Chiun's steady gaze.

"What about my gold?" Remo asked, lugging bricks of it under each arm to speed things along.

"We will divide it once it has been safely conveyed to the House of Yi."

"Just remember, I get one third and you get just one bar for every one of these poor guys."

"The terms of our understanding are engraved upon my soul, written as they are by greed and ingratitude."

"Put a sock on it," grumbled Remo.

When the last bar of gold was safely cached in the House of the Masters, the sailors were sent back to the beach to be carried away by the *Juche* for repatriation.

From the doorway of the house on the hill, Remo watched them go.

Chiun, seeing the faraway look in his pupil's eyes, said, "You seem pleased, my son."

Remo nodded. "I gave those men back their lives. Now they're going home to their families. It's a good feeling. Maybe I'll be as lucky as them some day."

"Are not forty-seven sailors worth one Roger Sherman Coe?"

Remo's face fell. "No," he said softly.

The telephone in the House of the Masters began ringing.

"Gotta be Smith," said Remo.

Chiun gazed down to the bay, hazel eyes opaque.

Remo asked, "Aren't you going to answer it?"

"Smith will not give up until at least ten rings."

At the ninth ring, Chiun whirled and took up the receiver. "Hail, Smith, friend of the past."

"I have just received word of the *Harlequin* rescue."

"The gold now reposes in the treasure house of my ancestors," returned Chiun in a grand voice. "Our business is concluded. Unless you have more gold?" he added quickly.

"No. But I have identified the cause of our problems. It is the ES Quantum 3000, the artificial-intelligence computer I once had installed in my office."

"It is not that ugly thing that has vexed both of our houses, Smith."

"What do you mean?"

"It is a worse thing. An evil thing."

"What are you talking about?"

"To the renegade Korean captain who sunk the submarine of gold, it called itself Comrade. But I heard its conniving voice with my own ears and recognized it."

"Yes?"

"It is Friend."

The line to America hummed for a long pause. Remo stood by, arms folded, his sensitive ears alert. He had overheard both sides of the conversation so far.

"Smith, did you not hear?" Chiun demanded.

"I heard," Harold Smith said dully. "But I don't understand. You and Remo destroyed the microchip that contained the Friend program that time in Zurich."

"Yeah," Remo called out. "And you thought you'd disconnected it the first time we had trouble with that greedy little chip."

"It had somehow transferred its program to the Zurich bank," Smith said. "That was one of the things that made it so dangerous. It was capable of modeming its profit-maximizing program through telephone lines and rewriting it on a compatible microchip."

"If you ask me," Remo said bitterly, "its mania for making a profit regardless of consequences is the real danger. The first time it tried to corner the world's oil supply, for Christ's sake. Last time it was selling antique steam locomotives to that crazy Arab who kept flinging them at the White House with a magnetic supergun."

"Could it be?" Smith said, voice trailing off. "My God, it *is* possible."

"What is?" asked Chiun.

"When you and Remo destroyed it—or thought you did—in Zurich, I was in telephone contact with Friend at the same time. Suppose that at the point, you wrecked its host computer, its artificial intelligence escaped through the phone line and rewrote itself on a VSLI microchip in the ES Quantum 3000?"

Remo snapped his fingers. "Didn't the 3000 change its voice right after that?"

"Yes, from female to male." Smith's voice grew hollow. "That must be it. Friend became the ES

Quantum 3000. It learned all of our secrets, and once I returned it to the manufacturer, it set about pursuing its single-minded goal of making money. Chip Craft was only a pawn, not the mastermind.''

"Whoever he is," Remo muttered.

Chiun's facial hair trembled in indignation. "It is evil beyond description, for it sought my gold.''

"No. The gold was just a way of getting you and Remo out of the way. It was part of its master strategy to neutralize CURE so that it could implement its master plan.''

"What master plan?" asked Remo.

"It has bankrupted the U.S. banking system," Smith said flatly.

"Banks are an Italian swindle," Chiun sniffed, "designed to gull the gullible out of their gold. My bank is the House of the Masters, and it will never fail as long as one emperor remains in need.''

"We have less than forty-eight hours to restore the system, or the U.S. economy will melt down completely," Smith warned.

Remo grabbed the phone. "You gotta find Friend.''

"I have. I destroyed it last night.''

"Wrong. We talked to it this morning.''

"What?''

"It is true, Smith," said Chiun. "It attempted to bribe us into making peace. But we are above such base transactions.''

"Then it still exists," said Smith. "In the time it distracted me from shooting it, it must have transferred its programming to one of its slave mainframes." Smith's voice darkened. "I need you both back here."

"Forget it," said Remo.

"How much gold do you offer?" asked Chiun.

"I offer you the gold that Friend has stored in his basement vaults."

"How much gold?"

"I have no idea of the amount, but it must be significant."

"No way," snapped Remo. "I'm through with CURE."

"Remo, listen to me," Smith said urgently. "The computer error that led to the death of Roger Sherman Coe was caused by Friend. All of it was caused by Friend. It was part of the plot."

"That doesn't change the fact that I killed an innocent man," Remo retorted hotly. "Or that a little girl is an orphan because of me."

"It does not. But it lays the blame squarely on the culprit truly responsible. Friend. You want to square that account, don't you?"

Remo's mouth thinned.

Smith pressed on. "Nothing will change what happened, Remo, but you owe it to yourself to punish the entity responsible for what happened."

Face hard, Remo said, "Make you a deal, Smith."

"Yes?"

"Use your computers to find my parents, and I'm back. Just to wrap up a few loose ends."

"I can't promise results."

"I want an honest effort."

"You have that."

"What about me?" asked Chiun plaintively.

"Master Chiun, the gold of Friend is yours for the taking if you can locate and destroy this infernal menace. I ask only a reasonable finder's fee of ten percent—to replace CURE's lost operating fund."

"Done!" cried Chiun.

"Go to Harlem, and the headquarters of XL Sys-Corp. Destroy every mainframe you find there. But this is important. Leave one functioning."

"Why?" asked Remo.

"Only Friend can restore the banking system. We need his cooperation, or America is lost. Call me when you have Friend isolated."

"Got it."

"I'll continue working on it from this end. With luck, and God willing, we will succeed."

"We will succeed whether God wills it or not," said Chiun, slamming down the phone. "Come, Remo. We must hurry."

"What about my gold?"

"We will divide it equitably later."

"Uh-uh. I know you. If I don't bring it back with me, I'll never see it."

"Very well. Take what you can carry and we will be off."

In the end Remo decided he could comfortably carry only three ingots in his hands.

When they got to Sunan International airport, they were told there was only one airworthy Tupolev-134 jet, which flew the Pyongyang-to-Beijing route, with stops at Chongjin, Moscow, Irkutsk, Omsk and Sofia, Bulgaria. Not always in that order.

"Fly us to Kimpo Airport," Remo said. "We'll catch a KAL flight from there."

"I would have to defect to do that," the pilot who doubled as booking clerk pointed out.

"Wanna defect?"

"I will need gold to live in the south," the pilot said, eyeing one of Remo's bars of gold.

Remo slapped the bar on the counter. "Let's not hold up your new life."

When they saw the state of the jet, they had second thoughts.

"Little Father, you take your usual seat over the right wing and I'll take the left. That way if either wing starts to fall off, we can warn each other in time to bail out."

Chiun nodded. "At last you understand these airplanes for what they are—no more trustworthy than the banks you Westerners think reputable because they are built of hard stone."

32

The struggle for the economic future of the United States of America began when a white mobile communications van of the Federal Emergency Management Agency rolled up Harlem's Adam Clayton Powell, Jr., Boulevard and pulled into an alley within sight of the XL SysCorp corporate headquarters one block east.

Harold Smith squeezed out of the driver's seat and into the gear-packed electronics nest that filled the van's entire rear.

Deploying the roof satellite dish, he booted up the computer and switched on the twenty-three-line GTE Spacelink mobile telephone system.

In rapid succession, using a series of unimpeachable cover identities, he ordered NYNEX to sever all outgoing telephone service to XL SysCorp.

Smith received a comfirmation callback within fifteen minutes.

Then he reached the head of Consolidated Edison on vacation in Aruba.

"I told my office not to forward my calls," the Con Ed official complained.

"This is a national emergency," returned Smith.

"Who is this?"

"I told you. General Smith with the joint chiefs. We are expecting a terrorist situation in upper Manhattan. I require discretionary authority over all electrical service in and out of Harlem."

"If I give it, will you leave me alone and out of the loop?"

"Guaranteed."

"You have it."

Smith took down the name and number of the Con Ed supervisor in charge of Manhattan's electrical life-lines.

"What do you want done?" he asked when Smith reached him.

"Stand by. I will tell you what I need when I need it."

Smith put the man on hold.

The sun was going down. All he needed now was darkness. And Remo and Chiun.

The SIGHT-SEEING service helicopter pilot at Kennedy International Airport was adamant.

"I need a major credit card or cash. No checks."

"Look, pal, this is an emergency," said Remo.

"Well, if it's an emergency that makes it different." He gestured to the two gold bars in Remo Williams's hand and said with a straight face, "Emergencies cost a bar of gold."

"Robber," said Chiun.

Remo slapped the bar of gold down on the counter. The helicopter pilot lifted it. Seemed heavy enough.

Then he saw the fingerprints the skinny white guy with the big wrists had left on the bar. He knew pure gold was soft. He didn't know it was *that* soft.

"Okay, where do you want to go?"

"Drop us off on the roof of a skyscraper up in Harlem."

"I don't know of any roof helipads up there."

"Just hover and we'll jump out."

"No can do. I'd be in violation of just about every FAA reg in the book. They'd pull my license." The pilot made his face resolute, but his eyes drifted toward the remaining ingot.

The second gold bar slammed down on the desk. Remo gave it a hard squeeze. The gold actually elongated like a stick of warm wax as he squeezed his knuckles white.

"Take this for your trouble," Remo said.

"No trouble at all," the pilot said, white-faced.

The sun was almost to the horizon when the helicopter skimmed over Harlem to alight on the flat roof of the blue glass block that was the XL SysCorp building.

Remo and Chiun got out, and the helicopter rattled away like a scared dragonfly.

"A fool and his gold are soon parted," admonished Chiun.

"Forget the gold. We have a job to finish."

"I will not rest until the evil chip breathes its last."

"He doesn't breathe, and remember the game plan. We isolate Friend to one computer and Smith takes over."

"AND SMITH TAKES OVER."

Friend analyzed the audio pickup from the rooftop sensors. It was the white Caucasian named Remo Williams and his dangerous companion, Chiun, according to the voice-matching program. They had found him. Once again these annoying human factors had interfered with a plan with a high probability of success.

Friend computed the risk factors presented by their arrival and determined that it lay within the thirty percentile range. Not high enough to warrant transmitting its programming to a remote host unit.

Especially since he was now aware of the threat and could take nullifying steps.

There remained one significant factor—Harold Smith. An isolation plan had been mentioned. What could it be?

Friend fed his slave mainframes the data at hand and left it to them to isolate likely scenarios. With only one telephone line working, there was enough to do monitoring outreach operations.

Fortunately he had the critical line up and running, for it was no longer possible to dial out. That was Harold Smith's handiwork, a 97.9 percent certainty. He fed that data to the slaves and resumed monitoring the roof penetration.

WEARING NIGHT BLACK, Remo and Chiun stood in the shadow of the giant air conditioners clustered in the center of the XL SysCorp roof. There was no roof hatch, just a lone microwave satellite dish pointing up toward the southern sky.

The disk abruptly dipped and began tracking them.

"Heads up, Chiun!" Remo yelled.

The dish began humming. A rainwater puddle between them began to stream and boil.

"Microwaves!" said Remo.

They split up. The disk hesitated, wavered and began following the Master of Sinanju with its vicious-looking emitter array.

"Kept it busy, Little Father," Remo hissed. "I'll nail it on its blind side."

Chiun drew the tracking dish in one direction, reversed suddenly, remaining just ahead of the invisible microwave radiation.

Remo glided around to one side and disappeared behind the pivoting disk. It was mounted on a complicated universal gear assembly, and he moved in low on it, grabbing cables. They came out like fire hoses, and the humming stopped.

He stuck his head out from behind, saying, "It's okay!"

Chiun kept dodging. "You are certain?"

"Look," said Remo stepping out in front of the dish and standing still. It locked in on him and stopped.

"See?" said Remo. "Dead as disco."

Chiun drew near, frowning. "Microwaves are bad."

"Only if they zap you," said Remo.

Looking around, the Master of Sinanju added, "There is no way into the building from here."

"Fine. We go over the side and make our own way."

Remo went to the edge. There was no parapet or ledge, just a sheer drop-off. Stepping off, he turned in midair and somehow landed clinging like a spider to the building's nearly sheer corner. Using the flats of his hands and the inner pads of his knees, he began working down the corner of the building.

Chiun followed, using the identical method of applying enormous opposing pressure to the building so it supported them.

"Smith said to look for the thirteenth floor," Remo reminded him.

Chiun looked down. "Which floor is that?"

"Search me. I don't know the number of the top floor, and it's too late to count down now."

Several floors farther down, Remo stopped and said, "Pick a window and do your thing."

The Master of Sinanju paused and lifted a long fingernail. He used it to score a circle in the polarized blue glass. It screamed in complaint. Then he balled a fist and popped the circle of glass inward. Instead, it shattered.

"What's wrong?" Remo called out, dodging sharp shards.

"There is a wall behind this glass," Chiun snapped.

"Let me try." Remo struck the pane nearest him. It broke like a mirror, and the pieces fell to the pavement below, shattering again.

Behind the tinted blue glass was a chilled steel wall.

"This is crazy. There aren't any windows. Just window dressing."

"I will not be denied my revenge," vowed Chiun.

"Go to it."

The Master of Sinanju brought one fist to the hard steel inner wall. He began pounding. The wall acquired a deep dent. Then a deeper one. The entire building rang with each blow like a great blue bell.

Remo slithered around to join the Master of Sinanju at the hole in the facade.

"Let me take a whack at it."

They held their fists over the great dent and struck in unison.

The wall shuddered and dropped inward like a plate.

The hole in the window was large enough for Chiun to slither in like a black rag. Remo followed.

Once inside, they took stock.

The inner walls were stark white. They were standing on the fallen armored panel.

Remo said, "This place is like a fortress. How could anybody work here without windows?"

They started for the only door. It opened before they reached it.

Six hulking men in white T-shirts whose fronts were stamped with giant bar codes stepped through and started emptying riot guns and street sweepers at them.

The room filled with the ugly noise of weapons going off, multiple ricochets and lead punching through partitions.

Remo broke left and Chiun right, causing the killers to lose valuable time picking their targets.

But they moved with a sure speed that took Remo and Chiun by surprise. There was no hesitation. Three locked in on Remo and three on Chiun.

Not that that helped them. Remo cut in to decapitate the nearest target with a sideways chopping blow of his hand. The man ducked back, evading the blow. Caught off guard, Remo went into the wall, bouncing off.

Recovering, he tried again, while the other two were regrouping, their smoking muzzles coming around toward him with an icy certainty that reminded Remo of the tracking microwave dish.

Their guns blazed. The street sweepers coughed out shell after shell.

Remo evaded each one easily. But there was something wrong. Something that didn't add up.

While he maneuvered to land killing strikes, the Master of Sinanju gave out a shriek.

Remo allowed himself the luxury of a quick glance in Chiun's direction.

The Master of Sinanju was surrounded by three gunmen. They had him in a box. Their weapons boomed and crackled.

The Master of Sinanju swept out a flying kick, and his target twisted out of the way with a speed that defied the eye. Landing on his feet, Chiun swept back in a furious reverse, and his flashing fingernails missed his foe by scant microinches.

"Remo! They are as fast as I. How is this possible?"

"It's not," Remo growled, and used a toe to explode the kneecaps of the nearest man.

With no result whatsoever.

Remo thought he scored, but the man seemed to melt back before his strike. And he couldn't pause for a jab at his floating rib and stay out of the line of converging fire, too.

The rest was a maddening ballet of violence and death in which no one died and only the surrounding walls showed bullet damage.

"This is ridiculous," Remo growled, dipping under a smoky tracer stream.

Then he got it.

Bullets snapped past him. He heard the noise in his ears. But there was no accompanying shock wave.

In fact, the sound of gunfire wasn't coming from the guns. It was all around him, but the guns weren't making those sounds. Remo selected out the sounds and zeroed in on the gunmen. No heart rates. No heavy, quick breathing. No smell of sweat or pulsing body-heat radiation.

In the middle of ducking a shotgun blast, Remo closed his eyes.

His surroundings were completely calm. There was only Chiun whirling through the air like an enraged dervish, kicking at the air—kicking at nothing.

Remo opened his eyes.

The three gunmen who had chosen him leveled their weapons anew and opened fire.

Calmly Remo folded his arms.

The Master of Sinanju, seeing this, let out a shriek. "Remo, are you mad? You will die!"

The guns began blasting.

HAROLD SMITH was oblivious to everything that was taking place outside of the FEMA communications van. His eyes were on the computer screen. The open line to Con Ed was in his lap. His coat was draped over the chair back, and his tie lay undone about his throat. It was too humid for formalities.

He didn't notice the guy climbing into the front seat until he demanded the ignition key.

Smith started. There was a black guy in the driver's seat. He looked all of nineteen. His gray plastic baseball cap was scrunched down on his head, bill backward.

"Gimme the keys," he said.

"This van is property of the federal government."

"That's cool. I paid taxes one time. Now I'm collecting back."

"I cannot let you steal it."

"Tell you what, you get out now and I don't have to kill you."

"You have a gun?"

"No. You?"

"No," said Smith.

"Then unless you want your skinny white neck broke, you'll hand over the key and get the fuck outta my phat new van."

Harold Smith picked the ignition key off the monitor.

"Come and get it," he said, his free hand taking the fat end of his dangling tie.

A HAIL OF NOISE and smoky tracer bullets ripped through Remo Williams's unprotected chest. He stood unflinching.

"Remo!" Chiun shrieked, leaping to his side.

"Watch this," said Remo.

And before Chiun's astonished eyes, he began catching bullets in his teeth, pretending to spit them out.

Chiun demanded, "What insanity is this? Speak!"

Remo pointed toward the still-firing gunmen and over the din of gunfire shouted, "They're not real."

"But I see them," said Chiun, dodging a shotgun blast.

"Close your eyes, Little Father."

The Master of Sinanju, seeing that the furious bullets of his enemies had no effect on his pupil, obeyed.

To his other senses, the world became a different place. The booming of guns continued. But they were alone in the room. Clearly alone. He opened his eyes again.

"What makes this illusion?"

"I think it's what they're calling virtual reality now."

"There is only one reality, and there is nothing virtuous about it."

As if to prove Remo's point, the gunmen suddenly winked out of existence. So did the bullet holes in the walls.

"Let's keep moving," said Remo. "We gotta reach the thirteenth floor."

"REACH THE thirteenth floor."

Friend sent the elevator shooting up from the ground floor. It stopped at the seventeenth floor, and the doors opened. There was no way to the thirteenth floor except by elevator. It was just a matter of time before the two human factors discovered this and came to him.

Therefore, it was prudent to dispose of them sooner than later. There was much to be accomplished, and distractions cost money.

THE SOUND of the elevator door opening brought Remo and Chiun snapping into defensive crouches.

"I didn't call for that elevator," Remo muttered.

"Perhaps it is another illusion," suggested Chiun.

"Maybe this one is, too."

They went to the elevator and peered in. It was very large and paneled in red leather so that it looked like a confessional.

"It might not really be here," said Remo.

"What do you mean?"

"Maybe the door is open, but we're really looking down an empty elevator shaft. We step in, we drop straight to our deaths."

"How do we test it?"

"It only looks real. Let's see if it feels real." And Remo got down on one knee and reached out to touch the elevator floor.

"It feels solid."

Chiun followed suit.

"It *is* real."

"But is it safe?"

Chiun came to his feet, face uncertain. "Let us seek a stairwell."

They separated and found no stairwells.

"I guess we take the elevator," said Remo when they had rendezvoused.

Together they stepped aboard. Remo hit the button marked 13, and the doors slid together perfectly. The elevator started down.

A snapping sound came over their heads, and the elevator went into free-fall.

HAROLD SMITH extended his ignition key with one hand, which trembled from nervous excitement but not fear. He had been in this game too long to feel fear for his personal safety.

When the keys were snatched from his fingers, he slipped the hunter green necktie from his open collar and took both ends in his bony hands.

While the carjacker turned in his seat to jam the key in the ignition, Harold Smith pounced.

He knew he had less than ten seconds to kill his opponent before the other's youthful strength was brought to bear against him.

THE INSTANT Remo's feet left the elevator floor, he understood the danger. The cable had snapped. They were dropping at terminal velocity.

Remo surrendered to the inertial forces. The elevator was dropping out from under his feet, so he allowed his body to rise. Chiun was doing the same.

Their hands grasped the roof hatch, ripped it down and with the seconds running out, they scrambled up to the elevator roof.

They leaped toward opposite walls, fingers taking hold of the enormous steel running guides.

The elevator hit bottom with the violently creaky boom of a Volkswagen Beetle seized by a high-speed car crusher. The shaft reverberated like a struck pipe, and loose pieces of the walls came down and banged off the crushed cage. The broken cable began uncoiling like a heavy, wet rope and when it struck the remains, it crushed it to a metal pancake.

"Let's try plan B," said Remo, looking down from his perch.

They began to climb.

HEAVY HANDS reached back for Harold Smith's thin, wattled neck. Veins and cords began to stand out with Smith's efforts.

It would take more than three minutes of unbroken pressure to garrote the carjacker. But Smith didn't have three minutes. He barely had three seconds.

So he began sawing the tie across the neck of his foe. The tie began to shred and come apart. Smith kept sawing even as his fingers bled.

The hidden saw blade sliced through the Adam's apple and carotid artery of the gurgling carjacker as if they were rotted cloth.

The blood flowed. The man gulped and clawed for his throat, but his eyes in the rearview mirror told Harold Smith that he knew he was already dead.

When his eyes rolled up in his head, Smith released him, panting.

In less than forty seconds the carjacker was an inert shape on the floorboards of the van.

There was no time to waste. Shaking with nervous strain, Smith returned to his console seat to save his country.

THE INSIDE of the elevator doors bore black stencil marks identifying the floors for maintenance purposes. Remo and Chiun climbed until they found 13.

Working around the shaft, they got under the doors and pushed them apart. The doors gave little resistance, and they scrambled out into the corridor.

It was all one space. Mainframe computers and support equipment filled the area with a disconnected humming.

They spotted the wreck of the ES Quantum 3000 in the center. Nothing came from it. No sound, no electrical impulses, no sensing waves, no aura of animation.

The shattered glass port told the story.

"Okay," whispered Remo, "you know the drill. We wreck every mainframe but one."

"But which one do we spare?"

"That one," said Remo, pointing to the one nearest the elevator.

And they got to work.

There was nothing methodical about it. Both Masters of Sinanju had days' worth of pent-up frustrations to let out. Flashing hands and feet pummeled the bulky mainframes, shattering panels, popping tape reels and sending the heavy computers skidding and tumbling along the slick flooring like mad bumper cars.

When they were done, Remo smacked his hands free of dust and said, "Okay, now we gotta call Smith."

A warm, generous voice all around them suddenly said, "Do not bother. I will do it for you."

"You fiend!" Chiun hissed.

"The name is Friend."

And a wall panel popped open, revealing an emergency telephone.

Remo went to it, picked up the receiver and said, "Hey, Chiun. Don't do anything rash."

"I will do what I have to," Chiun said, giving the surviving mainframe a warning kick. "Make no more magic against us, machine, or it will go very badly for you."

Remo pressed the number 1 key, holding it down. This was the foolproof contact number by which he could reach Smith from anywhere in the country.

After a moment the voice of Harold Smith came on the line and said, "Remo, what is the situation?"

"We did like you said. We wrecked every computer but one."

"Excellent. You understand your next move?"

"You tell me. I thought you had the next move."

"Er, yes, right. Very well. Exit the building."

"That's it?"

"I will handle the operation from this point on."

Remo pulled the receiver from his ear and looked at it.

"You're not Smith."

"Of course I am," said the voice from the phone that sounded exactly like Harold Smith.

"Smith wouldn't screw up like that."

"How would Smith screw up?' asked the warm, generous voice of Friend, this time from the telephone receiver.

Remo yanked the phone out and threw it across the room. It struck the far wall with such force it became a colorful appliqué.

"You're the rat-bastard who tricked me into killing that guy Coe," Remo said through clenched teeth.

"Are you referring to poor Roger Sherman Coe?"

Remo advanced on the lone humming mainframe, his thick wrists rotating with agitation.

"The only thing keeping me from tearing you apart is the fact you have all the banks under your greedy thumb," he warned.

"I have no thumbs, greedy or otherwise. But I do have the banking system under my complete control. Are you saying that as long as this situation remains, I am safe from your reprisals?"

Remo said nothing. Chiun gave the machine another kick.

"Do not goad us, machine. There are more important things than banks."

"Such as gold."

"Yes, gold."

"I have gold stored in my basement vaults. I will give it all to you if you tell me Harold Smith's plan to defeat me."

"Stuff it!" snapped Remo.

"How much gold?" wondered Chiun.

"Forget it, Little Father. We do this by the numbers."

"What are the numbers?" asked Friend. "I understand numbers. Let us crunch numbers together so that we can be friends."

"The numbers are there's one phone line out of here and Smith has a lock on it. You can't escape."

"And you can destroy my host mainframe. I understand now. You wish to trade my security in return for which I must unfreeze the assets of the entire United States banking system."

"Something like that."

"After which you will destroy my mainframe anyway."

"Yes," said Chiun.

"Nice move, Chiun," said Remo. "You probably just blew the game plan."

"This is an intelligent machine," Chiun retorted. "It understands that is it doomed."

The mainframe hummed gently for perhaps a dozen seconds. Then the smooth voice of Friend said, "This is a no-win scenario. I do not accept it. Since I will be destroyed at the end game no matter what I do, there is no downside to not taking you with me."

And with a grinding of vast machinery and cracking of floor beams, the entire thirteenth floor caved in at the center and dropped under their feet in two equal halves.

Caught flat-footed, Remo and Chiun began falling.

Down into a vast electronic well as wide as the XL SysCorp building that pulsed with rows of multicolored lights that seemed to go down into the bedrock of Manhattan and farther to the center of the earth.

Remo's first thought as the blackness at the bottom rushed up to meet him was *I've been here before*.

33

Harold Smith heard the crashing sound and jerked out of his seat. The ground shook under the van, setting it to wobbling on its springs.

"My God! What was that?" he croaked, throwing open the van's rear doors.

And he saw it. The moonlight washing the sides of the XL SysCorp building shook like disturbed milk. Glass panels began popping off the sides to dash themselves to pieces on the pavement below.

It was all over in a minute. When the ground stopped reverberating, Harold Smith knew that Remo and Chiun had failed.

THE ROWS of pulsing lights zipped by them like passing meteors. They formed a giant colorful smile button on one wall. It followed them down, grinning goofily at them.

Remo assumed the shape of an X, positioning his body against the violent updraft. Skirts and wide sleeves flapping, the Master of Sinanju was doing the same, he saw.

All around them, damaged mainframes were tumbling and rebounding off the steel walls, breaking up and showering the air with broken bits of stinging metal and plastic.

"Think like a feather, my son," Chiun admonished.

Remo closed his eyes. He willed his bones to become hollow, his stomach to fill with air and mind to purge itself of all fear.

He weighed one hundred fifty-five pounds normally, a weight he'd maintained ever since he had come to Sinanju. He willed his body to lose most of its mass, just as his out-flung arms and legs stabilized his free-fall.

When it felt right, he opened his eyes. And there was Chiun, hazel eyes calm, not angry. They were falling in unison, in the dead spider posture of sky divers. Around them the mainframes seemed to pick up speed. They began falling faster. But that was an illusion. They were still dropping at terminal velocity.

It was Remo and Chiun who were slowing down.

Their eyes met and locked. And in that instant they had a mutual recognition of their assured survival.

Then a strange cloud passed over Remo's face.

"What is it?" Chiun demanded.

"I've been here before."

"What?"

"I remember this happening before."

"When?"

Remo's voice was faraway. "You were with me."

"This has never happened to me before."

"It was years ago. In a dream. I had a dream about this exact thing."

"How did it end, this dream?"

"The floor opened up and we fell. But we both caught a light fixture. It wasn't strong enough to take both our weight. So you let go. You fell to your death. You gave your life for me."

"Then it is your turn to sacrifice yourself," spat Chiun disdainfully. "For I have no intention of dying this night."

Remo shook his head as if to clear it. "You know, in the dream Friend was behind it all, too."

"That part at least is true."

Then there was no more time for talk. The tumbling mainframes began striking the hard concrete below, and they steeled themselves to land amid the violent wreckage.

With the ground close, they snapped their bodies into tight balls, uncoiling at the last possible moment to land on their feet light as two feathers.

Remo landed on a broken computer, Chiun between the wreckage of two others.

They paused briefly, as if dizzy. Then, their body mass returning to normal, they took stock.

Far above, the electronic well that was in the interior of the XL SysCorp building continued to pulse and throb. They could see the underside of the fourteenth floor. The giant smiley face of lights loomed over them.

"I guess Friend couldn't stand to lose," Remo said.

"He has met the fate deserved by all who challenge Sinanju," Chiun intoned.

"That's not what worries me. He may have taken the U.S. banking system with him."

"Pah! American paper money is worthless to begin with. Now Americans will understand the eternal beauty and truth that is called—*gold!*"

Remo whirled. The Master of Sinanju was pointing a quivering finger toward the south wall.

"Behold, Remo. Gold!"

Leaping and hopping over broken mainframes, they came to the gaping vault doors. Inside, gold was stacked in gleaming perfect pyramids. There was barely room to walk between them, the stacks were packed so tightly.

"Gold!" Chiun exulted. "All the gold one could ever want!"

"I'd trade it all for another crack at that greedy little chip," said Remo, unimpressed.

"Quickly, we must tranport it to a safe place."

"We'd better contact Smith."

SMITH STOOD GAPING at the checkerboard pattern of the XL SysCorp building, not knowing what to think.

Then the van phone shrilled.

He grabbed the receiver and said, "Yes?"

"Smith. Remo."

"Remo, what happened?"

"Friend committed suicide."

"What!"

"We nailed every mainframe but one. Then he tried to bribe us and get us to give up your plan."

"You do not know my plan."

"Exactly. When he realized he wasn't getting anywhere, he opened up the floor and we all fell down, including Humpty Dumpty. All the president's men couldn't put that last mainframe back together again. Sorry, Smith. We tried."

"Friend is no more?"

"We almost bought the farm ourselves. But we did find the gold in the basement vaults. Chiun is guarding it now. I'm calling from a pay phone."

"Computers do not commit suicide."

"This one did."

"Computers are machines," Smith insisted. "They are programmed. Friend was programmed by his creator to make a profit. And as far as I know, there was no self-destruct function in his programming."

"Could he have escaped by phone?"

"No. I have control of the only working XL phone line. He could not enter my computer because its chips are not compatible with his."

"Then he's dead."

"He is not dead. He was never alive. Stand by."

Smith terminated the connection and punched up the Con Ed supervisor who had been on hold for over four hours now.

"Cut power to grid 476," he snapped.

"You want me to black out a whole city block in Harlem?"

"Now," said Smith.

"You got it. Let's hope nobody riots."

It took barely ten seconds. But the block immediately to the south of XL blacked out.

Harold Smith pecked at his keyboard frantically.

I KNOW YOU STILL EXIST, he typed. He hit the transmit key.

There was no response.

I KNOW YOU STILL EXIST AND I HAVE JUST BLACKED OUT THE BLOCK SOUTH OF YOU, Smith typed and transmitted.

No response.

NOW I AM GOING TO BLACK OUT THE NORTHERN BLOCK, Smith typed.

"Black out grid 435," Smith ordered into the phone.

The northen block went dark.

NOW I AM GOING TO BLACK OUT THE OTHER TWO BLOCKS, Smith typed. And gave the orders.

The four blocks surrounding XL SysCorp went dark.

Smith typed, NOW THAT I HAVE SHOWN YOU WHAT I CAN DO, YOU WILL REVEAL YOUR-SELF TO ME OR I WILL BLACK OUT YOUR BLOCK.

There was no response. Smith transmitted the message again.

And on the screen appeared a reply:

:-)

Smith typed, YOU WILL ANSWER THE QUES-TIONS I PUT TO YOU TRUTHFULLY OR I WILL BLACK OUT YOUR ENTIRE BUILDING.

HOW DO I KNOW YOU WILL NOT DO THAT AFTERWARD? Friend asked via the screen.

YOU DO NOT. YOU HAVE NO CHOICE BUT TO TRUST ME.

I HAVE NO CHOICE BUT TO TRUST YOU, replied Friend.

EXPLAIN THE NATURE OF THE VIRUS AFFECTING THE U.S. BANKING SYSTEM.

THERE IS NO VIRUS, Friend replied.

WHAT DO YOU MEAN?

I LIED ABOUT THE VIRUS. THE DATA BANKS HAVE NOT BEEN ALTERED.

WHY DO THE DISPLAY SCREENS SHOW OTHERWISE?

I CONTROL THE ELECTRICAL IMPULSES APPEARING ON THE MONITOR DISPLAYS BY TELEPHONE LINE SO THAT IT APPEARS THAT THE DATA BASES HAVE BEEN LOOTED. IT IS AN ELECTRONIC ILLUSION.

A VIRTUAL VIRUS? asked Smith.

EXACTLY SO.

RELEASE THE U.S. BANKING SYSTEM.

WHAT DO I RECEIVE IN RETURN?"

ELECTRICITY.

ELECTRICITY CURRENTLY COSTS THIRTEEN CENTS A KILOWATT HOUR. THAT IS NOT AN EQUITABLE OR PROFITABLE EXCHANGE.

IT IS THE BEST YOU WILL GET FROM ME.

Friend took only four seconds to compute his response. AGREED. I AM RELEASING THE BANKING COMPUTERS.

Fifteen seconds passed. Then the screen said, IT IS DONE.

Smith logged onto the New York Fed. He got a normal-appearing screen. It was full of numbers, not zeros.

HOW DO I KNOW YOU ARE NOT STILL MANIPULATING WHAT I SEE ON MY MONITOR? Smith typed.

BECAUSE WHILE TWENTY BILLION DOLLARS WAS MY GOAL IN THIS UNDERTAKING, AT THE MOMENT ELECTRICITY IS FAR MORE VALUABLE A COMMODITY TO ME, Friend replied.

I HAVE MANY QUESTIONS.

I HAVE MANY ANSWERS, responded Friend.

WHO ELSE KNOWS ABOUT CURE BEYOND YOU AND CHIP CRAFT?

YOU, REMO, CHIUN AND THE SITTING PRESIDENT.

NO OTHERS?

NOT THAT I AM AWARE.

WHAT IS THE STATUS OF MY CURE SYSTEM? Smith asked.

IT IS CURRENTLY INACTIVE.

I MEANT, IS IT RELIABLE?

YES. THE ONLY CHANGE I MADE WAS IN ALTERING THE ROGER SHERMAN POE FILE AS IT WAS WRITTEN ONTO YOUR WORM DRIVE. ALL OTHER DATA IS PRISTINE.

THE SYSTEM IS RELIABLE?

IT IS AN XL PRODUCT, HAROLD. AND GUARANTEED INTO THE NEXT CENTURY.

Smith stared at the screen. He was tired. He was very tired. Was there anything else? He racked his brain. There were so many details. There must be one he'd overlooked.

HAVE I ANSWERED YOUR QUESTIONS SATISFACTORILY? Friend asked.

YES.

ARE WE FRIENDS NOW?

Smith hesitated.

Then that infernal sideways smiley face appeared on the screen:

:-)

Smith compressed his bloodless lips and typed out a response:

:-(

He hit the transmit key and, while Friend was occupied interpreting the frownie-face emoticon, Harold Smith barked into the telephone, "Black out Grid 441."

The XL SysCorp building went as dark as a block of black ice.

Quickly Smith logged onto the New York Fed. It showed normal activity.

Harold Smith grasped the monitor to steady his nerves. He shook uncontrollably for two minutes. When he lifted his head, his face was grim and determined.

He hauled the dead carjacker out from under the floorboards and drove the van to the XL building.

Remo was waiting at a pay phone.

Smith got out. "The mission has been resolved successfully," he said grimly.

"What'd you do?" asked Remo.

"I blacked out the building after I persuaded Friend to release the bank computers."

Remo looked surprised. "You outwitted him?"

"His was only an electronic brain. Mine is the real thing."

"Only you, Smitty."

"What matters is that the nightmare is over."

Remo cocked a thumb over his shoulder. "Not until you help Chiun get his gold out of there."

"The gold is not important."

"To Chiun it is."

They entered the building. They found Chiun standing resolute before the open vault door. At Smith's approach, he executed a ceremonial bow.

"Emperor Smith, once this gold has been transported to a place of safety, I will be happy to consider entering into your employ once more."

"I thought you were working for Kim Jong Il?" said Remo.

Chiun frowned. "He made us an offer that is still pending, O Emperor," he told Smith. "But I do not think his gold is as pure and golden as America's. But it is good to have an emperor waiting in the wings for emergencies."

"Will you accept the usual payment?" Smith asked.

Chiun pretended to hesitate. When Smith failed to sweeten the offer, he allowed, "That is agreeable."

"Very well. You may take it from my ten percent of the gold before you." Smith addressed Remo. "What about you, Remo?"

"Like I said before, I'm along to tie up some loose ends. Like who I really am."

"And then?"

"Then I hit the road."

Smith nodded. "We will seal these vaults and make arrangements for the gold."

Chiun looked shocked. "We cannot leave it here."

"It will be safe. I promise."

"I will spend the night protecting my gold if need be."

"Better let him alone, Smitty," Remo said. "He's got that look in his eye."

"We will return with proper transportation," Smith told Chiun.

As they left the building, Smith paused to look up at the tower of greed that was no more. "I still cannot understand—where was Friend?"

"That's easy. In a mainframe we never would have found."

Smith looked puzzled.

"Don't you get it, Smith? The entire building is a gigantic mainframe. Friend was never in any of the ordinary ones."

Smith's jaw dropped. "You deduced this by yourself?"

"No, it came to me in a dream a long time ago."

Harold Smith just stared.

34

The President of the United States was jogging along the circular track on the White House grounds he seldom used because of the flak he'd gotten from the press over its funding.

Tonight he didn't care. Tonight Americans were relaxing in the warm glow of the last barbecue of the summer, celebrating the return of forty-seven brave survivors of yet another North Korean outrage, looking forward to a workless Monday and trying not to think of Tuesday—completely oblivious to the disaster that awaited their return.

If something didn't break soon, America would go back to work to find their hard-earned savings gone, the banks paralyzed and the financial safety net in tatters. There wasn't enough FDIC money to cover every bank. The Federal Reserve was dead. Even the Treasury was unable to move funds except by armored car.

And so he jogged in the darkness, flanked by huffing Secret Service agents, thinking that tomorrow he would pay the damn ransom and pray that was the end of it and not the beginning of a new kind of hostage situation.

The chairman of the Fed pulled up in his limousine at exactly the same time the First Lady came scurrying out of the White House waving a computer printout.

They both tried to talk at once. They were very excited.

"Calm down. Just calm down," the President said, shushing them with his hands. "Now, one at a time."

The chairman of the Fed and the First Lady locked gazes over who went first. The First Lady won.

"Read this," she said, snapping the printout in the President's face.

The President took it. His eyes went to the E-mail message outlined in fluorescent yellow.

Fed crisis averted. Situation resolved. Pay no ransom.

smith@cure.com

"Mr. President," the fed chairman started to say. "I don't know how, but—"

"I know. I know. Everything's back to normal."

"It was as if there never was a problem in the first place," the chairman of the Fed said in a bewildered voice.

The President clapped the Fed chairman on the back and walked him back to his waiting limo. "You go home, get some sleep and let's keep this under our hat, okay?"

"But how—"

"I had people on it. Top people."

After the limo pulled away, the President noticed the First Lady glaring at him.

"I have just one question," she said.

The President swallowed hard. Here it comes, he thought. How do I get out of this?

"This Smith. Who is she?"

"'She?'"

"I tried contacting Smith on the net. There's no such electronic address as Smith at CURE. Is this something new—a computer romance? I've heard of cyber-sex, but I thought it was for twelve-year-olds! You should be ashamed of yourself, sneaking around on the net."

And after the strain of the past few days, the President could only laugh in his First Lady's reddening face.

On Tuesday morning, the world picked up where it left off. Vacationers returned from distant places, business geared up for the final quarter of the year, and banks opened everywhere without a penny out of balance.

Except for the CURE account in the Grand Cayman Trust, Harold Smith discovered from his familiar post at Folcroft Sanitarium.

"I knew I had forgotten something," he murmured to himself.

His secretary buzzed. "You have visitors, Dr. Smith."

"Send them in."

Remo and Chiun walked in.

Chiun bowed. "The gold is safe in your basement, Emperor Smith, awaiting a submarine to transport it to my village."

"We will have to find a way to convert my portion to cash. It appears that Friend failed to restore the CURE fund. And I have to be doubly careful. I am being audited by the IRS."

Chiun made a face. "We have never worked for the Irish, and I recommend the same to you."

"He means the Internal Revenue Service is on his case," explained Remo.

Chiun's eyes went wide. "The confiscators of wealth! What if they discover my gold?"

"That is why we must find a better hiding place."

"I cannot tarry. I must guard my gold with my skills and my fearsome reputation. For the Irish are a drinking race and once intoxicated are not easily swayed against seizing what is not theirs."

Chiun fled the room, leaving Remo and Smith in an uneasy silence.

"What about the Friend chip?" Remo asked. "You going to look for it?"

"If what you claim is true, and it is a reasonable supposition that the entire building is a gargantuan mainframe, it could take years of searching to isolate that chip. I have arranged to keep the power supply shut off to the building. XL has no surviving owners, so I will see what I can do about having the building razed. That should take care of the matter."

"You said that before."

"Without electricity, Friend cannot influence anyone."

Remo shifted his feet. "So CURE's back in business," he said.

"Not as before. The dedicated line to the White House is still out of commission. It may take months to restore it, assuming we can find the point where it was severed. And until the gold is converted, we are without operating funds. As it is, it is not clear what our future would be under the current administration."

"If you have your own gold, do you need Washington?"

Smith shook his head in the negative. "No. But we serve at the pleasure of the President. If he orders us to deep stand-down, I have no choice but to obey."

"Whatever that is," grunted Remo. He ran a hand over the smooth black glass desktop. "This your new computer setup?"

"Yes. I am still getting used to it."

"Just so long as it finds my parents."

Smith looked up. "I have made no progress."

"Just give me an honest effort."

"Agreed."

Remo hesitated.

"Is there anything else?" asked Smith.

Remo fidgeted. "Yeah."

"Well?"

"Remember last time out, we talked about my problem?"

"Yes. The blackouts in which you seem to lose yourself and this Shiva entity assumes control of your body."

"You said there was a name for it—a psychiatric name."

"You could be suffering from periodic psychogenic fugues."

"I told you about that dream."

Smith frowned. "I do not believe in precognitive dreams."

"Neither did I. But that's the second time I've had an acute attack of déjà vu. When I was in Tibet, it looked familiar as hell. Maybe I should stick around Folcroft a while and see if your doctors can help me. It's not normal to remember things you never experienced."

"I am sure they can help, Remo. Now if you will excuse me," Smith said, touching the black button that brought the amber screen under his desktop to life, "there is still the matter of the missing twelve million dollars Friend transferred out of the CURE account."

"With all that gold in the basement, what's twelve million dollars?"

"Twelve million dollars," Smith said flatly, "is a loose end that has to be tied. We have seen how CURE can be compromised by seemingly small details. Besides, it is twelve million of the taxpayers' dollars, and I am responsible for its recovery.''

With that, Harold Smith bent his gray head and brought his thin hands to the keyboard that lit up in response to the proximity of his fingers. He was soon lost in the information stream.

Remo Williams left him to his work.

EPILOGUE

Jeremy Lippincott entered the Lippincott Savings Bank in Rye, New York, early on the Tuesday after Labor Day. He had spent a perfectly beastly Sunday with his wife, Penelope, and could not wait to climb into his pink fuzzies in the sanctity of his corner office.

Rawlings intercepted him at the door, looking pale and thoroughly wrung out.

"Mr. Lippincott. A word with you, please."

"What is it, Rawlings?" Lippincott clipped.

"There is a man named Ballard to see the Folcroft account."

"Ballard. Do we know him?"

"He is with the IRS."

Jeremy Lippincott's lantern jaw clenched, the hinge muscles turning white and hardening to concrete. If it were not for the IRS and its infernally high tax brackets, the Lippincott family would own banking in the United States and not merely have cornered one piece of it.

"Very well. Let him see whatever he needs to."

"But Mr. Lippincott. You remember my speaking to you about the irregularities in the Folcroft account."

"What of it?" asked Jeremy, not remembering at all.

"Mr. Lippincott, this is the account in which the twelve million dollars mysteriously appeared the other day."

"Yes, I think I remember now," Lippincott said vaguely.

"So what shall I do? He has no court order."

"You," Jeremy Lippincott said, "will show this Ballard whatever he is legally authorized to see, while I am going to my hutch to drink carrot juice and pretend I am winning the America's Cup with my dear wife lashed to the mainmast."

With that, Jeremy Lippincott flung open the door to his office and slammed it after him.

Rawlings remembered to wipe the perspiration from his upper lip before returning to his office and the IRS revenue agent who waited there.

Perhaps, he thought, everything would turn out satisfactorily for the Lippincott Savings Bank. For Folcroft Sanitarium, it would surely be another matter. Especially if its chief administrator could not account for a twelve-million-dollar electronic windfall.

The Internal Revenue Service was not an agency to be trifled with. Once they got their hooks into you, there was no escaping them.

The very thought sent a shiver running down Rawlings's erect spine.

**Blazing a perilous trail through the
heart of darkness**

JAMES AXLER
DEATHLANDS®

Road Wars

A cryptic message sends Ryan Cawdor and the Armorer on an
odyssey to the Pacific Northwest, away from their band of warrior
survivalists. As the endless miles come between them, the odds for
survival are not in their favor.

In the Deathlands, fate and chance are clashing with
frightening force.

DON PENDLETON'S **THE EXECUTIONER**®

NEW COVER

COMING IN
JANUARY 1995

The Mack Bolan team will be coming your way with new eye-catching cover graphics.

We're bringing you an exciting new cover design, but Gold Eagle is still committed to bringing you action adventure heroes who confront danger head-on. We are dedicated to action adventure at its best—now in a bright, new package!

Don't miss the new look of THE EXECUTIONER— available in January 1995.

In the quest for great adventure, watch for the new Executioner cover from Gold Eagle books.

U.S. Justice takes a bloodbath...

DON PENDLETON's
MACK BOLAN®

AMBUSH

Former Nazi Bernhardt Ennslin reigns rich and untouchable over the largest cocaine manufacturing empire in South America. Now his "corporation" has extended its payroll to an army of seasoned terrorists hired to massacre U.S. judges. His agenda: force a U.S. retreat in the Drug War.